Lucky Strike

by

Thomas Fenske

Lucky Strike

"So, what do we have," Lance said. "Two gold coins from Italy, and some Italian guy snooping around. 'Course we have no way to connect them."

"Yeah, but we also know Loot and Smidgeon's father joined the army together and this Italian, what was his name?"

"Cerides, I think," Lance said.

"Cerides indicated he knew them from their army days."

Lance swallowed his last bit of burger. "And they both served in North Africa?"

Sam tapped the rim of his glass, deep in thought. "Yeah. If they joined together, they most likely served together. We know Joe was wounded in North Africa and we know they were together for a picture. And Cerides mentioned North Africa, too."

"I don't know where all Loot ended up going, but my daddy never got any further than North Africa. And the note," Smidgeon added. "Don't forget the note."

"Note? What note?" Lance asked.

Sam continued his tapping, "Remember the cigarette tin?"

"Oh, that's right! The Lucky Strike box from inside the wall. Something about south of Valentine."

Sam mused, "Might be time to take a little road trip."

What They Are Saying About Lucky Strike

This time out, a treasure found a continent away and decades ago, brings the wrath of one man to Sam Milton and Smidgeon Toll's doorstep, leading one on a cross-country search for clues as the other suddenly disappears. Meanwhile, a hidden cache lay hidden, perhaps protected by an old curse of the ghosts who fell to its pull.

In *Lucky Strike*, Thomas Fenske uses his signature style to its best advantage as mystery, mayhem and murder meet small town ingenuity with the help of ghosts from the past!

—Tome Tender Book Blog
http://tometender.blogspot.com

Changing focus from the lost gold mine to a mystery buried treasure from World War II, Fenske steps it up in the complexity department. I'm impressed by his ability to weave together so many disparate parts into a coherent whole, slowly revealing bits of information both about the resolution of the mystery and about the characters we've met through the first two books. World War II, deserters, and buried treasure; international criminals, kidnapping, and murder. Oh, and our friends the ghosts, who once again play a pivotal role in the resolution of the key drama.

—The Edifying Word Book Blog
https://theedifyingword.com/blog/

The war wasn't over for Cerides, an Italian defector, who felt cheated by the soldiers who had rescued him. A decades-old grudge reignited an internal war within Cerides as he set out on a vendetta to the small Texas town of Van Horn to find his enemies and reclaim his lost treasure. Sam Milton once again finds himself in the thick of things after a clue is found during the reconstruction of the Mossback Café.

Thomas Fenske weaves together an intriguing story full of suspense, mystery and murder, with an added paranormal twist.

—Marianne Reese Books
https://mariannereeseauthor.wordpress.com

Lucky Strike
Traces of Treasure, Book 3

Thomas Fenske

Mystery Novel

Published by Thomas Fenske

Copyright © 2019 by: Thomas Fenske
ISBN: 979-8-9928799-2-6

Originally published by Wings ePress, Inc.

Edited by: Jeanne Smith
Copy Edited by: Rebecca Smith
Executive Editor: Jeanne Smith
Cover Artist: Trisha FitzGerald-Jung
Cover image Credit: ID 11490173 © Piotr Marcinski | Dreamstime.com

Published In the United States Of America

Acknowledgments

I would like to thank Marianne Reese, Ginger Millican, Carol Bonomo, Debra Ferguson, and Janet Peri for reading early versions of this novel and offering valuable insight. Bob Elkins provided valuable technical input as well. I would like to further thank Mirella Branca for her assistance with some Italian outbursts and Mr. James White for his gracious permission to mention both Brite Ranch and the Lucky Strike well in this novel.

Lucky Strike is also a cigarette trademark owned by the British American Tobacco Groups.

Note: This is a work of fiction and places like Brite Ranch are privately owned and mentioned only for realistic accuracy.

Dedication

This book is dedicated to my mother and father, gone but never forgotten.

One

North Africa, 1942

Another German 88mm shell screamed overhead and exploded about a hundred yards in front of the idling half-track armored vehicle. Loot revved the engine as he and the major studied several depressions in the sand indicating an apparent fork in the lame excuse for a road they were trying to follow. The lumbering behemoth shuddered with each press of the accelerator.

"What do you think, Loot? Which way?" the major shouted over the persistent rumbling of the mechanical beast.

"I've got me a feeling, sir," he said as his eyes darted between the two options.

Major Elkins shot him a quick glance. "I'm open to suggestions."

In the distance, even above the noise of the vehicle, he could hear the unmistakable booming of artillery and Loot Meldings gulped hard. "Left, sir."

The major tapped the young soldier's helmet and pointed left. "Go."

The M3 half-track lurched as it accelerated to the left. Behind them, the Germans unleashed a barrage of hell in their wake as a line of explosions continued along the right fork of the road. Loot secretly hoped the rear idler wouldn't break again, at least until they got to some cover. Those idlers had been a persistent problem with the M3s since landing in North Africa.

Major "Satch" Elkins shook his head and chuckled nervously as the blasts continued behind them. He yelled to make himself heard over the racket. "Good call, Loot!"

German 88s and mechanized armor didn't get along. A hit from one of the big shells could turn the hulking metal brutes into explosive bonfires.

Hours later, the platoon of five half-tracks halted in a depression of North African desert; they each turned to form a crude circle that provided some protection on the inner side. There was evidence of a previous encampment.

"Looks like somebody else thought this was a good refuge," the major said. "Probably an Italian patrol," he added. "Dig in, keep any fires small and inside the circle." Elkins jumped from the vehicle and went to find the radioman so he could report.

Usually, they were part of an armored group including tanks, jeeps, and support trucks, but for this trip, they had broken off as a company on patrol. When the major was out of earshot, Loot walked to what had been the last vehicle in the group and whispered loudly, "Digly!"

A scraggly youth emerged from the dark confines of the half-track behind the 50 caliber machine gun, dressed in a hodgepodge of military and civilian clothes. Loot had found the boy in the remains of a village a few weeks earlier, half-starved and happy to do anything as long as it kept him fed. He spoke a smattering of English and was a fast learner.

Loot was pretty sure most of the officers knew about the boy, but the men in the company looked out for him and didn't flaunt his presence. They had tried to leave him behind when they started this patrol, but the kid insisted on coming along. There was rarely time to argue when they were given the order to move out. He hid while traveling and emerged only at night.

The boy told them he was a nineteen-year-old Italian army conscript, but he looked much younger. He insisted his father was Cypriot, not Italian, and he had had enough of *Il Duce* and the Italian army. Loot, always looking for the easy way in Army life, readily adopted him as a general helper to the group.

Delbert, Scooter, Joey, and Babe all conspired with Loot to help Digly dispose of his ragged Italian uniform and somehow found him some ill-fitting replacements. There was no shortage of refugees, so they tried to pass him off as one. It was not unusual for locals to come around and try to work for handouts. Even in better times it was a hard place to live, and the realities of war only made it more difficult.

All five of them liked the kid, and he was a boon to the exhausted soldiers, who willingly accepted his aid, which consisted primarily of digging foxholes and fetching water. They knew bringing him along on a patrol was dangerous, and they all, including Digly, accepted the fact that if the army found out about his status, he'd be made a prisoner of war. They also knew a deserter like Digly had little chance of survival even if he made his way back to the Italians.

"Let's get to it," Loot said.

"*Si, signore*," came the reply, and Digly quickly produced two shovels from nooks and crannies of the vehicle. He handed one to Loot.

As usual, the boy did more than his fair share of the digging for the group. His given name was Indigo, and it seemed to reflect both his Greek heritage and his sun-darkened complexion. Loot had coined the nickname Digly as a supposed extension of the kid's presumed new occupation among his American friends.

"Ain't nothing a soldier hates more than digging foxholes," Loot said, "but there ain't nothing a soldier appreciates more than a deep one." He cackled like an old man at his joke.

Bright white teeth flashed back at him as the boy continued chipping away at the hard earth. When Digly finished the first hole, he started on a second, and followed with a third.

"Is easier, this one," he said, still smiling.

"Looser dirt?" Loot asked.

"*Si*...how you say, loose," Digly said, as he stabbed at the ground with an earnest pace.

The rest of Digly's new family converged on the new foxholes. Scooter jumped into one, while Joey and Babe jumped into the other one and made themselves at home. Delbert started digging another one. Loot rested his arms on the edge of his and watched Digly work.

In the distance, they could hear the renewed thunder of artillery, an occurrence so common no one much noticed until the resulting explosions came closer. Tonight the carnage seemed far away, but the dull booming in the background could not cover the sound of Digly's shovel ringing with the distinct "CLANG" of metal on metal. Five grimy faces twisted to the figure holding the shovel; he returned their stares, wide-eyed with surprise.

"What'd you hit?" Loot asked.

"*Non lo so*," the boy mumbled.

"Huh?"

"Not know," he corrected. He disappeared into the hole, and five weary, helmeted heads appeared at the edge of the foxhole to watch as the boy scooped mounds of dirt away from a buried metal box.

After several minutes of such digging, he managed to grasp the edges of the box and work it loose from its tomb. Loot reached down and helped Digly hoist the container. It was a lot heavier than Loot had imagined such a small box would be and they both struggled with it until finally Loot lifted it over the top and dropped it a few feet beyond the hole, where it landed with a dull thud.

Scooter looked around and made sure no one else had heard. Joey, Delbert and Babe joined Loot in dusting caked dirt off the box. Digly scampered out of the foxhole.

"Heavy," Loot said. "Too heavy for its size."

"The coast is clear," Scooter said.

A rusty padlock secured one side of the box and Babe dispatched it with the butt of his M1. Loot gingerly opened the box.

5

It was full of gold coins. Loot extracted one and examined it in the light of the full moon.

"*Madonna santa,*" Digly whispered when he saw the coin.

"Looks like a danged treasure," Babe added.

"Yep," Loot said, "You're right. I'd say it is indeed a danged treasure."

He returned the coin and closed the box.

"This needs to be our secret, the six of us," Loot continued. "We'll divvy it up later, but if the major gets wind of it, he'll confiscate it and turn it over. We found it fair and square, so keep yer yaps shut, got me?" All six men nodded in agreement.

Van Horn, Texas, summer, 1983

Sam Milton gently revved the Volkswagen's engine while Lance Norton limped around the yard chasing his dog and shouting, "Prewash! Git on in that house, you hear?"

Sam opened the car door, "Come here, girl."

The dog ran to Sam, and he grabbed her collar.

"She's just playing," Lance panted as he approached. He clicked a leash in place and began to lead her away from the car. "Come on now, let's git in the house."

Prewash glanced back at Sam with dark, soulful eyes.

"Sorry I can't help you, girl."

After depositing the dog and locking the door, Lance hobbled to the car. "Chasing the danged dog ain't good for this bum leg."

Sam tried to stifle a laugh. "Yeah, I was really feeling for you, buddy. You were quite a sight, stumbling around chasing her. She knew what she was doing."

"Ain't had much time to play with her since I got shot." Lance winced as he maneuvered into the passenger seat. "Let me get my hind leg in. Hey, thanks again for letting me shack up in Loot's old house."

"Well, he left the place to me in his will, and I'm staying with Smidgeon so it's been sitting here empty. You didn't have a place to stay after Tim MacGregg let you go from the ranch, so it works out for the both of us. Well, we best get on to The Mossback. Smidgeon is over there waiting for us. The sooner the repairs are completed, the sooner we start working again."

"I'm hoping we can settle into a nice routine. I ain't worked food service since college, but I'm no stranger to it." Lance adjusted himself in his seat and glanced around nervously. "Hopefully people around here are getting more used to seeing a black man riding around in a danged vee-dub with a white boy."

Sam chuckled as he backed out the driveway, "Yeah, some peace and quiet will be nice. When I first started nosing around in the desert out here looking for that gold mine, I never knew it would end up causing so much trouble."

"You and me both. I'd heard my grandpa's stories about Slim and Scamp looking for that mine my whole life. It's what they called him back in them days, Scamp...he was just Grandpa Thad to me. I don't know how a city boy like you got away with trespassing and hiking on ranchland for so long. At least I was a city boy who went to college in west Texas. I had some time to adapt to country life. You came out here cold from Houston and Austin."

"Yeah, I guess I got used to it. Hah, that's the first time I heard the name Scamp. Before we met, I thought I was the only one who knew about the mine. When Slim died in my arms, all he had time to tell me was the clues to it in his riddle." Sam winked at Lance. "Ya gotta follow the devil until you see the table, then—"

Lance continued, "Turn around, and you'll see the why of it. Yeah, and we both found it, too. You were lucky and found it first."

"I don't know if I'd call it lucky. I'd searched for years, spending long weekends hiking cross-country in the dark. But I got overconfident when I thought I had solved the devil part of the clue. I made mistakes and almost lost my life."

"But you found it anyway."

"Yeah, but not until MacGregg's ranch hands found me, beat me up, threw me down a ravine, and left me for dead. After I came to, I knew I had to figure out some way to escape. In the process, I stumbled across the table-shaped rock the same way you did, walking up that little side arroyo."

"Yeah, I walked down and saw a crazy flat rock...it stopped me in my tracks. Then you popped out of the hole on the other side." Lance slapped his good leg. "Pretty much scared us both silly."

"Yeah, I couldn't believe it when I saw you standing there. Of course," Sam continued, "later, things started getting interesting."

"Who could have figured the woman would go plumb crazy?"

Sam furrowed his brow and sighed. "I don't know what happened to Moll. She'd been one of my best friends for years, but I guess maybe grief made her snap. Whatever it was, it cost too many lives. Worst of all was Loot. You know, he had pegged me early on as a prospector. And I tried to ignore him because I never thought I needed help, but he ended up being a great friend."

"Yeah, grandpa knew him, but he mostly remembered him as a drunken old cuss ... 'course, he *did* save grandpa's life."

"Yeah, Slim's, too. They were both caught trespassing out on Diablo Rim, out on the MacGregg ranch same as me. MacGregg beat them badly before dumping them in town. Loot came across them and tried to get them help. There was a glimmer of good in Loot even when he was blind drunk."

"Grandpa said he broke a window on the Mossback out of frustration. Probably why Smidgeon's dad took such a dislike to him."

Sam frowned. "I always figured it went deeper, but that incident sure didn't help. And my friendship with Loot was a sore spot between Smidgeon and me for a while, especially when we first realized we liked each other."

"How'd you meet her anyway?"

"The café. I usually ate there after spending weekends poking around. It was part of my routine. I liked to eat a good breakfast before driving the ten hours back to Austin. But early on, it was just light-hearted stuff. It got more real when she picked me up out on the highway."

"Oh, when you was escaping after finding the mine, right?"

"Yeah, it was like fate or something. She showed up right after I started trying to hitchhike back to town. Loot had dropped me off because I was hiking so far back into the hills. After MacGregg's men found me, I knew I couldn't get back to the spot Loot and I had agreed on, and I had no way of contacting him, so I decided to hike east, to the highway. I took a chance on the first car and stuck out my thumb and it stopped. When I opened the door, I stood there with my mouth open for a second; it was Smidgeon. It shocked her, too, but she wouldn't budge until I told her what was going on. Afterward, she did everything she could to keep me safe."

"Dang, boy, it worked out good for you, though," Lance snickered.

"I'd say it has worked out for all of us, don't you think?"

"Well, at least maybe I'll have a job if they ever finish repairing the burned part of The Mossback."

"Yeah, that was all Moll's fault, too."

"Danged woman tried to kill the MacGreggs and tried to kill Smidgeon by burning down the café; I lost count of the other people she killed. All for what?"

"Sometimes nothing can explain evil, Lance. She had lost her husband—heck, his death hit me hard, too—he was one of my best friends. For some reason, I guess she kind of fixated on me. Grief can do strange things to the mind."

"But did she think murdering people would get her what she wanted?"

"Maybe. I don't think she was thinking clearly, but it seemed like she wanted to remove everyone else from my life except her."

"Let me use some of my college psychology class to at least try to rationalize her pattern. I think maybe she targeted Loot because he was helping you. And as for those friends of yours from Austin, Sally and Bob, maybe she was trying to wipe away fragments of your past life."

"She could have been afraid they might spot her. Sally had met her before."

"Okay, but why the MacGreggs? They had nothing to do with you. I can tell you, Tim was completely smitten with her and she was leading him on big time, all the while poisoning him and his mom. She was even a mite forward with me."

"For her, I think it was all means to an end. I think maybe she wanted the mother out of the way, then thought perhaps she'd save Tim, at least long enough to get some control over the ranch. She probably thought it would help her to exert more power over me. Because Moll had been my friend, she knew it was on the MacGregg ranch somewhere, but she didn't know the exact location."

"But why kill that Loretta woman?"

"She knew Loretta and I had spent some time together. I think it was a combination of jealousy and revenge. It hit me pretty hard when Loretta left me and Moll knew that. Who could have figured Loot would leave Loretta anything in his will? And I sure didn't expect her to show up and it put her pretty much in the wrong place at the wrong time. I think at some point, Moll decided to kill anybody she felt might stand in her way, Loot, Sally, Bob, Loretta, Tim, his mom, and Smidgeon."

"So she kidnaps you. But why did she take you out to the mine?"

"To her, it was the ultimate symbol of control over me. Once out there, she proceeded to give me an ultimatum. She was ready to destroy the mine either way, and if I didn't go with her, she planned on destroying me along with it. But she didn't figure on you, my friend."

"Or on Smidgeon," Lance added. "She and her cousin showed up just in time to save you."

"It got really crazy, shots flying all over. I was so sorry one of the slugs caught you."

"Could have been a lot worse. I'm even sorrier for poor Hez."

"Yeah, Hezekiah had been a big help to me. He was the only other person who knew where the mine was. That's why Smidgeon called him. But once the bullets started flying—"

"So, I never right out asked you," Lance was looking intently at Sam as he drove. "You think she blew herself up? Like on purpose?"

"I don't know, Lance. She didn't seem the type to kill herself. And even if she did, I think she'd be more likely to include me in her plan."

"But you and Smidgeon had won, right?"

"She wasn't beaten, Lance, not by a long shot. We both got out of the mine and had the darkness on our side, but at the time, I thought it was far from over. I knew we had to get away from her, and we had you to worry about and Hez, too. We didn't know he was dead."

Lance feigned an explosion with his hands. "Then, BOOM."

"Yeah, it was quite a boom, too, threw both of us off our feet. She was most likely fiddling with the dynamite and it went off."

"It can be a mite tricky to deal with sometimes. I just wish it all hadn't ended there. Sad to think all that history with Grandpa, Slim, and Loot pretty much blew up with the mine, you know?"

"Yeah, sometimes I sorta felt like Slim and Loot were still there looking after me...silly, I guess. Hey, we'll be back at The Mossback in a few minutes. At least maybe that part of the story has a happy ending," Sam joked.

"Yeah, and like I said, if they can ever finish the repairs, we can all settle down to living and working like regular folks."

"One can only hope," Sam muttered.

Two

The noise of the crash was heart-sickening. Smidgeon nudged herself a few inches behind builder John Mason and held her breath as a substantial section of wall crumbled and fell at their feet.

"Will this ever be over?" Smidgeon Toll coughed and waved dust from her face as she glanced up and down at the spots of bare wood framing along the back wall of her restaurant, The Mossback Cafe. She walked back and forth, peering into cracks and crevices. She picked at pieces of the scorched wall and tried to wipe the soot off her fingers. She squinted back at John, who was staring intently at his clipboard.

The contractor looked up and responded, "Miss Smidgeon, a fire in an old building is one of the worstest things they is." John Mason was a tall man, his face tanned and leathered from years of working outdoors. "They's always things we didn't see at the first looking. And old construction, well things crop up, old damage, old repairs, and even old damage that warn't repaired. This old gal," he patted the wall gingerly, "mighta served you okay for ten or twenty more years, but your fire, it opened up a can of worms for us to fix."

"Oh I know, John, I really do. I'm just anxious to get open again. Money's going out, and there isn't any coming in."

"I understand, Miss Smidgeon. Give us a couple of more weeks, and we should be downwind of this thing." He turned his attention back to his work.

Smidgeon put her hands on her hips as she again strolled along the wall, stopping at the spot where the fire had started. She thought back to the night when Sam had returned to the mine against her wishes.

"He thought he was protecting me by heading out to confront the killer," Smidgeon softly whispered to herself. "But leaving me here alone almost sealed my fate."

The plan was more devious than any of them had imagined. The fire Moll set on the back wall of The Mossback was designed to smolder unnoticed while Smidgeon was alone in the building, then flare up after the killer had left to confront Sam in the desert.

Smidgeon shook her head at the memory. "What would make someone go so crazy?"

Something in the debris of the recently collapsed wall caught her eye; she bent down and picked up what looked like a small metal box. She was holding it in her hands when she heard a familiar puttering sound approach and saw Sam's dusty Volkswagen Beetle pull up and park near her.

Two figures emerged. The driver smiled as he walked to her side and gave her a light kiss.

"Looks like they're making progress."

"Sam, you're way too optimistic."

The passenger, a young black man walking with a limp favoring his right leg, joined them.

"Naw," Sam said. "What do you think, Lance?"

Lance Norton closely examined a section of new construction, pushing and tugging at the boards. "I guess the fire coulda been worse, but it's always tough to repair old buildings."

"Yeah, that's what Mr. Mason was saying," Smidgeon said. "Where you boys been?"

"Getting Lance squared away over at Loot's old house."

"Still moving a might slow," Lance said. "Been hurt a few times in my life but ain't been gunshot before. I guess it sorta took it out of me."

"Still can't believe Tim MacGregg fired you," Sam said. "Geez, you saved his life."

"Don't know about that, but heck, I guess I *did* kinda take the job with ulterior motives."

"Yeah, but you told him to get to the doctor. That should stand for something. Besides, he hired *you* with deceitful motives in mind as well. And heck, Lance, you did a good job for him."

"Maybe, but it was all pretty complicated. Sure, I told Tim what was up, but he paid attention too late to save his mom. I think he was more irate because of the whole deal of me conniving with Sam about the mine. He saw it as thieving."

"Yeah, but there really wasn't much to steal, at least not yet. And anyway, I'd worked that one spot for over two years before you even got there. Maybe I should go over and tell him you didn't have anything to do with it."

"Don't bother, Sam, trust me...he blames you the most. *Your* friend Moll killed his mom and danged near killed him. And even worse, I think he was jealous she was using him to get at you."

Sam nudged some of the debris with the toe of his boot. "Well, the mine's gone now, at least as far as we're concerned. Still, wish I'd gotten farther down the collapsed shaft."

"Can't say I'm sad about the mine," Smidgeon said. "And now he's already started excavating the thing. I've heard there is a lot of heavy equipment out there digging every day. Do you think he'll find anything?"

"Dunno, honey. It was so unstable, I never got down as far as I planned, and I never found more than a trace of gold. He might find a fortune, but I think it's more likely it might just be a dead end." Sam looked down at his feet and added, "That's pretty much what it was for me."

Smidgeon blew a kiss. "Aw, sweetie, you've still got me."

"I'd say I got the better end of the deal."

Sam glanced down and noticed the box in her hands.

"What's that you've got?" he asked.

Smidgeon handed Sam the container. "They knocked down part of the wall a few minutes ago and I found this in the mess."

He closely examined the dusty artifact. "It was in the wall?"

"I guess so. I've never seen it."

He handed it back to her, "Looks like it must have been stuck in there a long time ago. I guess it could have been accidentally left by a worker...or maybe your dad hid it away for some reason."

Lance had been a few feet away, examining some of the repair work, when he returned and said, "Lucky Strike

Green!" Lance said, adding a faint whistle under his breath. "Ain't seen one of them cans in a long time. They used to pack cigarettes in them years ago. My grandpa Thad still had a couple sitting around. They're nice to store little whatnots in."

"I know the brand," Sam said, "but I thought their packaging was white."

"Redesigned the packs in the forties," Lance said. "Green is vintage. Grandpa always said they ruined 'em when they switched over to white. He changed to Chesterfields, which I always thought was odd since they have a white pack, too. Where'd you get it, Miss Smidgeon?"

"It was in one of the walls," she said.

"Wonder what's in it?" Sam asked.

"I had just found it when you two drove up...I'm a little scared by it. Never much liked secrets."

Sam laughed. "I know you don't!"

"Well, it's an old secret," Lance said, "so there should be no harm to anyone now. Heck, it was probably dropped by a workman or something."

"Guess we better see." Smidgeon led them around the front of the building to the dining room where they sat at one of the dusty tables.

They all took turns examining the box; it was dirty and smelled of smoke, but it was otherwise intact. The green paint and logo were still quite visible. "Lucky Strike," she said to herself as she traced the red circle surrounding the words. She pointed at the other words on the top. "Flat Fifties?"

"Came with fifty cigarettes," Lance said.

Smidgeon ran her fingers over the edges of the box.

Sam said, "It's hinged on the back."

"Right." She used her fingernails on the front side to wedge the top and bottom apart until the dimpled clasp made a slight 'pop' and she was able to raise the lid with a slight creak.

Inside there was a bundle wrapped in three small plastic bags. She unwrapped the package, and a slip of paper folded around a photograph fell to the table. Sam could see what looked like three soldiers. Smidgeon picked up the photo and said, "Daddy, and..." She handed it to Sam.

"Loot," Sam said.

"Who's the other guy?" she asked.

Sam flipped the photo over and read, "Joey, Loot, and Babe."

"Who the heck is Babe?" Lance asked.

Smidgeon said, "I never knew Daddy and Loot served together. As for Babe, I have no idea who he is. Never ever heard Daddy mention him. He didn't talk about the war at all. I mean, I knew he served in North Africa and was wounded. I asked my mom once, and she told me to let it be."

"War affects people differently," Lance said. "Some can't shut up about it...some can't say a thing."

She said, "They're standing next to some kind of army vehicle."

"Looks like a half-track," Sam said. "Loot had a picture of one, too."

"Armored Infantry," Lance said.

Smidgeon unfolded the paper and breathed deeply as she read it. "It's not Daddy's handwriting; I don't know what it means."

Sam took the paper from her. "Looks like directions...but to what?" He strained to read the words. "Valentine?" he said and looked up at Smidgeon.

"Southeast of here. Toward Marfa," she said.

"Oh right," he continued as he traced the words with his finger. "S Miller Ranch Rd - Old Brite - 16 miles," Sam looked up again and said, "... and there's this triangle with an X along one side of it."

"X marks the spot, I guess," Lance said. "Just what we all need, another ding dong dang mystery. Why was it stuck in the wall?"

Smidgeon stammered. "I—I have no earthly idea."

All three of them stared at the note and the tin for several minutes in silence until she took a deep breath and returned the note to the tin and put it in her purse. "I can't deal with this now."

"Yeah, it's been in the wall for a long time. It's likely nothing. You're right," Sam said, "we have too much to do...we can worry about it later."

Lance stood up, a bit unsteady on his game leg. "Sounds good to me, and anyways, I need to get home." He turned to Sam. "Can you haul me back to the house?"

"Sure, Lance," he said. He asked Smidgeon, "You headed back home?"

"Guess there ain't much more for me to do here today," she said with a sigh.

Sam and Lance waved back at her as they drove off in a cloud of dust.

"Hope we have enough money left over to pave the danged parking lot," she said as she fanned her hand in front of her face and coughed.

~ * ~

Once she got back to her house, Smidgeon sat at the kitchen table and removed the metal cigarette tin from her purse to examine the contents again. The picture of her dad with Loot Meldings was even more perplexing than the slip of paper.

"You hated Loot," she whispered to herself as she outlined her father's face with her finger. "Why would you have his picture? And who is Babe? I never heard you mention him."

Her thoughts were interrupted when she heard Sam's car in the driveway. She returned the items, closed the lid, and deposited the can on a nearby shelf, wedging it on top of a stack of books. She was in time to meet Sam as he came in the door.

"Got Lance all squared away over there?" she asked as she pecked at his lips.

"Yeah, he'll be okay once he's settled in."

"Still think he ought to pay more than just the taxes," she said, "we're going to need the money. Either that or you ought to sell the place."

"I'm not ready to let all of Loot's legacy go, at least not quite yet. We'll do okay. The Mossback is coming along, right? Did John give you any idea of when they will finish?"

"A couple of weeks is all he said. And we still have equipment and furniture to buy."

"Sweetie, the insurance paid more than you expected, and we still have some of Loot's nest egg to take care of the rest."

"Sam, did Loot ever say anything about him and my dad in the war?"

"Loot never much mentioned the war," he said.

"Neither did my dad. And all my life, he pretty much hated Loot."

"It was not unusual for friends and neighbors to join up together. They also form lifelong friendships after serving.

Soldiers always seem to have a certain brotherhood. But I've heard of deep grudges coming out of combat, too. Something must have driven them apart. Any family around who might know something more about their past?"

"There's my cousin Mildred, you know, poor Hezekiah's mom. She's pretty much my last living relative around here. I owe her a visit, too...I haven't seen her since the funeral."

"She didn't look well," Sam said.

"No, and she..." Smidgeon sobbed, and Sam drew her to him and hugged her tight. "I think she blames me for what happened."

"It wasn't your fault,"

"I took him out there," she said.

"He was loyal to both of us. He went out there to help you and to help me. I feel guilty enough for the both of us."

"It was *that* woman," she said, her voice trailing off.

"I'm not sure what drove Moll to do what she did. It was a crazy situation."

As he said that, his thoughts turned to the small good luck piece given to him by the *bruja*, the old witch woman. He credited it for his luck in surviving the attack in the desert and for finding the mine, but he also blamed it for changing Moll. He lost it at her house after Godson's death. In his heart he knew it had infected Moll somehow after she found it and it cursed her, turning her into what she had become. He also knew better than to mention the stone to Smidgeon; she hated it and made him keep it hidden.

"Well, maybe Hez's mother will be willing to talk. It will be good for you to get things out in the open, and maybe she knows something. Gil might know something, too."

"Oh, Gil. Right. Maybe we can ask him at the café...if we ever get it open again."

Sam continued, "Still, I wonder what those directions mean. You know, on the slip of paper."

"Who knows? It was yellow with age. One thing is certain...the box must have been hidden away on purpose and forgotten."

"Still, there had to be a reason, but then again, out of sight out of mind, right?"

"You said there was another photo of Loot...from the war."

"Yeah," Sam said, "it was in a small box of mementos." He hesitated as he thought for a second. "It was in the same closet where I found Loot's cash. He hid the cash under the floorboards, but the other stuff was on the shelf. The entire house was crammed full of stuff but oddly, nothing else was in the closet."

"I wonder if his box of cash is connected somehow to all of this. The note Loot put in with the cash mentioned a connection to Army buddies. You think this Lucky Strike box has something to do with Loot's box?"

"Seems a stretch, honey. We've got way too many mysteries to contemplate on an empty stomach, don't you think?" A slight rumble from Sam's abdomen was right on cue.

"I guess you're right. I'll go find something for us to eat." She patted him on his rear as he walked past her, then giggled as she added, "And after dinner, I might have a surprise or two you might like."

Three

"I need some help out here...can one of you come out and bus a couple of tables? I got people standing in the doorway waiting." Smidgeon lingered at the kitchen door after calling out.

Sam was up to his elbows in dishwater and Lance was doing some prep work. They both looked up.

"I got it, Sam." Lance grabbed a tub and disappeared into the dining room.

"Thanks, buddy," Sam called behind him.

Several minutes later, Lance returned with a tub full of dirty dishes, and he proceeded to rinse them in an empty sink next to the one Sam was using.

Sam said, "The place is running a little smoother now, but it took us a week to get the kinks worked out. Looks like the local folks have really started to come back. I guess we have to get used to working again."

"I know, but I love it. I don't much care for sitting around. It's nice to be busy."

"Now, Lance, when have you not been busy? You've been fixing up the house almost nonstop for weeks. I hardly recognize the place now."

"It's shaping up, but you did most of the heavy lifting before I got there. Well, I better get the rest of the tables," Lance added as he picked up the tub.

He rushed past Smidgeon as he hurried to the dining room.

"Thanks, Lance."

"You bet, Miss Smidgeon."

She dropped off an order with Chuy and joined Sam at the sink.

"Lance seems to be fitting in like he's been here for years. I was surprised to find out he even knows his way around the flat grill. I've caught him helping cook a couple of times. His bad leg is still slowing him down a little, but he's getting stronger every day."

"Getting shot was...well, it's never a good thing. I'm glad we can help him out. He's a good man."

"And, seriously, Sam, we owe him big time."

"We sure do." Sam smiled as he kept washing dishes.

"I still feel responsible for him getting hurt." Smidgeon looked down and her eyes teared up. "And Hez, too."

"Ah, honey," Sam said as he half embraced her with his upper arms and shoulders, holding his wet hands away from her body. "I've told you a dozen times, it wasn't you. It was Moll. She was the one who was doing everything...the killings, the fire, kidnapping me, those were all on her. You and Hez were both just trying to save me."

The conversation was interrupted by a faint bell.

"More customers," Smidgeon said, and she headed back out to the dining room.

Sam finished washing the latest load of dishes, and as he dried his hands, he turned to Chuy and asked, "You need anything else?"

"Naw, Mr. Sam, I'm all set...for now."

Sam grabbed a broom and dustpan and went out into the dining room and began gently sweeping the area around the front door and between the tables. The dry west Texas air made for a lot of dust, and there was always something to sweep up in a busy cafe. The bell on the door rang again, and Sam looked up to see a stranger in the doorway. A short, older man came in and looked around hesitantly. He had an odd, salt and pepper goatee, and Sam thought to himself the gentleman looked a bit like a villain from an old movie.

Sam said, "Sit anywhere you like, sir."

"Yes, of course, thank you." The newcomer shuffled to a table.

The accent seemed familiar...perhaps Italian, Sam thought to himself. He swept a small pile of dust, French fries, and wadded up sugar packets into a dustpan, and dumped it in a can by the kitchen door. After washing his hands at the sink near the drink station, he grabbed a menu before approaching the stranger.

"Coffee?"

"*Si*, er yes, please."

The stranger's eyes darted around the dining room as if he were looking for something specific. Sam observed him while he poured the coffee and walked back over to the table.

Sam placed the cup on the table with a few packets of creamer. "Passing through?"

"Yes and no. The owner here, he's Joey Toll, no?"

"Joe passed away several years ago. His daughter owns the place."

"Of course. Death takes us all one by one, no?"

"It does indeed. Do you want to talk to her?"

"Perhaps another time. I had some acquaintance with Mr. Toll several years ago. I was curious to, er, see if he was still around. Breakfast is my goal for today. Is good, yes?"

"Best breakfast around here," Sam said.

The man looked around as he said, "Very clean for an older place."

"We had a fire and it closed us for a while, but we just reopened. Didn't much burn here in the dining room but it's got a fresh coat of paint and new floors."

"Ah, a fire is always a mess with smoke and water, but it is a cleansing process in the end."

"Yep."

The stranger ordered a standard breakfast, and as Sam took the order to the kitchen, Lance joined him, carrying a tub full of dirty dishes.

As he was rinsing the dishes before putting them into the dishwater, he said to Sam, "Funny little guy. Foreigner?"

"Yeah, Italian, I'd say. Asked about Joe Toll."

"Smidgeon's dad?"

"Yeah, called him 'Joey' which is something I've never heard around here."

"The picture we found in the box labeled her dad Joey," Lance said.

Sam's face flashed recognition. "You're right, I had forgotten."

"He looks well-worn like he's had a tough go of life."

"Well, he's an older guy, Lance."

"Sure, but I know the look, Sam, he's got an odd pallor about him like he's been in prison or something. It's a gut impression, but I'd say he's come from someplace where you have to work hard."

"Breaking rocks like in the movies?"

"Maybe. Keep an eye on him," Lance said. "I will, too."

"Well, I'll size him up again when I take him his food," Sam said as he handed Chuy the order.

When Sam brought the plate to the bearded stranger, he asked, "Will there be anything else?"

"Ah, I forgot. Is it possible to get some hot peppers for my eggs?"

"Jalapenos okay? Chopped?"

"Yes."

"Sure, I'll be right back," Sam said.

When he returned, the stranger took the small bowl and said, "Thank you so much, young man. I am afraid I have acquired quite a taste for these in my time away from my home country."

"Italy?"

"Close enough. My accent has betrayed me?"

"A bit."

"Ah, but I've been on this side of the Atlantic for many, many years. I lived for a long time south of your border, but I spent time near here as well."

"Near here? In Texas?"

"Yes," he hesitated, "I spent some time a bit north, near Hereford, and later, close to Marfa."

"Is that how you knew Joe?"

"No, I knew him from the war. North Africa. He and several friends paid me many kindnesses. Ah, but difficulties arose and we lost track. This is inevitable in war, and in life, too, I think."

"So you knew Joe in the army?"

"Ah, so many questions. It was a long time ago, and Joey is, as you say, gone now. My food is getting cold."

"Of course, I'm sorry. Please, I'll leave you to your breakfast, Mr—"

The man stood and extended a hand, "Cerides...Indigo Cerides."

"Sam Milton. I'm sorry for bothering you, Mr. Cerides, enjoy your meal." As Sam shook the hand, he was taken aback by the hardened texture of the palm. He thought back to what Lance had said.

"Is no problem at all. Thank you, young man, er, Sam," he said with a slight smile.

Later, in the kitchen as Sam was washing what seemed like the morning's twelfth load of plates and silverware, Smidgeon came up to him.

"You waited on the funny little guy with the foreign accent?"

"Yeah. He said he knew your dad back in the war. Indigo Cerides is what he said his name was."

"Really? Never heard Daddy mention him. He didn't say anything when he paid me. Hardly said thank you. But there was something peculiar about him...as he ate, I could *feel* him watching me."

"What?"

"Yeah. It was uncomfortable. Oh, and he paid with *this*." Smidgeon handed Sam a twenty dollar bill from her apron pocket.

He examined it and said, "It's old, like Loot's stash."

"Yeah, I thought so, too," she said. "He gave me the shivers. It wasn't like he was ogling me, I don't think it was sexual, at least I hope not, but it was like he was looking at me clinically, you know? It's hard to explain. It was like he expected to discover some deep dark secret from watching me. I didn't like it."

"From what you say, I don't think I like it either. Still, I talked to the guy a little and he seemed harmless. Maybe a little unusual but harmless."

~ * ~

After work, Lance was relaxing on his couch, listening to Willie Nelson singing "Pancho and Lefty" on a small radio. His dog, Prewash, was lazily sleeping at his feet when she suddenly raised her head and let out a curt "woof."

Almost immediately, there was a light tapping at the front door. Lance warily got up and approached the door. Prewash was at his heels. The house was off the main road, and he didn't have any friends in Van Horn except for Sam and Smidgeon, so he was a bit nervous at the prospect of a visitor. As he approached the door, he thought back to the first time he had come to this house to see Loot Meldings. He had never forgotten being greeted by the long, double barrels of a shotgun with old Loot peering from behind them. When he moved in, he had placed his own shotgun by the doorframe, and he considered repeating Loot's welcome, but instead anxiously inhaled and held his breath as he opened the door.

The short figure he encountered seemed innocuous standing against the darkness. Lance recognized the man as Sam's Italian customer.

"May I help you?"

"I hope you pardon the intrusion. My name is Indigo Cerides. I am trying to find information on Kelvin Meldings. I was given this address some time ago by mutual acquaintances."

"*Kelvin?*" Lance said, momentarily confused. "Oh, wait, you mean Loot?"

The gentleman beamed broadly, showing a prominent gold tooth, "*Si*, Loot, Mr. Loot Meldings. This was his house, yes?"

Lance shook his head. "Sorry to say Loot passed away last year. Sam Milton owns this house and is renting it to me."

"Sam, oh, the gentleman from the café?"

"Yes. Loot left the house to Sam in his will."

"I see. I am very sorry to hear about Loot. He was, well, I knew him many years ago."

"In the war?"

"Ah, yes, the war. Such a long time ago." The man dropped his gaze as if in deep thought. He raised his head again, and his eyes darted around quickly. Lance got the impression the man was sizing up the place, and he didn't like it.

"You need something else?" Lance felt a shiver run up and down his spine as the dark eyes met his again with an intense stare he returned for a few seconds before continuing.

"No, no, no, I think I have taken too much of your time."

Cerides turned and, with his odd limp, scurried away, heading down Tesoro road toward the main street.

As Lance closed the door, he muttered to himself, "Twice in one day. Grandpa Thad would call it a bad omen. And no car, either. Creepy."

Prewash had already returned to her station at the couch but raised her head and looked at him quizzically as he sat. Then she settled back down to her important evening nap.

Lance thought about calling Sam but decided it could wait until he saw him at work.

Four

Chuy had just disappeared into the walk-in cooler and Lance took the opportunity to share his latest encounter. "Your little guy with the goatee showed up at my house last night looking for Loot."

"Are you serious? He went all the way out there?" Sam was wide-eyed. "How did he even know where it was?"

"Said he'd had the address for a while. I told him Loot had passed away."

"He's sure being nosy. What would some foreign guy from the war want with Loot and Joe after so long? I guess they could be army buddies, but what if—"

"What?" Lance stopped sweeping the kitchen and stared at Sam.

"Well, I was thinking, what if he was from the *other* side?"

"Oh, you mean like an Italian soldier or something?"

"Maybe. I don't like it. It's downright creepy."

Lance leaned the broom against the wall, "I said the same thing last night. I tell you, he made my skin crawl, tromping all the way out to my house, with no car or nothing."

Chuy returned from the cooler with several heads of lettuce and they both turned back to their work.

Later, during a lull in the morning rush, Sam told Smidgeon what was going on.

"I don't like it, Sam. There's something not quite right about it. And the man looks odd. I mean those hard, dark eyes and his crazy beard. Should I ask Clay about him?"

Sam shook his head. "No need to bring the police into it. I mean, he hasn't actually done anything except ask about a couple of people. And if ordering breakfast is suspicious, well most of the town is guilty."

"Maybe you're right. I guess I shouldn't be paranoid." She winked and added, "We get plenty of strange people in here, right?"

~ * ~

Sam worked the evening shift at the Mossback, allowing Smidgeon to enjoy some alone time at home. She cherished her few moments of private contemplation and used the time as an opportunity to straighten up around the house while she thought about things. As she dusted the shelves, she noticed the small Lucky Strike tin poking out on top of a stack of books. It had been a curiosity when it turned up during the renovations of the café, and after the initial excitement of the find, she had placed it there as a convenience. It seemed to fit right in with her mother and father's various possessions from the same era. Her mother had kept those items on display, and they were still peppered around the living room and den. She remembered the excitement of the box's discovery, but it had also left her with mixed feelings. She had put it aside because she wasn't quite ready for another mystery in her life, but today she seemed compelled to take another look; she carried the small box to the couch and opened it. The picture and the folded sheet of paper were still there. Her heart raced when she saw the previously unknown image of her father, and she touched his young face on the photo.

Smidgeon sobbed quietly. "Oh, Daddy, I still miss you so much. I think you'd be proud of the things I've done."

Her father rarely mentioned the war, but she knew he had lost several close friends. He was wounded seriously enough to bring him back to the States. He recovered, but she knew he had scars and he always complained he knew when stormy weather was coming.

She glanced at another nearby picture of her parents as she said, "You and Momma would always argue about it, but the weather would almost always change and bear you out."

She glanced at the paper again. The handwriting was blocky but legible. "I wonder who wrote it and what it means? It's not far, but I can't imagine there being anything to find after such a long time. Is it even worth heading out there?"

She shook her head as she refolded the paper and returned it and the picture to the tin. "It's silly. I have a business to run, and there won't be anything out there but rocks and scrub and a broken axle."

She resumed her dusting but didn't get far before the timer chimed in the kitchen.

"Lordy, my cakes."

After she checked the cakes with a toothpick, she pulled the two pans from the oven. Then she gasped as she remembered Hez's mother.

"I plumb forgot!" she blurted out. She had told her cousin Francine she planned to visit; she thought for a moment and decided she could do it while the cake cooled.

She removed the two cake layers from the pans and put them on a rack to cool, grabbed her purse, and headed out the door.

The last time Smidgeon had driven to Mildred Taynor's house was the night she had picked up Hezekiah. She needed his help to follow Sam to the mine; Lance was going out there the back way, and Hez was the only other person besides Sam and Lance who knew the mine's location. Tears welled up in her eyes as remembered the night he died.

Mildred and her daughter Francine were Smidgeon's last living relatives. Mildred was her mother's first cousin. She had been in poor health before the shooting, and her son's death had left her weaker than ever.

Francine answered the door.

"Hi, Jo, come on in. Mama will be happy to see you."

"I hope so. I still feel so guilty."

"She doesn't blame you. Hez had been traipsing off to those hills almost all of his life. We know he was the only one you could turn to. It wasn't *you*, Jo, it was that crazy woman, shooting at anything she thought she saw. It's been tough on Mom, but she's still holding her own."

"I appreciate it, Francine. I'll come by and visit more often, I promise."

"We know you've been all busy with the café and such."

Mildred was sitting in her bed, propped up with pillows.

"My sweet, dear Jo. Come here and give your cousin a hug."

After their brief embrace, Smidgeon sat in a chair by the bed. "I'm sorry I haven't visited. I've been feeling guilty about Hezekiah and all. If I hadn't got him to take me—"

Mildred's eyes were filling with tears as she grabbed Smidgeon's hand and said, "Shush your nonsense, Jo. You needed his help, and Hezekiah, well, he loved you and would have given you his left leg if it would help you. You said you needed him, and he was out the door. We all understand. It's been tough, but I know my boy and know he would have gone to help you no matter what. He always helped anybody he could." She dabbed at her eyes with a tissue. "How's your young man, oh, and the café? I hear it is back up and running."

"Sam? He's...uh, we're doing fine. Yes, The Mossback is back, a bit cleaner, but pretty much the same old place. Business as usual."

"What a relief. Joe put his heart and soul into it. I still can't believe everything that crazy woman did." She sobbed as she lingered on the memory of her son. "I need to stop this...I swear I've cried enough for two lifetimes," Mildred said, wiping away another tear. "Now why haven't you come to see your cousin?"

"Like I said...I just didn't know what to say to you."

"You know I always loved you like another daughter. Heck, you and Francine were always like two peas in a pod back when you were youngsters."

"Yes. I remember. I've been silly. I'll keep up, I promise. The reason I called, though, is that I wanted to know something about Dad. Do you remember when he went into the army?"

"Lord, child, it was such a long time ago."

"I know. We found a picture of him from his army days, hidden in the wall. He hardly ever mentioned the war, and I wanted to see if you might remember anything about those days."

"Hard times then. A bunch of local boys joined up right after Pearl Harbor. Straight out of school, most of them. Your dad and Kelvin, and Delbert. I dated Delbert a little back in those days."

Mildred sighed and looked down, "I always wondered what happened to him." She refocused on Smidgeon and said, "Joe and Kelvin were best friends before the war, but when they came back, they were like oil and water."

"Kelvin...you mean Loot?"

"Yes, I always hated that fool nickname. When he came back, he was a shiftless drunk. I heard he mended his ways, but I think deep down, nobody much changes."

"So, they had a falling out?"

"I don't rightly know what happened, but Joe got wounded, and they sent him home. He wouldn't talk about it. Kelvin served until the end of the war. There was definitely some troubles going on between them when he came back. I know Kelvin tried to patch things up with Joe a couple of times, but by then, your daddy had married your mama and started up the café, and I always figured he didn't want nothing to do with a low-life drunk. I never much blamed him."

"I do know Daddy always had a bad taste in his mouth about Loot, and I guess it sort of rubbed off on me."

"Kelvin was always an odd sort of guy, but back before the war, he had a good heart. Alcohol isn't picky. It grabs the good and the bad. Least ways, he wasn't a mean drunk."

"So you think there were any secrets between them?"

"Lordy, child, so many questions," Mildred said with a laugh. "But it's funny you ask. I always had a feeling they both brought some dark secret back from the war. They were as different as night and day after they returned. It went far beyond Kelvin's drinking, if you ask me."

Mildred coughed, and Francine approached the bed. "I think Mama's getting tired."

"Right," Smidgeon said. "I'm sorry. Mildred, you've helped a lot."

Mildred took Smidgeon's hand, "Sweet Jo, I wish I could be more help. It was all so long ago. And so much has happened." She closed her eyes and turned a cheek to her pillow.

Smidgeon kissed her on the forehead and started to leave.

"Wait, honey, there was one odd thing I remember. Something that happened at the café," Mildred said with a start. Smidgeon stopped and turned around.

"At the café?"

"A bunch of rowdies came in one day. I was there having lunch. Old army buddies, I think. Delbert was with them. Last time I ever saw him. He didn't even notice me. There was a guy named Scooter and I remember a quiet guy named Babe, too. At first, they were hooting and hollering and said they wanted to get Loot and all go out and find a bar. They kept trying to get your daddy to go along. I remember them mentioning unfinished business and an acquaintance named 'Digly'—I remember it because they kept saying the name like it was something important. They were so loud! I also recollect something about revenge and some deal that had gone wrong for Delbert and Scooter down in Mexico. I think they were on the run. But your daddy, well, you know he wasn't a drinking man, and once they mentioned the name Digly, Joe changed from being civil and friendly with them to almost angry. He finally chased them all out and told them never to come back. Digly, that was the name. It was so unusual...it sort of stuck in my mind all of these years. Whoever Digly is, your daddy didn't like hearing the name. No, not one bit."

"Did you ask him about it?"

"No, it seemed to be pretty much his business, and I let him keep it to himself. He didn't want those fellows around anymore, so he chased them out. I assume they found Loot and probably did all sorts of carrying on. Never saw any of those three again. No, wait, the quiet one, Babe, he came around one Christmas a while later. I seem to remember him doing some work for Joe. So long ago."

Mildred gently exhaled and put her head back down and whispered to herself again and again as she drifted off to sleep, "Digly...Digly."

Francine tugged at Smidgeon's elbow, and the two women retired to the hall. "Let her sleep. You plum tuckered her out. I don't think I've ever heard her mention any of those last bits."

"I never heard those stories either. I never imagined Daddy and Loot were ever friends."

"Me neither, but folks often get at odds over the years, usually over some foolish thing."

Francine hugged Smidgeon tight.

"Like me, Jo. I admit it. I guess I've been kind of holding Hez's death against you, but no more. He went with you of his own free will, and he always helped anybody he could. He loved you, and he liked Sam a lot, too, looked up to him like a brother. There was no way he wouldn't help you and Sam if he could. It was..." Francine stifled a sob, "*her*, that crazy woman shooting blindly out in the darkness. Odd how it always seems to be a stray bullet that kills somebody close."

"Could have just as easily been me," Smidgeon whispered.

"He worshiped the ground you walked on. You were almost a better sister to him than I was."

39

"Aw, Francine, don't say that."

After a brief cry, they both made their way to the door.

"Don't make yourself so scarce, Jo, you hear?"

Smidgeon hugged her again and said, "I won't."

~ * ~

Sam was home when Smidgeon returned, and he met her at the door.

"Where you been?"

"Oh, I decided I needed to visit my cousin Mildred."

Sam looked down for a second, with a slight frown, "Oh," he said, "...Hez's mom. How's she doing?"

"Weak, but pretty good. We had a nice chat. It was tough. I still feel so guilty about Hezekiah."

"Me too, sweetie," he said and pulled her to him, hugging her tight.

"Thank you, Sam."

"For what?"

"For being so good."

"So good?   I don't know about good, but I'm hungry...what's for dinner?"

"You goof. Sandwich night, I guess, since I didn't cook us anything. Unless you brought something from the restaurant."

"Hah, I called earlier, and you didn't answer, so I figured something was up. I brought us some burgers. They're probably cold."

Smidgeon said, "No matter, I'm hungry enough to eat anything, even a cold burger."

While they ate, she told Sam about her meeting with Mildred.

"So did she have anything more to add to what we already know?"

"Well, she did say Daddy and Loot were good friends growing up, but thought whatever bad blood they had between them must have happened during the war. They joined up together, and Daddy was injured and came back first. By the time Loot came back, things were cool between them."

"So it wasn't just the incident with Slim and Scamp."

"Guess not, but it was surely amplified by any bad feelings they already had."

After they had eaten, Sam said, "don't forget you have a cake in the kitchen. You want me to put some icing on it?"

"I haven't made the icing yet. Let me finish up my dusting and I'll whip some up and finish it."

Sam worked on the dishes while Smidgeon continued dusting. After a few minutes, he heard the sound of glass breaking and a resounding "No!" coming from the living room. He hurried in to see what was wrong.

Smidgeon was crying. "I can't believe I broke Daddy's medal case."

Sam often looked at the small shadowbox frame on one of the shelves. It displayed Joe Toll's Purple Heart and other service medals, all of which were scattered across the floor along with the slivers of broken glass and splintered wood.

"Aw, honey, we can get another frame. I'm sure of it."

"I know, it's just...well, it hurts to think I broke something Daddy put together. I don't know; it makes me feel like I lost another little part of him."

"It's only a thing. The memories are still there...we'll fix it up, good as new."

Sam crouched down and picked up the faded velvet backing and flicked away a few shards of glass.

"Be careful, don't cut yourself."

Sam smirked up at her, "I know, I know, I'm trying to find everything," he said as he started to pick up the medals.

He paused when he spotted something shiny on the floor; it seemed out of place.

He held it up so Smidgeon could see it and asked, "What's this?" It was round and golden and surprisingly heavy for its size.

"Ain't never seen *that*," she said. "What the heck?"

Sam stood and handed it to her. "It's a coin. Gold, I think. It must have been in the back of the frame."

Smidgeon turned the coin around in her hands. "Looks Italian...one hundred *Lire*."

"Why would it be hidden? It has to be worth some money, don't you think?"

"Must have meant something to Daddy. I don't know." Smidgeon handed the coin back to Sam and said, "Well, let's clean this mess up."

Sam wrapped the coin and medals with the velvet and put them in Smidgeon's sock drawer in the bedroom before sweeping the remnants of the frame into a dustpan.

After she had frosted the cake, they both enjoyed a piece and talked about what they had found.

"I was wondering...first, a strange Italian guy shows up asking about my dad, and now we find an Italian coin."

"It's only a coincidence, I'm sure."

She shivered a bit. "I guess you're right."

Five

Smidgeon turned the front door key, and the deadbolt's distinctive sound resonated through the empty restaurant. She beamed as she spun around. "Six weeks!"

Sam was balancing the day's receipts at the cash register. "What?"

"It's been six weeks since we re-opened."

"What's all the shouting about?" Lance asked as he walked in from the kitchen.

"We've been open six weeks now," she said.

Lance whooped and put down a tray of salt and pepper shakers he was carrying. "Six weeks? It's seemed a lot longer. Congratulations!"

Smidgeon hugged Lance. "To all of us! You're a big part of it, too."

"I never much thought I'd like working in a restaurant again, but this has been a good experience for me."

"We should have planned a party or something," Sam joked.

Smidgeon hugged Sam as well. "I remember thinking if we could make it six weeks and still be standing, we'd be all right. When I locked the door, I realized today was the day."

"Why'd you settle on six weeks?" Sam was still busy with his small stacks of cash.

"Don't rightly know. It seemed like a good number. Maybe a throwback to school report cards or something."

"Wish we'd left the grill on," Sam said. "I was joking before, but maybe a little celebration *is* in order, you know?"

Lance said, "The grill *is* on. After Chuy left, I put some foil over it to burn it off a little. A place I worked when I was in high school used to do the same thing, so I do it once a week and scrape it off real good with steel wool."

"Lance, you amaze me sometimes," Smidgeon said. "I can only imagine how good you were at managing the ranch."

"My grandpa Thad always kept after me to stay busy. That's how I found this." He reached into his pocket and pulled out a glittering gold coin.

Sam gasped. "Where'd you find it?" He looked over and saw the shock on Smidgeon's face.

"I was cleaning out one of the kitchen cabinets, you know, like behind the drawers...found it there. It looked like it had been there a while. Don't think anybody had pulled all those drawers out in a really long time."

Sam looked down sheepishly. "Yeah, not something I ever got around to."

Lance guffawed. "Heck, man, I didn't mean you! Anyways, I don't know if it was Loot's or not. It might have predated him, too, but it was definitely hidden." He held the coin up.

"Is it gold?"

"I reckon it is," Lance said, and he started to hand it to Sam. "Figure it's rightly yours since it is from your house."

Sam took the coin and examined it. Smidgeon leaned in for a closer look as well.

Sam murmured, "It definitely looks gold. Italian." He raised one eyebrow as he caught Smidgeon's eye again, and he handed the coin back to Lance, "Finders keepers. It's yours, Lance."

"You sure?"

"Yes, I'm sure. Besides," Sam paused a moment as he looked at Smidgeon again, and she nodded slightly, "we already have one. We found another one exactly like this hidden in a picture frame back at the house."

"No kidding? Tell you what, I'll rustle us up some burgers and let's talk about it."

"Great idea," Smidgeon said. "We'll finish up out here, and then we can eat. Is the fryer still on?"

"Naw. I filtered the grease and shut it off, but I could slap together a couple of salads."

Sam said, "Sounds good to me. Smidgeon?"

"I think I'll just have the burger."

Lance nodded and disappeared into the kitchen.

"What do you think?" Sam asked.

Smidgeon frowned. "I don't know what to think, but there must be something to it, some connection. There has to be. I feel it, you know? It has to be part of the connection between Loot and my dad."

"Yeah, I was thinking the same thing. Let's hurry this work up before Lance brings the food."

While Smidgeon finished sweeping the floor and arranging the tables and chairs; Sam worked on the day's receipts. By the time they were finished, Lance appeared at the kitchen door with a tray of food.

"Lance, what have you done with them? They look wonderful."

"Added some of your great pimento cheese, a little guacamole, and topped it off with some hot peppers and bacon," he said.

Smidgeon brought them all soft drinks, and they sat at one of the tables.

Lance held up his glass and said, "To six weeks!"

They touched glasses, and started to eat.

Smidgeon took a big bite and looked up, surprised. "Lance, I might need to put you on the grill. I have to say, *this* is the best-danged burger I've ever eaten!"

"I think we should put it on the menu," Sam said.

"Maybe we will," Smidgeon said.

Lance struggled to talk through a mouthful of food, "Well, I don't think I'm quite as efficient as Chuy." He swallowed and changed the subject," So, you have another Italian gold coin?"

"Yeah. Smidgeon's dad had a small frame with his war medals in it. The other day, it fell off the shelf and broke, but while cleaning it up, we found a similar coin. It must have been hidden inside the frame." Sam had been speaking, but Smidgeon nodded her head in agreement as she chewed another mouthful of her burger.

"Can't help thinking about the strange little dude who's been nosing around. You know, Italian coins, Italian dude." Lance took another bite and pensively chewed.

Sam said, "We thought the same thing. Probably a coincidence."

"I don't know. Coincidences seem to abound in your life, Sam."

"Welcome to my world," Smidgeon laughed.

~ * ~

Three wispy figures hovered nearby watching Smidgeon, Sam, and Lance talk.

"Coincidence! Hah. Loot, the boy thinks it's a *coincidence.*"

Loot nodded. "Yeah, Slim, it's been a slow job getting them on the right track, but I'm learning...I'm learning—"

Scamp chortled, "I thought she was going to jump clear out of her skin when you tipped that there frame off'n the shelf."

"Warn't no other way. She got ever so close, but never seemed to break it on her own even though I kept whispering into her ear, trying to sway her."

Scamp giggled again. "Yeah, I've had an easier time trying to get Lance to do stuff. He's a good boy, always did take direction well."

"Still don't rightly know what this is all about, Loot, but it's a heckuva lot more fun than just being dead," Slim said. "I figgered we was gone for good after we helped them with that crazy woman at the mine."

"I don't know...got me a feeling this is what we need to be doing. It's like it's something I forgot about when I was living, but—"

Scamp hovered closer to Loot. "So you think this's maybe why we gots pulled back this time?"

"Maybe, maybe...I'm thinking we get drawn to them when they're going to need our help, but I don't know exactly why yet."

~ * ~

"So, what do we have?" Lance said. "Two gold coins from Italy, and some Italian guy snooping around. 'Course we have no way to connect them."

"Yeah, but we also know Loot and Smidgeon's father joined the army together and this Italian, what was his name?"

"Cerides, I think," Lance said.

"Cerides indicated he knew them from their army days."

Lance swallowed his last bit of burger. "And they both served in North Africa?"

Sam tapped the rim of his glass, deep in thought. "Yeah. If they joined together, they most likely served together. We know Joe was wounded in North Africa and we know they were together for a picture. And Cerides mentioned North Africa, too."

"I don't know where all Loot ended up going, but my daddy never got any further than North Africa. And the note," Smidgeon added. "Don't forget the note."

"Note? What note?" Lance asked.

Sam continued his tapping, "Remember the cigarette tin?"

"Oh, that's right! The Lucky Strike box from inside the wall. Something about south of Valentine."

Sam mused, "Might be time to take a little road trip."

"Café's doing pretty good, but we can't all go," Smidgeon said. "I don't have Hez to call in to help anymore."

"Well," Lance said, "At least one of us could take the drive."

"A lone black stranger on a deserted west Texas back road probably isn't a good idea," Sam said.

"I could do it," Smidgeon said.

"You know anybody over there?" Sam asked.

"South of Valentine? Not really. I know of them. Miller Ranch and Nancy Ann Ranch, and 'old Brite' road must mean Brite Ranch. All of those are old spreads...they've been there forever. But it's far enough away...I don't know any of the ranchers."

"I dunno, I'm thinking it might be dangerous for a single woman, too," Lance said. "I'd feel better if you went, Sam."

Smidgeon frowned. "I don't like it. Sam's luck has to be running thin. The last time he did something like this, he was kidnapped. Right under your nose, too, Lance."

"Well, I doubt anything like that could happen this time, and I *am* the one with the most experience in this sort of thing. As for luck, I think I have it covered." His mouth curled into a sly grin.

Smidgeon glared at him. "You know I hate that darned thing!"

"I didn't even mention it," Sam said with a laugh.

"I guess I'm not in on this joke," Lance said.

"It's about a little good luck piece of mine. I'll tell you about it some time," Sam said. "But, seriously, I think, if anybody is going to go out there, it's got to be me. At least the first time, just to see what we're dealing with. Poking around is one thing I know how to do."

He was interrupted by headlights in the parking lot. Smidgeon stood up and looked out the window.

"Sheriff's car. Probably Clay, wondering why we're still here."

As the deputy approached the door, she unlocked it and let him in.

"Evening folks, everything okay?"

49

"Hey, Clay," Sam said. "We decided to have a little celebratory meal...it's our six week anniversary of being open."

"Well, I thought I had better check it out. There's been some stranger going around asking questions...a little guy with a funny beard. Have you seen him?"

"Yeah, he came here. Seemed harmless enough," Sam said. "Wanted to know about Smidgeon's dad."

"Came out to where I'm living, too, looking for Loot," Lance said.

"Interesting. Have any idea why?"

"Not really. Said it had something to do with the war." Lance rubbed the back of his head.

"What war?" Clay asked.

"World War Two. Both Loot and Joe Toll were veterans," Sam said.

"After all this time? Well, if he comes back, call us. We'd sure like to get to the bottom of this. It's probably nothing, but we don't want to take anything for granted, especially with crazy outsiders. Tourists passing through don't much bother me, but strangers hanging around asking questions? Well, I have a few questions of my own I want to ask."

Smidgeon unlocked the door and said, "Thank you, Clay. Have a safe night."

"You, too, Miss Smidgeon, Y'all don't stay here alone too long, you hear? Good evening, folks."

"Things must be looking up...he didn't focus on me at all," Lance snickered.

Sam replied, "When you first came out here people always concentrated on you for some reason."

"Especially the police. I ain't complaining, mind you, but it does get tiresome. I guess Clay is getting used to having me around."

"This is no laughing matter," Smidgeon said. "If that Italian guy comes in here again, I want to know about it."

"Yes, Miss Smidgeon," Lance said. "He did seem pretty harmless, but underneath the surface, well, something didn't seem quite right about him. He was polite and all, but, well, he just seemed off somehow."

"We'll have to keep an eye out," Sam said as he stood and gathered the dishes. "I guess we better clean up and clear out like Clay said. Tomorrow morning is going to come way too early."

~ * ~

Back at the house, Sam had gone to bed almost as soon as they got home. Smidgeon sat for a long time with the cat purring in her lap.

"Somehow all of this fits together, but I can't quite figure out how the pieces go," she muttered to herself.

She got up and rummaged in a hall closet until she found a tattered cardboard box. Her mind had turned to it when they found the other items, but she had stifled the impulse. She had a lot of practice ignoring the painful memories the box contained. She brought it to the kitchen and opened it, revealing a variety of folders, papers, pictures, and quite a few letters.

"Daddy," she murmured as she fingered the contents, remembering the days after his death when she threw almost every memento of her father into the box before packing it away.

"Smidgeon?" Sam was blinking at her in the hall doorway. "Can't sleep?"

"Aw, you know how I get sometimes."

"What you got there?"

"Box of Daddy's papers and such. After he died, I barely glanced at things before I stuffed them in this box, and I've just let it sit at the bottom of the closet ever since. It's been a lot of years. I was wondering if any of this might shed some light on either the stranger or the coins we found."

"Seems to be a pretty tall order for one box." Sam laughed.

He walked over and hugged her. She closed her eyes and relished the warmth of his body against hers. She shivered as he ran his fingers up and down her back before breaking the hug. He kissed her, and for a moment she was overwhelmed with the closeness she felt for him.

Sam yawned, "So, why don't you come on back to bed? We have to get up early."

"Every danged day," she said. "Sometimes I regret rebuilding the place. Up early every day and never time to take a vacation."

"We've talked about it—"

"Sure, we always say we'll do it when we get ahead enough and we feel like we can close up for a week or two. But I've been running the Mossback for so long, and that day never seems to come."

"I know, but business has been good since we reopened. We'll get there, I promise." Sam poked at the items in the box. "So what *is* all this stuff?"

"Just Daddy's old stuff. A few pictures. He never was much for pictures, not even of me. He had the same problem, no time. The Mossback *was* his life."

"At least he closed on Sundays."

"Mama insisted."

"We could try...it would give us a day off."

"I've thought about it, but I've got mixed feelings. Travelers need a place to stop and eat. And really, Sundays are a big day for us."

"I know they are. But at least you go on to church."

"And Father Charlie asks about you every week."

"I never should have told him I was raised a Catholic." Sam drew Smidgeon into another hug. "And what does he say about us living in sin?"

"Nothing," she smirked as she pushed him away, "but that don't mean he's not thinking it."

Something in the box caught Sam's eye. "What are these letters? They're old."

"Haven't looked through them yet."

Sam pulled out several of the envelopes. "Postmarks from the late forties and early fifties. Here's a couple in the sixties."

"Wow, three cent stamps!"

"I know. Rates keep going up and up."

Sam opened one. "Hard to read this handwriting. From somebody named Delbert." As Sam squinted at the faded pencil marks, he mumbled, "talks about 'it' a lot. Nothing specific. 'Got to do something about it'...here's a mention of 'if he shows up' and some mention of threats. Oh, here he mentions something about Babe, I can't quite make it out."

Sam opened another envelope. "Delbert again. At least he wrote in ink this time." He winked at Smidgeon. "Looks like more of the same. Something here about some deal in Mexico with Scooter. Oh, and mentions 'Babe' again. Another mention of the mysterious 'he' being on his trail and 'wants his share.' Here's a couple from Babe, rambling about something being 'not quite right.'"

Smidgeon grabbed the letters and put them back in the envelopes and stuffed them in the box.

"Enough of this, Sam. I should never have thought about this box. I was hoping it might have some answers, but now I'm more scared than ever."

"Still, who the heck are these people? Delbert, Scooter, Babe."

"Delbert was from around here. My cousin told me about him. I have no idea about the others except maybe they were army buddies. Now I'll never get to sleep. I may never sleep again," Smidgeon said as she sat and put her forehead on the table.

"Remember the note from Loot? He mentioned something about his money belonging to some army buddies running away from some failed scam in Mexico."

"I mean it, Sam. I've had enough for tonight." She grabbed the box and put it back in the closet.

"You know, you're cute when you're freaked out," he said, gently moving the stray strand of hair that always seemed to fall across her face.

She shivered again as his finger barely touched her skin. She pulled him to her in a tight embrace and whispered in his ear, "I think we had better head down the hall."

"I thought you'd never ask."

Six

Smidgeon pulled a fresh batch of Apple Thangs from one of the ovens. The fruity pastries were a weekend staple at The Mossback Café.

"Smells good," Lance said. "I surely do love them Apple Thangs."

"Now you know how they got their name. On Sundays, I almost can't make enough of them, especially with you trying to filch them!"

She didn't know where her mother had found the original recipe, or even what they were originally called, but she knew better than to take them off the menu.

Lance grinned as he chewed a portion of one. "Sort of a cross between a muffin and an apple fritter or something."

"Save them for the customers," she said.

Sam brought a tub of dishes from the dining room and set it near the sink.

"I think we're past the rush. Maybe it's a good time for me to head down the road toward Valentine. You sure you're okay with me driving out there this morning?"

"I don't know. It's only you and me and Lance. I never know what a Sunday's going to bring, customer-wise."

"That's for sure," Lance said as he pretended to reach for another Apple Thang.

"I told you...those are only for the *paying* customers!" Smidgeon had her hands on her hips.

Lance snickered. "I know...I was just yanking yer chain."

Sam laughed as he gathered up a bag of trash. "Maybe tomorrow would be better?"

"I don't know why, but you're right; we aren't near as busy on Monday. It might be better, Sam."

"Plus we'll have more help," Lance said.

"But you should get out there early," Smidgeon added.

"Okay, delay one more day and head out really early," he said as he reached to open the door. "Probably nothing out south of Valentine but scrub and brush."

As the door closed behind him and he approached the dumpster, Sam was startled by a sudden voice. "Mr. Milton?"

Sam dropped the bag and spun around. It was Indigo Cerides, the small goateed Italian man.

"You ought to know better than to sneak up behind a person," he said.

Cerides sneered. "I'm sorry if I startled you. I was hoping we might have a short conversation."

"The police were asking about you, I think they'd like to have a short conversation with *you*," Sam retorted.

"I've done nothing wrong, Mr. Milton. I've only been making a few inquiries regarding old friends."

"Everyone around here is a bit suspicious of strangers poking around."

"Ah, yes, I heard about the recent unfortunate events. You and your supposed lost gold mine, I believe. It is of no concern to me."

"Well, I have work to do. What do you want to know?"

"You were friends with Loot Meldings, correct? Everyone says so. He even left you his house after he passed away, no?"

"Yes, it's no secret, we were friends. You went out to his house, said you knew him in the war."

"Ah, you have been talking with the black gentleman. Yes. Loot and others befriended me when I was at, er, how do you Americans say, at a loose end?"

"So you knew Joe and Loot in North Africa. Were you in the army, too?"

"In a manner of speaking, I was indeed a soldier, but perhaps not as you are thinking. I was but a boy, a conscript into the crumbling remains of Il Duce's forces in the Northern African campaigns. Rescued, as it were, by your Loot and his friends. As I said, I was befriended and traveled with them for a brief time. It was a better option for me. I had been stunned and rendered unconscious...left for dead by my comrades as they retreated. I hid for a while, foraging for what food I could find. German forces had moved in but I knew they would provide no shelter for me, and by that time I would have been treated as a deserter by my own people."

"So what does any of this have to do with me? Loot and Joe are both dead. His daughter said Joe never talked about the war. Loot didn't either, at least not to me."

"And you've found nothing related to their service?"

57

"Nothing but pictures and old uniform medals. What are you looking for?"

"Something that belongs to me."

"You would have to be more specific."

"Yes, but I am afraid I cannot, as you say, be more specific at this time."

"Look, Mr. Cerides, am I remembering your name correctly?"

"*Si*, Indigo Cerides."

"I did you a favor by not giving the sheriff your name. I don't know what this is about, but I'm sure the answers you're looking for aren't around here anymore. I think it would be best if you just move on. If I see you again, I'm afraid I'll have to tell the police."

"There is no need to bother them, Mr. Milton. Perhaps you are right. It seems you don't know anything of interest to me."

"Good, then we understand each other."

"Perhaps one more question. What is it you expect to find south of Valentine?"

Sam felt his face flush. Cerides had apparently been listening at the door. His heart was racing, and he stammered as he answered, "S-something to do with the café, private business."

"Ah, yes. Odd location for a business transaction though, no?" The contemptuous smile behind the scraggly goatee unnerved Sam.

"I have work to do...I suggest you leave."

"Until next time, Mr. Milton."

"I doubt there will be a next time. There's nothing for you here."

"Perhaps not. Ah, but we shall see, yes?"

Sam brushed past the smallish man and was surprised to feel hard sinew and muscle on the diminutive frame as he reached for the trash bag. Cerides backed away slowly as Sam deposited the bag and turned to return to the kitchen. As he opened the door, he glanced back, but Cerides was gone.

The smell of bacon snapped Sam back to reality.

"You ain't smoking behind the new dumpster, are you?" Lance was laughing. "You sure were out there a while."

"Ran into our Italian friend; Cerides."

"What? Again?"

"Yeah," Sam said. "Don't tell Smidgeon about this. I pretty much told him to forget everything and head out of town."

"Did you tell him the police were looking for him?"

"Yes, but he didn't seem to care. Found out something else interesting...he wasn't in the army, at least not in *our* army."

"No?"

"I think he was like a deserter or something. Said he was 'befriended' by Joe and Loot, and he's looking for something he says belongs to him."

"Interesting," Lance said, as he flipped bacon slices on the grill. He stopped and looked at Sam. "But I don't like it, Sam. There's something not quite right about all of this."

"I know. I go out the door with the trash bag, and suddenly Cerides pops up? I almost jumped out of my skin."

"I'll keep an eye out. I don't like the idea of somebody lurking around back there. Ain't no way we can protect ourselves if..." Lance mashed down hard on the bacon with his big kitchen spatula, "...well, if he or someone else was up to no good." He walked over and locked the door. "Small town or no small town, I'm keeping this door locked."

"Really?"

Lance returned to his griddle and flipped another slice of bacon. "And. I'm thinking this trip out south of Valentine isn't a good idea either."

"Maybe not, but I think I've got to check it out anyway. I'll be okay."

Lance smirked and continued to work on his bacon. "No, sir, uh-uh, don't like it at all."

~ * ~

Sam and Smidgeon arrived at the café early the next day.

"Hate this place when it's dark like this," she said.

"Every place is spooky in the dark."

"There's more to this, Sam. I had the same feeling before the fire, you know, like something's getting ready to happen. What do they call that?"

Sam pulled her into a hug. "Foreboding?"

"Right. I have a sense of foreboding. I don't want you to go out there. Let's forget it."

"What? Don't be silly. I probably won't find a thing. Anyway, I'm sure I'll be okay. Don't you want to know if the note meant anything?"

She stuck out her bottom lip in a fake pout, and he kissed her forehead.

She sighed loudly. "I guess you're right. Well, at least help me get the place ready to open before you go."

They turned to the window when they saw headlights in the parking lot.

"Must be Chuy," Sam said. "Let's get to work."

Later, the aroma of bacon and coffee filled the air and Smidgeon turned the "Open" sign to face outside.

Sam removed his apron, "I guess I had better head out before it gets too late."

"Sam, I changed my mind again. Don't go."

"Don't be silly. I can take care of myself. It's best to get this over with."

"I know, I know."

"I'll be fine," he said. "I'll probably be back before lunch."

"You've got the shovel?"

"Yes, stuffed into the back of the clunker."

"You remember the note?"

"Miller Ranch Road then sixteen miles out, Old Brite."

"You know where it is?"

"I asked Billy over at the garage. He makes tows all around. Miller Ranch Road goes south just outside Valentine and becomes Old Brite. He said it's a long rough road, but it's made him some good money with wheel and axle damage."

"Some of those old roads are pretty ragged. People drive up and down them all the time, though."

Sam kissed her and said, "I better get out there."

Smidgeon nuzzled into his neck and reached up to kiss him again.

"You be careful, you hear me? Now that I've got you, I don't aim to lose you."

"I'll be careful. You don't have to worry about me."

Seven

Mulvihill "Mule" Hollis sat in his car and continued to peruse the lonely intersection of two farm-to-market roads. He sipped at a cup of tepid coffee and considered his options as he watched a battered Pinto pass by the dusty crossing and drive southwest, heading out of town.

"Dang, do people still drive Pintos?" He chuckled and resumed his reconnaissance. "I can see why Cerides would pick a place like Imperial," he mused to himself. When he first arrived, Mule wondered if the town had perhaps been decimated by a tornado or something, but the mixture of old and new buildings indicated this small town was naturally flat and desolate. But people lived there; there was even a high school. Of course, he hadn't seen a soul since he pulled into town, except for the lone Pinto.

He looked down at his map. "Only about thirty miles from Interstate 10," he muttered.

He checked his small notebook. He had received a tip informing him an older Buick sedan would meet with another car at 7 a.m., in the parking lot of the high school. From this vantage point, he could see intersecting traffic from both highways. The high school was on FM 11. There were few obstructions, so he had a clear view beyond the intersection to the high school. His information indicated a supposed money exchange. Mule knew one of Indigo Cerides favorite businesses in the US was money laundering.

Mule didn't expect to see the man himself. His criminal operations in Mexico were extensive, and he rarely ventured forth on petty errands.

"I couldn't get that lucky," he mumbled.

Mule Hollis had worked as a private investigator since retiring as a law enforcement officer. His current contract was with the Mexican Federal Police. Cerides had undertakings on both sides of the border, and they had hired Mule to help them track the criminal's movements in the US. He looked over the dossier provided by his employer.

The Mexicans were not thorough; there were many vague references in the report, which Mule thought odd, considering the fact Cerides had done quite a bit of time in Mexican prisons. Cerides was thought to be approximately sixty years old, born in the early 1920s. His nationality was also vague; different documents indicated Italy or Cyprus as a birthplace. His tracked criminal activity in Mexico seemed to begin in the late forties.

"A bad guy for over thirty-five years," he mused. "Someone is usually either really good at it or dead after such a long time."

63

Mule had yet to run a check on Cerides' record in the US because he knew he would need to enlist the help of local law enforcement contacts. He wanted to save such a big favor for a more proper time; namely, when he could connect the man to specific crimes. If things worked out, he hoped to collect from both the Americans and the Mexicans. As near as he could tell, Cerides had flown under the radar in Texas, at least so far, but he also heard the man had suddenly become much more active on this side of the border.

"Buick," he whispered to himself; he pulled out his camera.

Using the telephoto lens in the viewfinder, he watched it pull into the parking lot. Moments later, a black Chevy pulled next to it with the drivers' side windows facing each other; the cars were inches apart. Mule clicked the shutter again and again as he watched packets pass back and forth. He made sure he got both license plates in the photos as well.

"Probably stolen," he muttered. "Hell, the cars are probably stolen, too."

Automobile theft wasn't his problem. He wanted to follow the Chevy. *That* was his target.

Both cars sped off in opposite directions. Mule put the camera aside, started his car and followed, making sure to keep the black Chevy in view.

"They'll make me," he said to himself, "but it's probably why Cerides set this up in such an open area. Ain't nobody else around, so I'm sure to stand out like a sore thumb."

~ * ~

Sam felt refreshed as the early morning air whooshed through the windows of his old Volkswagen.

"The car's a bit musty," Sam said to himself. "It feels good to blow it out."

The engine sputtered a little as he tried to accelerate down US Highway 90, but once he was up to speed, the car settled into a comfortable cruise.

There was not much to look at. US 90 paralleled the railroad tracks, and except for an occasional house in the distance and the barbed wire fences, the road stretched into an uncertain horizon. Sam sipped coffee and glanced out at the flat scrubland vistas on both sides of the car; a sprinkling of distant hilltops broke through in the distance.

"Just like old times," he said over the constant wind noise.

He was reminded of his many long drives in search of the Sublett mine. According to the rumors floating around town, Tim MacGregg was digging out the location Sam had found with heavy equipment.

"He should have hired professionals to scout it out before digging. Although I found traces, I never found anything good, and I doubt he will either." Sam shook his head. "Still, it's a shame." He had invested ten years of his life to his search, including two years on the spot MacGregg was intent on excavating. The terrain in the Arroyo was treacherous, and he'd heard the operation was plagued with problems.

"*His* problems," Sam thought to himself.

Suddenly he saw a group of buildings coming at him fast and he slowed down.

"It must be Valentine," he whispered.

He was only a little over thirty miles away from Van Horn and found Valentine to be a tiny collection of houses and other small structures. To his city eyes, it was hardly a municipality at all, more a conglomeration of dwellings, but in the sparse expanse of Texas, any accumulation of life qualified as a town. He was almost all the way through the place before he remembered his instructions.

"Head to the far end of Valentine," Billy had said, "and the road right before the house with a windmill is Miller Ranch. It's a straight shot south. It ain't clear where it becomes Old Brite, but it's pretty much the same road."

"That must be it," he grumbled as he saw a weather-worn shack with a windmill alongside. He slowed and pulled onto the graded road. It looked as if it were sometimes blocked off with fencing but, thankfully, it was open this morning.

Sam glanced at the odometer and made a mental note of the mileage.

"Sixteen miles," he reminded himself.

The road was rough, but it looked like it was regularly maintained. Sam kept his pace slow because the car was kicking up a lot of dust. He remembered using dust clouds to alert himself to approaching vehicles in his many forays into the wilderness to search for the mine. The flat road stretched ahead of him, the landscape featureless except for some faint bumps of mountains in the distance.

There was nothing to see out there except an occasional path branching off going who knew where. There were also cutouts angled into the roadbed almost like exit ramps. Sam had seen those before and once asked a rancher about them.

"They help channel off runoff when it rains...keeps the roadbed from eroding too much and allows more of the rain to feed the land," the rancher had said.

He speculated about the people who regularly drove on this road and commiserated with them because the jarring of the rough roadbed wore on his nerves. He looked down at the odometer again.

"Only two miles!"

He tried to coax a little more speed out of his aging VW, but he worried at the wear-and-tear on his tires and suspension and backed off a little. He knew he was going to have to be patient.

"Ranchers are used to this road so they can likely go a little faster, but I don't want to chance a broken axle," he muttered.

There were no markings on the occasional turnoffs, and Sam wondered to himself how people knew where to go. He reasoned they were aware of subtle differences in the landscape. There *were* recent tire tracks, so it was evident people did drive out there. He also pondered another question as he drove: What would he say if he were confronted by someone while driving this desolate road? When he had asked at the garage about the location of the street, Billy had shared a tidbit about the Brite Ranch.

"There was a famous Mexican bandit raid down there back around 1920," he had said. "Killed three people!"

It wasn't a surprise to Sam since he had read about *villista* raiders during the Mexican revolution. Border attacks were not uncommon.

"Guess I could say I'm hunting history," he murmured to himself, "and wanted to see the location of the famous raid." If he were asked to leave, he figured he'd turn around and head back.

"My VW stands out like a sore thumb out here," he added. "But it gives some credence to the notion I might just be a wayward tourist."

He noted the mileage again. He had gone almost a quarter of the way. He passed what looked like a sort of corral, probably a way-station for loading cattle, he thought to himself. But for the most part, the only breaks in the monotony were the frequent turnoffs. He reached down and grabbed a gallon water bottle he had brought and sipped from it. The dust and the strain were getting to him as the miles ticked off.

A truck approached from the south, kicking up a powdery cloud in his path. He rolled up his windows and watched the driver as they approached each other. The man lazily raised a forefinger from the steering wheel in the standard west Texas wave, and Sam returned it like nothing was out of the ordinary. He glanced at his rearview mirror, making sure the truck disappeared into the dust swirls in his wake. Sam rolled his windows down again as the dust settled, but a faint hint of powder coated his nose and mouth, and he lifted his water bottle for another soothing drink.

After about fifteen miles, he noted a larger turnoff to the right and saw a severe gash cut into the countryside; he recognized the outline of what looked like a landing strip.

"Out here?" he said to himself, then he remembered Lucius MacGregg's plane and realized it wasn't unusual for owners of remote ranches to use airplanes. He assumed this meant he was close to a ranch headquarters house or something. Sam hoped he would find what he was looking for soon.

Ahead, he could see his road was about to be divided by a sizeable triangle, what would have been called a median in the city. Sam remembered the triangular shape scribbled on the note and assumed this had to be what it meant. He had driven almost exactly sixteen miles from the turnoff. He eased to the side of the graded road and let the haze settle before exiting the clunker. He pulled out his wallet and slid it under the seat. "Old habits die hard when prowling around in the desert," he quipped.

Outside the car, he listened for a minute. There was no sound but a slight breeze and a chirp or two of birds. It was a bright, quiet morning. He hoped he'd be able to hear someone coming long before he saw them. He walked around the perimeter of the triangle, examining the ground. The spot wasn't big, but except for rocks and some dry scrub, there wasn't anything out of the ordinary. He was used to searching for something that might not be obvious and was again reminded of his search for the clues to Slim's riddle while he looked for the Sublett mine.

"Gotta remember the note," he muttered, "it should be along over here."

He looked around again, slowly walking, examining the periphery.

"I guess it should be almost due southwest; it's how it was marked. Whoever might have buried something here probably wouldn't want to make it too noticeable."

Sam retrieved his compass and shovel and eased around the edge until he found what he figured must be a southwestern point and began to dig. The ground was hard

"I should have brought a pick," he said, grimacing as he tried to force the leading edge of his spade into the hard dirt, finally creating a small hole. As he reached a depth of about six inches or so, he widened the gap, gradually picking at the sides to enlarge it until it was about two feet across before he started chipping down again. The hole was about a foot deep when he heard a faint sound of metal on metal.

"Bingo."

He dropped to his hands and knees and scraped at the ground until his fingers ached, and slowly the earth gave up its secret. It was green, red, and gold.

"Another Lucky Strike box!"

As he examined it, he realized the arid climate had done its job; the box seemed fully intact.

Sam opened it and found a piece of paper wrapped in three plastic bags. He unfolded the paper and read:

"Duke Chapel—Savonarola—lower back."

Sam folded the paper and put it back in the box. "Duke Chapel?" he intoned. "And what the heck is Savonarola?"

He looked around as if to find an answer from his surroundings, but the warm breeze yielded no secrets. He was alone except for the solitary hawk soaring high overhead. There were no cars and no other sounds except the wind. He dropped to his knees and began to fill in the hole.

"Best get on my way before someone comes by," he mumbled.

He slipped the box under the driver's seat before he started the car, turned it around, and began driving north again.

"I don't know what to make of it, but at least I found *something*. It's definitely weird."

His return trip was uneventful except for a different truck passing him, heading south. He returned the predictable index finger wave and kept on his way. Eventually, he saw the outlines of the windmill, and he knew he was close to US 90.

As Sam began to brake, he noticed a car parked toward the left on what appeared to be a cut-through from the highway. A man was leaning against the fender, staring down the road in his direction. He slowed as he approached and the figure waved at him through the settling clouds of road dust. Sam assumed the man had car trouble, so he pulled over. The car was a battered and rusty Ford Pinto, and the outline of the figure came into focus as he pulled close. It was Cerides. He was holding a gun.

"Ah, welcome, Mr. Milton." His scraggly goatee betrayed a malicious smile. "I am so glad you could join me. Did you find what you were looking for?"

"I don't know what you're talking about. I was running an errand."

Cerides shook his head, "You must think I am a fool," Cerides said as he stooped to look into the car, still holding the gun on Sam. "I see a dirty shovel. Burying a body perhaps?"

Sam flushed. "What do you want?"

"Ah, there is much that I want, but we can leave such things for later. Get out. Please." Cerides waved his gun for emphasis and opened the driver's door. He waved the gun again. "My car, please. You will drive. I will direct, yes? Now, out!"

Sam did as he was told and got out of his car. Cerides stood beyond an arm's length, knowing the gun gave him the advantage. Sam decided to bide his time. He locked the door as he got out, thankful he had already rolled up the windows during the dusty ride.

"What about my car?"

"Ah, yes, your cute little commercial tribute to Herr Hitler. Leave it."

Cerides directed Sam to the driver's seat of his blue Pinto, and he got in the passenger seat. As Sam started the engine, he managed a sidelong glare at Cerides, who kept the firearm trained on Sam's head.

"Is a good American car, not too big, but, thankfully not German," he said, almost spitting disdain as the last word left his mouth.

"Where are we going?"

"I will direct you; we have many miles to go. Head east for now, that way," he said, pointing momentarily with the gun. "Relax and drive. I hear you like to drive these long Texas highways."

Eight

"Always feels good," Lance said to himself as he flipped the closed sign in the café window. "Some of these days are way too long."

He busied himself with the final duties of closing the restaurant and ran through the mental checklists he had devised to keep himself organized.

"Let's see, the salt and pepper shakers are done, the ketchup is filled and put away, the napkins are stocked, the coffee is set up for the morning..."

"Who you talking to, Mr. Lance?"

"Just me, Chuy."

Chuy laughed. "Like Mr. Sam, he's always yakking to himself about something."

"I guess we're both pretty comfortable in our own heads."

"Hah. Maybe. I'm all finished up in the kitchen, so I guess I'll be going now, unless you need me for something else."

"That's fine, Chuy," he said.

Some lights flashed in the parking lot as he said that, and he turned to look out.

Chuy noticed it, too. "Miss Smidgeon," he said. "You expecting her?"

"Not really, but sometimes she comes to help close."

Lance let Chuy out and held the door for Smidgeon. Chuy waved at them both as he drove away.

"Is Sam here?" she asked as she approached the front door.

"No, ma'am. I figured he finished up his chore and headed to the house." He locked the door behind her.

"It's been over thirteen and a half hours, Lance."

"How far is Valentine?" Lance asked, scratching his chin.

"About forty miles."

"And how far did he need to go once he got there?"

"Sixteen more miles, according to the note."

Lance waved Smidgeon toward a table and held a chair for her before sitting across from her.

"Maybe he had some car trouble. He don't call his car 'The Clunker' for nothing. Never much trusted them vee-dubs."

"Those roads out around those ranches can be pretty rough. They look deserted, but people drive on them pretty regularly. I'm sure if he had car trouble somebody would have picked him up. He'd have called by now."

"Seems so," Lance said. He rubbed a temple with one hand as he furrowed his brow. "I'm thinking maybe we should go out there."

"With night coming on? There ain't nothing in Valentine. It's a tiny place. They'd roll up the sidewalks in the evenings if they had any. And the land out south of there where Sam was headed would be black as coal at night."

More headlights flashed on the walls. Smidgeon stood up to glance out the window and said, "Sheriff. That can't be good." She sat down hard, stared straight ahead, and with a trembling voice said, "Lance, can you get the door?"

Lance felt his heart begin to race as he limped to the door and unlocked it. It was Clay, the sheriff's deputy.

"Evening, Lance," he said, and his eyes darted over toward the table, "Oh, and Jo. Good. You guys are closing up for the night, I guess."

"Yeah," Lance said.

"Sam here?" Clay asked.

"What's wrong?" she asked.

"Presidio County Sheriff's office found his car—"

Lance interrupted, "Near Valentine?"

Clay jerked his head toward Lance. "Yes, on the edge of town. What's going on? It's obvious you both know something's up."

Lance motioned to the table. "Have a seat, Clay. As a matter of fact, we were just talking about Sam."

At the table, Clay looked at both of them in turn before he started talking. "So, again, what's going on?"

"We found a hidden box during the renovation," Smidgeon said. "We didn't think much about it until recently when we found something else at the house, hidden in an old picture frame. The first box had a note that mentioned a spot south of Valentine, out Old Brite Road."

Clay sighed and shook his head. "You people and your mysterious goings on."

Lance spoke up, "Hey, Clay, this ain't like the shootings out at the mine. Ain't like it at all. Fact is, we didn't know what to make of the danged note, but Sam, well, he decided to go check things out."

"So he heads out into the boondocks south of Valentine, and now his car is abandoned there. Was it someplace he could walk? I mean, could he be out hiking in the scrub or something? Like maybe he's lost out there?"

"Note's at the house," Smidgeon said, "but it only mentioned going down Old Brite sixteen miles."

"I can't believe you've got me mixed up in another one of your crazy capers." Clay took out a handkerchief and nervously wiped sweat off his face. "Well, it's likely nothing. At least I hope so. When did he leave?"

"This morning about eight," Smidgeon said.

"We generally wait twenty-four hours before we really start worrying. I reckon Sam will show up before too long. But Presidio wants to know about the car."

"Maybe I should go down there tomorrow and get it. He has a spare key at the house," she said.

"Best wait and see if we hear from him," Clay stood and continued, "You know, in case ... well, anyway, let me know if he shows up and I'll radio it in."

As Lance walked Clay to the door, the deputy glanced at Smidgeon and whispered to Lance, "You don't think maybe he's got some girl over toward Valentine or Marfa do you? Wouldn't be the first time I've seen—"

"No," Lance interrupted. "I'm sure this is nothing like that."

"Well, okay," Clay said. He turned to Smidgeon and said aloud, "I'm sure it's nothing, Jo. I'll come by tomorrow, and we'll figure it out. Sam will have likely shown up by then."

Smidgeon didn't raise her head; she responded with a weak wave of her hand.

Lance locked the door and returned to the table and took Smidgeon's hand in both of his.

"You best get on home. I agree with Clay...Sam will be back soon, and we'll all have something to laugh about."

"I don't think so. Something is wrong. I feel it. Sam's in big trouble. I knew it the night he disappeared out at the mine, and I know it now." She let go of Lance's grip and stood, slapping her palms on the table.

"I going to go grab the key and get his car."

"But Clay said..." Lance started.

"I don't care. I think Sam drove down that road and found something...then somebody took it or him. We'll be weeks waiting for the police to figure out anything. They don't get excited until they find a body. No way I'm waiting for them."

"I haven't even closed out the register yet," he said.

"Leave it," she said, "Let's go. You follow me to my house."

"Can I at least run by my house and let the dog out?"

"Yes, then drive over to meet me."

~ * ~

As she sped home, Smidgeon's mind raced, thinking of all the bad things that could have happened to Sam. She imagined him bleeding to death out in the desert with no one to help him.

"Why did I let him do this alone? I must have been crazy."

At the house, she found Sam's spare key. He had given it to her when he first moved in. Every time she thought of him, her eyes started to tear up, but she stopped and set her mind on what she needed to do.

"No, not now," she said to herself, fighting back against the dread and fear welling up in her heart. "I can cry when I have something to cry about and the time to do it. Sam needs me right now."

The cat curled around her legs, patiently purring, so she sprinkled some dry food into her bowl. Smidgeon reviewed the cryptic note.

"Not much to go on," she said. "Can't go check it out in the dark, and his car isn't out there, it's in town. I think he went out there and came back."

She heard Lance's truck pull up and went out onto the front porch. Lance motioned for her to come over to him.

"I'll drive us over, and you can drive Sam's car back, okay?"

Smidgeon nodded and climbed into the passenger seat.

"Lance, you need to clean up this dog hair...I'll be covered in it."

"Sorry about the mess. Prewash has taken to looking out the window."

"Well, I guess a little dog hair is the least of my worries today."

As he drove, Lance nervously made small talk. "Ain't never been down to Valentine," he said.

"Tiny place, but there's not much there. Went to a service at a nice little old church there once," Smidgeon said. "What do you think happened?"

"Well, I figure somebody followed him, most likely on his way back. Maybe they took some offense to him nosing around out there. Guess there's always the possibility he broke down. His old vee-dub has a lot of miles on it."

"Maybe," she said, "but we would have heard from him by now, don't you think?"

"Hard to say. I don't think he woulda run into trouble if he broke down. Most folks are nice and helpful. Somebody would have helped Sam make a call; heck, most woulda hauled him back home and invited him to dinner."

"That's what I was thinking." Smidgeon furrowed her brow. "What about the strange little man who's been hanging around?"

"Cerides? I think Sam could easily take him out. Besides, why would he want to kidnap Sam?"

"I don't know, but it's the only thing I can figure."

"Well, we'll see when we get there. Maybe we'll see Sam walking down the highway."

"You think so?" she asked.

Lance inhaled deeply and let out a sigh. "Wishful thinking," he said.

Smidgeon looked out the dark window. "I hope we figure out something."

The rest of the trip passed quickly until the silence was broken by Lance. "Lights ahead."

"It's Valentine. Slow down. I think the road we want is on the far side."

There was little activity around the few buildings in what passed for the town. They spotted Sam's white Volkswagen on the far side of town.

"There it is," Smidgeon said.

Lance slowed and pulled over at what appeared to be an unofficial cutover to the graded ranching road. Smidgeon got out of the truck before Lance even set the emergency brake, key in hand. She tried the door.

"Locked," she said.

"Houston boy," Lance retorted as he joined her, a small flashlight in his hand. "Locking doors is a way of life back there."

She inserted the key and popped the door lock. Smidgeon held her breath as she opened the door. She didn't know what she was expecting, but all she got was a musty car smell.

Lance shone a light around the front and back seats. "He likes it messy."

"I've been after him for a while to clean this out," she said.

"Nothing obvious is in plain sight, so we try the next most obvious place," he said, reaching under the driver's seat. "Bingo." He pulled out the small box and flashed his light on it.

"Exactly like the one from the café," Smidgeon said.

"Yep, Lucky Strike," Lance said. He held the small light in his mouth as he opened the box cautiously. Inside there was a note wrapped in three old plastic sandwich bags.

Smidgeon picked up the paper and read it in the dim light. "I can barely read it, but it looks like it says 'Duke Chapel—Savonarola—lower back.'"

"Duke Chapel?" Lance asked.

"That's what it says. I don't know any Duke Chapel."

Lance picked up the paper and read it. "The only Duke Chapel I know about is at Duke University. I got some cousins in Durham, North Carolina. I've been there. Nice place."

"North Carolina? What the heck is going on here?"

A passing truck blared its horn.

"Don't rightly know, but we best be on our way. I hope the car starts."

She put the paper back in the tin and took it from Lance. As the tin snapped closed, she said, "You're right. Start it up while I get my purse." She handed Lance the key.

The car was puttering when she returned. "Looks like there's plenty of gas...you're all set," Lance said. "I'll follow you back to your house."

Smidgeon sat in the car and re-familiarized herself with the controls.

"I only ever drove this thing one time when mine was in the shop," she muttered to herself.

She fumbled with the release under the front seat and her heart skipped a beat when she found something else. "Sam's wallet!" She remembered he had said he always took it out when he hiked. She slid the seat closer to the steering wheel so she could press in the clutch. Lance pulled his truck around behind her, and she slowly moved the car over onto the highway.

Her mind was racing as she drove back to her house, and the trip was made even lonelier by a profound realization.

"I can still smell Sam in this car...where are you, honey?"

~ * ~

Mule Hollis mumbled to himself as he drove west down Interstate 10.

"Well, I knew they would figure out I was following them, but I didn't expect them to give me the slip so easily. I might as well head back to Fort Stockton."

He had followed the black Chevy from the rendezvous in Imperial, but once they both closed in on Fort Stockton, the other driver had made good use of a sharp turn in the highway to slip him. As soon as he hit the curve, Mule realized the car was gone.

"Danged fool mistake," he said as he approached an exit for US Highway 67. The exit sign mentioned Alpine, and Mule changed his mind.

"Maybe I'll head over there instead."

About thirty minutes down US 67 he noted an approaching railroad crossing; it was at the first curve he'd encountered. Something black on the side of the road caught his eye. It was at a spot where a graded road connected with the highway. Mule slowed and pulled to the left where a familiar black Chevy was parked. He drove past it but saw nothing. He parked and walked over to the car, placing his hand on the hood as he walked past it.

"Still warm," he said.

He stooped down and looked inside. The car was empty. Mule stood upright and looked all around but saw nothing until a Department of Public Safety trooper pulled up and parked.

"Need some help?"

Mule showed his identification. "Private investigator, former sheriff's deputy. I had been following these folks, but they gave me the slip. What's this road?" he asked, pointing down the graded road.

"That's the Old Alpine Highway," the trooper replied.

Mule kicked at the gravel, "Some highway," he said.

"Well, it's paved about halfway back to Fort Stockton. Even this last bit is pretty well maintained."

"Maybe so, but they sure used it to give me the slip. Engine's still hot, too...they must have had another car waiting."

"They wanted or something?"

"Not yet, at least as far as I can tell. I'm doing a little work for the *Federales*, investigating a gang starting to work this side of the border. I guess I just missed them."

"Well, I'll call this in, get it towed off. You need anything more from me?"

"No, sir. Appreciate it."

Mule returned to his car and waved to the trooper as he got in and headed south.

"My old cop instincts were right, even if I was a little slow. Going to head to Alpine and get my bearings," he said. "Just a little too slow."

Nine

Lance approached the door to Smidgeon's house feeling a bit of trepidation. She had driven ahead of him and the trip had given him time to ponder the situation. He had initially disagreed with her plan to check out Sam's car, but now he could see it was the right choice. He had hoped Sam was close by but that expectation diminished when he saw the abandoned vehicle. He hadn't known Smidgeon a long time, but he already knew her well enough to realize she was prone to decisive action and he had a pretty good idea of what she was planning to do. He hoped he could talk some sense into her. The door was open, so he peeked in.

"Guess it's okay to come on in?"

"Of course, Lance."

Smidgeon had placed the two metal boxes on the dining room table. There was a gold coin between them.

"There certainly is a pattern," he said. He dug into his pocket and pulled out the coin he had found at Loot's house and put it next to the other one.

"Yeah, I'm sure the coins are part of it, too," Smidgeon added. She picked up the second note.

"You say this Duke Chapel is in North Carolina?"

"Yes, in Durham," Lance said.

"How many miles away?"

Lance whistled under his breath. "Gotta be sixteen hundred, seventeen hundred miles, maybe more. Long drive. You aren't thinking of going there, are you?"

"I think I have to. Sam found this tin," she said, tapping the second, dirtier box, "and I think it has to have *something* to do with his disappearance."

"Yeah, but Smidgeon, it's so far away. How can it...?"

She interrupted. "I don't know, Lance, and I don't care. It's like a puzzle and to solve it we need *all* the pieces. I've got to find Sam, and if this is a clue, I need to find out what it means and see where it takes me."

"So you think it's another clue?" Lance traced the edge of one of the tins with his finger as he said, "Probably just a wild goose chase."

"You said it yourself, what we have here is a pattern. I'm pretty sure we have several more steps to follow before we find out what it's all about."

"But if this leads to Sam, why did they leave the tin?"

"Who?"

"The person or persons who took him."

"They probably didn't find it when they grabbed him. Lance, it's got to be related, all of it. I'm betting on Cerides. He was asking about me, right?"

"Well, your dad," Lance said.

"He probably thinks he can get to me through Sam. He must be convinced I know something."

"But you don't, right?"

Smidgeon tapped her fingers nervously on the table. "Not until I figure this out."

"Cerides was weird, but he seemed harmless. Remember, I talked to him at the house. I could've squashed him like a bug if I had wanted to. And anyway, he was asking about Loot, not your dad."

"And he probably knew Sam and Loot were thick as thieves. There was a roughness to him, Lance. I see a lot of folks in the café, and I think I am a pretty good judge of people. You and Sam are good examples. I liked you both from the start. This guy? Not at all. There was something almost evil about him...I am *sure* he has Sam, and Cerides is not going to let Sam go until he gets what he's looking for."

"Maybe so, but to drive all the way to Durham would take you three or four days each way. What about the Mossback?"

"You can run it for me while I'm away. You know the routines. The cooks all like you. The customers like you. You've been filling in more and more. You're more than capable, and I trust you, Lance."

"I don't know. Maybe I should be the one to go to North Carolina. I've got a cousin there. Maybe I could call him, and he could go check the Chapel."

"No, Lance. I've got to do this. I think it's up to me and I'll tell you another reason I feel this way. I'm pretty sure it means my daddy was mixed up with something shady...I don't know what it is, but deep inside, I know I have to make it right. I can feel it here," she said, tapping her chest, "and in the same way, I know it's probably the only way to save Sam, too."

"Shouldn't we tell Clay what we think?"

"Tell him what? We don't have anything to go on but the feeling in my gut. He ain't going to care about my intuition. I'm going, and that's that."

~ * ~

Sam had been driving for hours and barely noticed the sign looming ahead of the car.

BIG BEND NATIONAL PARK

"*Cavolo ti sei dimenticato di girare!*"

"What? I don't understand what you're saying."

"You have missed the turn!"

"You didn't say anything," Sam said. "I turned south on US three eighty-five like you said."

"I don't want to go into this park. Turn around and go back. It is not far, not far."

Sam complied, carefully made a U-turn and headed north again. They approached an intersection with a ranch road. Sam remembered passing it.

"Turn right here. It was not your fault...I am afraid my mind wandered for a moment."

Shortly after he turned on Ranch Road 2627, Sam noted a small mileage sign. "La Linda?"

"*Si*. Drive." Cerides waved nonchalantly with his gun.

They passed many miles of monotonous landscape, interspersed with an occasional dwelling or, more often, a contemporary ruin of some sort. Eventually, they approached a small bridge. Sam had kept track of direction as best as he could, and although the ranch road had curved a few times, he knew they had generally been continuing south.

"Keep going. Across the bridge."

"Mexico?" Sam was guessing.

"Yes, we go into Mexico."

The lonely bridge across the Rio Grande was unlike any other border crossing he had ever seen. There were no guards and no customs agents on either side; it was just a bridge in the middle of nowhere. There was a sharp turn, and down the road, he could see what looked like a tiny town made up of a few houses.

"La Linda," Cerides snickered. "Keep driving but please to be careful...the road is rough."

~ * ~

"You sure this is what you want to do, Miss Smidgeon?"

"Yes, Lance, I need to do this." Smidgeon busied herself with paperwork in the small office in a far corner of the café's kitchen. "I don't think I'll be gone for much more than a week. Three days to get there, you said."

"Yep," Lance said. "Three long days there...and three more days back."

Smidgeon frowned. "I understand. We get used to making long drives out here, but I've never driven across the country before. I've never been out of Texas except maybe a day in Juarez."

"I been up to Durham a couple of times but mostly when I was a kid. Last time was a couple of years ago when my aunt passed. It ain't a particularly bad drive, but it takes a while. I guess I'll be okay here for a week or so."

"You'll be great."

"What about bills and such?" Lance asked.

"I've paid what I could. I didn't have time to set you up on the accounts or anything, but I talked with the bank. They know you from making deposits, so you can go talk to

Mike down there and they'll draft the account to pay any critical bills. Most of the suppliers will run on credit, but you can pay out of receipts if you need to."

"Well, okay, I guess. I'll keep the place going as best as I can."

She finished organizing stacks of papers on the desk and took a deep breath. "I think that's everything for now. I better get on the road."

"I'm gonna ask you one more time. You sure this is a good idea? I could still get my cousin to go up there."

"Lance, if this was Sam instead of us, like if he was faced with the decision to save you or me, there would be no question about it. He'd already be on his way there right now."

"You know, it could be he is."

"And not tell me or you? Not to mention leaving his car? How would he have gotten there? And he didn't take the note with him either. No, Lance, somebody grabbed him, and I'm sure this is the first step to getting him back home."

"I guess you're right. Unless...well, it could be somebody *forced* him to go there."

"Think about it. The tin looked like it was right where he had left it. No, somebody grabbed him, and they didn't know about the tin. But I bet they know something. I think everything is related, and I'm hoping we know more facts than whoever took him. I want to keep it that way."

Lance nodded as Smidgeon stood.

"Take care of my place, Lance. I'll check in when I can."

She hugged him tightly.

"Don't worry about it, Miss Smidgeon. I'll hold down the fort."

He walked her out to her car. The sky was beginning to brighten.

"Gonna be tough driving east, at least for a while. The sun will be brutal."

"I've got a few more things to take care of at the house," she said. "Oh, and thanks for keeping MamaKat."

"Prewash will appreciate the company," he said, "especially with me working extra-long hours."

Smidgeon's eyes began to tear. "I'm so glad we all became friends."

"Y'all saved my life, Miss Smidgeon. It sort of goes with the territory."

"More like we almost got you killed."

Lance tittered. "Well, you've got a point there, but Sam and me, well, we had already developed a certain affinity for each other before all that tension started. There was no way I was letting y'all deal with that situation alone, and anyways, I was in it as deep as you were. I figure we both had no choice."

"Still, this is a really big favor."

"I gots this, don't worry."

He patted on the car's roof as she closed the door and started across the parking lot. She glanced back and waved to Lance. She fought back a tear as she drove down the main road toward her home. "Sam, Lance, and The Mossback are all I have in this world," she said to herself.

Smidgeon retrieved some of Sam's hidden cash. They had spent most of it on the building repairs, but she hoped what she was using for this trip would be put to good use. She looked around the darkened rooms, trying to make sure she didn't leave anything she needed.

"Seems so lonely and depressing, not even the cat purring," she mused.

She went into the kitchen, made several sandwiches, and refilled an old bottle of water she kept on the counter. She noticed a bag of lemon cream-filled sandwich cookies in a corner.

"Sam's," she whispered. "He won't mind if I take them for a snack." She teared up again as she imagined his response.

In her mind, she could almost hear him joking, "Sure, I've heard they still have them at the store."

She loaded two bags in the trunk of her car and placed a few other items she thought she needed on the passenger seat. As she was heading out the door one final time, she paused and went back into the bedroom.

"I need my own pillow," she mumbled to herself. "I can't abide by motel pillows."

She looked up at the sky after she locked the door. "The sun should be high enough now to not bother me too much," she said.

She pulled out of the driveway and was on her way.

"I hope I'm doing the right thing, sweetie," she said to herself.

Ten

Cerides pointed to a rutted trail leading up to a small rundown shack, somewhat hidden from prying eyes.

"Pull in here."

Sam was relieved. He was exhausted after driving for hours, much of the time on rough paths, some of which barely resembled roads. His captor had chosen their destination well; this remote outpost somewhere in rugged northern Mexico seemed to be a perfect hiding place. They had passed a smattering of buildings close by, but this one was protected by a barrier of vegetation.

Cerides reached over and retrieved the car keys. "Would you like to relieve yourself?"

Sam nodded, and he was directed around the back of the shack to a privy. The old man held a steady aim on Sam while he fumbled in the pocket of his coat with his free hand, eventually producing a pair of handcuffs.

"Your right hand, please." Sam complied.

His captor secured one shackle on Sam's wrist and the other through a large bracket on the wall.

"This will have to do for now," Cerides said before he entered the small enclosure. When he emerged, he said, "Now, for you, your left hand behind your back." Sam again complied, while Cerides removed the cuff from the bracket. He locked the cuff to a similar bracket in the door and pointed inside. Sam entered and closed the door, breathing through his mouth to avoid the stench.

Soon Sam said, "Done," and Cerides carefully opened the door just enough to remove the restraint and held onto the chain as he pointed with his gun.

"Inside, please."

They entered through a back door and Sam scanned the place. It was late in the day, and the room was only illuminated by dim sunlight filtering through a dusty sheet hung over the single window. He was not surprised by the Spartan accommodations, given the remote location, but it did show signs of recent occupation. The first room had a small bed, a bucket, a table, and what amounted to a kitchen. There were large bottles of water on the floor adjacent to a table with two chairs, and a small wood stove in a corner. He had no view of the adjoining room. Kerosene lanterns and candles were evidence the structure had no electricity.

"Sit," Cerides said, again pointing with the gun. Sam complied. Cerides fastened the handcuffs behind his back and through a slat in the chair.

Sam decided he had held his tongue long enough.

"Why are you doing this? I'm just a guy who works in a café. What good am I to you?"

"Oh, you are much, much more than that, my friend. What were you looking for down such a desolate road?"

"What business is it of yours?"

"Oh, I believe I have a vested interest in most things involving Joseph Toll and Loot Meldings."

"They are both long gone, along with any secrets they might have had."

"I am not so sure. Once again, what were you looking for out there? Did you find this thing you were looking for?"

Minutes passed as Sam glared at the old man. They both began to sweat as they sat facing one another.

The old man eventually cracked a sly grin. "No matter, all in due time. I am a very patient man. I have been waiting for almost forty years...a few more hours or days will not matter to me."

"Forty years? This goes back to the war?"

"Ah, yes, as you say, the war. Understand, young man, there is a lesson there, too. You see, a military life teaches one patience...it is not all fighting battles. No. In an army, it is the waiting, always the waiting. And, of course, the busy work...there is always work. It makes one hard, inside and out."

"I still don't see what this has to do with me."

"You were friends with Loot, no?"

"Yes, we were friends."

"And this café woman, Miss Toll, she is Joseph Toll's daughter."

"Yes. Why does this concern you?"

"I find it, ah, how do you say," he paused and looked aside as if struggling for a word. He mumbled, "*ironico*" under his breath. "Ah, *si*, of course, it is the same...ironic."

"What in heaven's name are you talking about?"

"Many things. Yes, it *is* quite ironic that one's friend and the other's daughter have ended up together. Both of these men took something from me, the least of which was my freedom. I spent years in prison, first as a prisoner of war until I escaped to Mexico where my situation became quite desperate. I was young. I made mistakes and spent many years in prison here in Mexico as well."

"And you blame them, Loot and Joe, for all of your troubles?"

"Not them alone. There were others as well. I looked up to those men. I almost worshipped them. Then they turned on me, took something from me, all of them, and cast me out to the wolves. Ah, but I've outlived them all. And I know some of what they took still exists, and I want to find it."

"I still don't know what any of this has to do with me, or with Joe's daughter."

"All in due time. First, we eat, eh? You must be hungry. Unfortunately, there is not much available here. I hope you do not mind simplicity."

Cerides lit one of the kerosene lanterns before fumbling in a nearby box. He produced a sleeve of crackers and two tins of potted meat. It wasn't one of Sam's favorite foods, but it was always one of his emergency staples on his long hikes. Cerides disappeared into the second room and returned with two bottles of Coke.

"Not cold, I am afraid, but you would no doubt find the water here less agreeable."

"How am I supposed to eat and drink handcuffed?"

Cerides struggled with a can opener on one of the tins. He took the cap off one of the Cokes and sat. He wiped a spoon fastidiously with a handkerchief.

"I will eat first then I will allow you to eat while I keep watch on you with my gun here."

"This is fine. I don't care about the food, what I want to know is why I'm here."

"Ah, well," Cerides began before pausing to take a sip of the drink. He stared at Sam and spread a small quantity of potted meat on a cracker with the back of the spoon. He slowly chewed the bite, and followed up with another sip of the drink.

"I will tell you a little tale of Joe and Loot. They were soldiers during the war. I was a soldier as well."

"In your home country."

"It is complicated. As it happens, when I met these gentlemen, I had recently been serving *Il Duce* in *Libia Italiana*. My mother is Italian, and my father was a Cypriot who found work in Italy before the war, so I grew up in *Italia*. When *Il Duce* and *Signore* Hitler both decided to complicate everyone's lives, my father wanted no part of it, but he was forced into the Army. He died in Ethiopia. My turn came when I became a conscript. I had consoled my mother when my father died, and so I was already tired of the war before that phase of my life had even started.

"I was sent to Libya, and it was an awful place, worse than this. When the Americans and British began to fight in earnest, we were never a match for them, so Hitler sent Rommel, and we became the supporting players...we were mere pawns on his chessboard. Neither the Germans nor the Allies ever cared for the caliber of the Italian soldier, which I can tell you is a bit unfair, but in my case they were right.

"I had no stomach for battle, and I soon deserted. Well, in truth, we were overrun, and most of my comrades were killed so I saved myself. Some time passed before I encountered a few American soldiers and saw an opportunity, and you might say I volunteered to help them. Luckily, I knew a little English. As you can see, I am small and at the time looked much younger than my nineteen years. They treated me like a boy. I didn't care, I was eating, and I was protected."

"So you were a kind of mascot?"

"Yes, a mascot. I helped dig foxholes, a duty the soldiers particularly hated. And what they called latrines. They called me Digly, a sort of joke on my name of Indigo. I detested the name but accepted it along with my situation. The officers ignored my presence."

"Okay, so what does this have to do with me?"

"Loot was my primary benefactor. He was the one I found first, and he helped to hide me. I grew to love Loot like a brother. I learned more English quickly. In addition to digging, I translated where necessary. Traveling with them was sometimes terrifying, especially if we were under fire from the German artillery. One day we survived a particularly brutal barrage when Loot drove us to relative safety, and we made camp." Cerides stroked his beard as he remembered. "I found it while digging."

"Found what?"

"A box containing a fortune in gold coins. A cache someone had buried. I have no doubt a corrupt Italian officer had stolen it and hidden it, but...I found it. Of course, Loot, Scooter, Joe, Babe, and Delbert all claimed it. At first, I was certain I would get a share and was fine with a fair portion. We were comrades, after all. But eventually, I came to understand I was not going to be a partner in what I had found."

"They cut you out?"

Cerides raised one eyebrow. "Ah, so you understand. Yes, I was sure they indeed planned to, as you say, cut me out."

"Tough. What we say is...all's fair in love and war."

He gave a sly smile. "Perhaps, but I had done a good job working for them. I thought I was part of their group. I *found* this thing. I could not tolerate their greed. I grew depressed and lost my enthusiasm for digging, for helping. They called me lazy and threatened to turn me in if I did not continue my work as before. I decided to leave, but..." Cerides paused for a sip.

Sam interjected, "You decided to take it all."

His eyes brightened. "Yes! I made plans to leave, but I was going to take the money, *my* money. I found it. I had been most content to share it with my comrades but...now I knew I wasn't one of *their* comrades. They kept it hidden from all the other soldiers in the platoon, but the six of us were together all the time, and I knew where they kept it hidden. It was heavy, but I was strong. I had deserted from the Italian army...I would desert again and take what was rightfully mine."

"Tough to do."

"*Si*, it was very tough. I could not carry such a box far. I planned to sneak out one night and dig a new hole to hide it, after pocketing enough coins to sustain myself for a while. Late one night, I took a shovel and walked out about a mile from our camp and dug a deep hole. It was in a place I knew I could find again. When I returned to get the box, Joey discovered me carrying it. We fought, and the resulting noise alerted the others. Delbert fired his rifle, as a warning, I thought, but he hit Joey. Then he fired again and hit me.

Loot and Scooter took the box back before others in the platoon arrived. The medic treated me...my wound was minor, but Joey was seriously injured. They took him away. I was, of course, blamed for everything. The officers could no longer look the other way. I was treated as an intruder and became a prisoner of war. I was eventually sent to a camp for Italian prisoners in Hereford, Texas."

"Really?"

"Yes, but my stay was unpleasant. I don't know how, but it became known I likely deserted and so I was considered a traitor. I was eventually removed for my own protection and sent to a camp for German prisoners in Marfa, Texas. The Germans have no respect for Italians, but at least they did not know of my desertion. I kept to myself and worked on local ranches where I also learned some Spanish. Eventually, I managed to escape, and I fled into Mexico."

"So you are an escaped prisoner of war?"

Cerides delicately dabbed a handkerchief at the corners of his mouth. "Perhaps, but I don't think anyone cares much now."

The older man opened the second bottle of Coke, picked up his gun, and used one hand to unlock the handcuffs. He motioned for Sam to eat and drink.

"So," Sam said as he reached for the bottle, "you continued to live in Mexico?" The warm drink was a relief to his parched throat.

"I had received word of my mother's death during my captivity, so there was nothing for me in Europe. I knew I was destined to be an outcast no matter where I went. I resorted to petty crime just to survive. This is where the story becomes somewhat more, as I said before, ironic. I happened across Scooter and Delbert in Mexico."

"Oh, from the old unit?"

"*Si*, the same. They had fallen to hard times and had fled the United States due to some legal issues of their own. The world of crime often follows similar tracks, so it was perhaps inevitable we would meet."

"But didn't you say Delbert shot you?"

"Yes, but it had been the result of confusion. The wound to Joe was much more serious. I later enlisted them in one of my many business ventures. They double-crossed me and fled back into Texas with more of my money. They suffered serious consequences for this, perhaps a story for another time."

Cerides paused when Sam began to cough on a cracker crumb.

He continued, "Now when I asked them about the money we had found, they told me they had squandered their shares, and they knew Joe had used his share to build a café. They weren't sure about Loot, but Babe, they said, had kept his share and hidden it. He felt guilty about it, and became paranoid. He eventually traveled the country like a vagabond, but they knew he spent significant time in Texas and often visited Joe and Loot. Delbert and Scooter were both certain Babe had shared the location of his part of the treasure with his old friends."

"And this is what brought you to the café?"

"Due in part to you, my friend."

Sam bristled when Cerides said that.

The Italian continued, "Through news reports, I became aware of your recent experiences, even in Mexico. I noted the mention of Loot's name as a victim. And, of course, the name Toll was also cited, associated with a café. So, you see, these newspaper accounts drew me to the area and I made inquiries. I am quite thorough when I am on the track of something I consider to be my own. I heard of a box found during recent construction."

"How would you ever hear about something like that?"

"There were workers all around the building, yes? People talk about unusual things. I listen. I wanted to find my money."

"I noticed you always return to the subject of what you call your money."

"Yes, my money."

"It's a long time to hold onto a grudge. The war is over."

Cerides looked at his watch. "Ah, but yes, it is time for me to leave. I must find Miss Toll and see what else she can tell me.

Sam flushed. "Leave her alone. She knows nothing about any of this."

Cerides flashed a smile. "We shall see. She will be most worried about your well-being, no? Perhaps this will make her more cooperative." The Italian picked up the handcuffs. "Your hands, please."

Eleven

Smidgeon was weary of the road after three days of driving and struggled to keep herself awake but was pleased to see she was almost to Durham.

"Lordy," she said to herself. "But at least I'm finally almost there."

She checked into a small motel in Durham. It was early evening, but she thought she'd try to find Duke Chapel. She got some vague directions from the desk clerk and headed to Duke University. It was dusk, and in the distance, through a break in the trees, she spotted a gothic spire illuminated by spotlights.

"That's got to be it," she whispered.

She navigated a maze of streets until she finally figured out the right path to the front of the structure. The campus was almost dead, and she saw a parking place near a small plaza in front of the chapel.

"This is amazing," she said as she tilted her head back to survey the high tower before approaching the doorway. She pulled at the handle; it was locked. Six statues, three on either side of the entryway, stared at her as she pondered her next move.

"Miss? Can I help you? The chapel closes at eight unless there is an event scheduled."

Smidgeon was momentarily startled at the intrusion. It was a young man, a student, she guessed.

"Oh, thanks," she said. "I was curious about something called Savonarola."

The man laughed. "You're standing right next to him," he said pointing to her left. "He's the first one, holding the cross."

Smidgeon looked up at one of the three statues on the side of the entranceway. "I'm glad I asked. I would never have found this. I mean, there aren't labels or anything."

"Oh," he said, "they are supposed to be symbolic. This side has influential reformation leaders, Girolamo *Savonarola*, Martin Luther, and John Wycliffe. The other side has some prominent Southerners, Thomas Jefferson, Robert E. Lee, and Sidney Lanier."

"You seem to know a lot about it," she said.

"I'm a graduate student in Divinity, but I have to confess, I love the chapel and I am a stickler for historical details. Why are you interested in Savonarola? He was a fascinating figure in religious history, quite controversial in his day. Most people have never heard of him."

"Oh, nothing really, a friend mentioned him to me and told me to check out his statue here. I'm just visiting from Texas on my way somewhere else."

"Well," he said, tapping the base of the statue, "that's him! God bless you and have a safe trip," the young man said, and he hurried off.

After he left, Smidgeon looked around to make sure no one else was watching and reached up around the statue's sandaled feet. She had to raise on her toes to reach behind the figure. There was something there. She felt around the edges. It felt like metal, not stone.

"Don't think it's part of the statue," she grunted under her breath.

She found she could barely grasp the object and tugged hard at it; Smidgeon thought she might dislodge the statue, but it stood firm. She pulled again with a little more force and, finally, the object released its hold on the stonework.

She glanced at it in her hand and saw it was a small box about the size of a pack of cigarettes. She put it in her other hand and reached up again but could feel nothing else.

"I better get going before I draw any attention," she said to herself.

She quickly crossed the lonely plaza and got back into her car. She dropped the box on the seat and drove away. Glancing down at the small rusted metal box as she drove, Smidgeon could make out some prominent words showing through some mottled rust: *Lucky Strike*.

Back at the motel, as she examined the box, she turned it over and laughed out loud.

"Gum! This thing was stuck on there with gum!"

She worked at the box to loosen the rust and managed to pop open the hinged top revealing a yellowed piece of paper wrapped in three plastic bags. She read the note and gasped.

"What have I gotten myself into?"

~ * ~

Lance locked the front door of The Mossback. Smidgeon had been gone for three days, and he was already starting to regret his decision to take over the café. Although business was good and he knew the place well enough, he felt out of his element. To his surprise, people readily accepted his explanation of a family emergency leaving him in charge.

"Not sure for how long, but so far so good," he mumbled to himself.

He took the receipts into a little office off the kitchen to close the register.

Manny, the night cook, came in. "What's the special tomorrow?"

Lance glanced at a list Smidgeon had taped to the wall. "Looks like it's time for King Ranch Chicken. We have everything?"

"Yeah, I think we're good. I'll do some of the prep for it and finish cleaning up. You okay in here?"

"I'm fine. Thanks, Manny."

"When's the boss coming back?"

"Not sure," Lance said. "She had to go a long way, but I'm hoping she'll call pretty soon."

It was not a lie. He had been worried about both Smidgeon and Sam. He had faith in Sam's ability to take care of himself, but he was afraid Smidgeon was out of her comfort zone.

His thoughts were interrupted by the phone.

"Mossback," he said.

A voice on the line asked him to accept a collect call.

"Lance, it's me." Lance felt a wave of relief when he heard Smidgeon's voice. "Any word on Sam?"

"Nothing," he said, adding, "I'm glad you called, though, I've been worried. Are you okay? Did you get to Durham?"

"Yes, and I've already been to the chapel. I'll start back in the morning."

"Did you find anything?"

"Another one of those Lucky Strike tins. A different one, kinda like a cigarette pack. Smaller. Stuck up behind a statue with old gum. Can't believe it held there."

"Ever try to get the gum off the bottom of our tables?"

She giggled. "You know, I didn't even think about that."

"Anything useful in it?"

"A note with more directions. I'm looking at a map now. The note said 'Lawrenceburg Tenn Bumpass Cem. Center back Samuels '70'...nothing more."

"Wait, where the heck is Lawrenceburg?"

"Lawrenceburg, Tennessee, is on US Highway sixty-four. Looking at the map, US sixty-four cuts right across the entire state of North Carolina. It looks like a long slow haul through the mountains, but I bet it's a pretty drive. It's hard to get used to all the trees."

"Oh, yeah, they got a lot of nice trees there. Quite a change from here. So what do you think 'cem' means...cemetery?"

"Pretty sure, but if it is a cemetery, Samuels is likely a grave...maybe from somebody who died in 1970. It's the only thing I can imagine."

"Smidgeon, couldn't we leave this to later? What does this have to do with Sam? I was hoping he somehow headed out there and you'd catch up with him. He obviously hasn't been there. This sounds like some kind of crazy wild goose chase."

"I don't know, but I have a gut feeling I have to follow any clue I find. I think this has everything to do with the reason he's missing."

"I don't like it. Sounds risky."

"Well, it's sort of on the way home...at least I'm headed west. But I wish it was faster, like the interstate."

"Might be part of the point, off the beaten track."

"Maybe. Or maybe there wasn't any interstate highway when this was set up."

"It's possible. Parts of it were slow to complete. I don't know US sixty-four...does it come to Texas?" Lance asked.

"It heads west across North Carolina and Tennessee. I need more maps. I'll decide what to do after I find whatever is there. Well, I better go. Any café business I need to know about?"

"Everything is running smoothly so far. Business is steady. I'm telling everybody you are on a family emergency."

"That's what I told the bank. I said I had to go out of state and might be away even as much as a week or more. With Sam missing, it really ain't much of a lie."

Lance said, "No, it isn't. Don't you worry, I got this. You can count on me." Lance hoped he wasn't lying.

"I know I can, Lance."

"You just be careful, you hear me?"

"I will, Lance, I promise. I'll let you know what I find in Tennessee. Bye."

Lance sighed as he hung up. "Tennessee," he whispered before his thoughts were interrupted by Manny.

"Mr. Lance, I'm done now. You okay? I heard the phone...did Miss Smidgeon call?"

"Yeah, she's fine. Should be back in a few days." Lance stood, "I'll let you out."

After Manny left, he finished balancing the day's receipts and did one final pass-through before locking up. He knew he'd be back bright and early the next morning. "Sam and Smidgeon kind of split opening and closing...these are long days for me," he said to himself.

Back home, he called out, "Prewash!"

The old dog had snuggled herself on the couch with MamaKat.

"Look at you two. Thick as thieves! Come on, girl, you gotta go out."

They both jumped down, and the dog lumbered to the open doorway. She hesitated momentarily and caught Lance's attention with a guttural growl. She went on to take care of her business. He was momentarily startled as he squinted into the darkness and said a single word in a low tone. "Cerides."

A lone figure unexpectedly emerged from the shadows. "Mr. Norton, can we speak?"

The older man was already moving toward the door when Lance raised a hand.

"We can speak out here."

Prewash moved past the two men back into the safety of the house, where she turned around and stood behind Lance.

"Of course." Cerides at first seemed preoccupied with the dog. "She seems like a good dog. I have had some unpleasant experiences with dogs...they don't seem to like me."

"She'll be fine. What do you want?"

"I note both of your associates at the café are away. I hope nothing is wrong."

"They're fine. Family emergency. What can I do for you?"

"I was hoping to speak with Miss Toll. Do you know when she will return?"

"Can't say when she'll be back. Why did you come here? You could have asked me at the restaurant. In fact, I'd prefer it. I like my privacy out here."

"I do not like crowds. It is my nature."

"You did fine coming in there before. Listen, Mr. Cerides, don't take this wrong, but I don't much like you. I'd prefer you not come out here like this. I'm not sure what it is you think you want, but I'm pretty darn sure I can't provide it."

Cerides took a step back. "Oh, I'm sorry. I mean you no harm. These are private matters best discussed in privacy, you see."

"Maybe you don't like witnesses." Lance leaned a few inches back into the doorway. His shotgun was just within arm's reach.

Cerides stared nervously. "Well, my business is with Miss Toll. I will await her return, no?"

"You didn't mention Sam. Maybe he could help you." Lance was fishing for a reaction.

Cerides was stone-faced. "No, Miss Toll is the person I need to speak with. As I said, I'll talk with her when she returns."

The little man turned and disappeared into the moonless, pitch black west Texas night.

"Again, no car," Lance thought to himself as he strained his eyes to look down the road. Prewash turned and disappeared into the house.

~ * ~

In Alpine, Mule saw a pretty young woman standing outside a dark green Mercury Cougar; she had stopped on the side of the road and was holding a baby he estimated to be about one year old. She vaguely reminded him of his daughter-in-law Michelle. His old cop instincts kicked in and he pulled over.

"Having some trouble?" he asked.

"I've got a flat tire. I was just going to change it but my daughter started crying."

Mule noted her eyes were red. "Is that all? Need some help?"

"With the tire, the baby, or with my idiot husband?"

"Let's start with the tire. Pop the trunk so I can get the spare and the jack."

He loosened the lug nuts and jacked up the car.

"I appreciate it. I probably could have managed."

"No problem. These nuts were on really tight, you might have needed some help with them anyway. What's up with your idiot husband?"

"Oh, he's in jail. We'd been on the outs and he came here to start over and convinced me he'd changed. It's obvious he hasn't. Maybe I'm the idiot."

Mule replaced the tire and started tightening the lug nuts. "Where'd you come from, I mean, to help him start over."

"California."

Mule lowered the car, gave each nut another tug with the tire iron and stood. "Here's what you do. Leave him. Get this flat fixed first, then you and your daughter head back to California. Like you said, he hasn't changed. I'm an ex-cop, I've seen this same situation hundreds of times." He hoisted the flat into the trunk and replaced the jack and tire iron.

"You're not the idiot, you seem like a really nice lady. Have a nice day, you hear?"

"Thank you so much," she said, "for everything."

"All in a day's work, ma'am. But don't forget to get the tire fixed."

Mule returned to his car. Helping the young woman reminded him he needed to check in with his daughter-in-law Michelle, so he found a pay phone about a half-mile away and called her. She took messages for him when he was working a case.

"Hey," he said, "it's me. Any messages?'

"Hi, Pops," she said. "Your friend in the *Federales* called. Dario?"

"Yeah, what did he want?"

"Their contacts say Cerides was likely operating near Van Horn. Hey, did you catch the money drop?"

"I managed some pictures before they took off. I lost the varmints though, down south of Fort Stockton. Van Horn, huh? Well, I'm not too far from there. How's everything else?"

"Okay. Mike's at work and little Junior is at school."

"Give everybody my love. I guess I'm still tracking until I find this guy."

When he hung up, he hesitated for a minute. He didn't have a real office, but Michelle had offered to take messages for him. His son Mike had followed his footsteps into law enforcement but left the sheriff's office when Mule was let go.

"It was a matter of time," Mike had said at the time. He was working in the oil industry, but it was tough, and Junior had recently recovered from a broken arm. Mule was drawing a good pension but hoped he'd be able to help his son's family when his investigator contracts started paying.

He sat in the car and reviewed his notes and his maps.

"So I guess I better head to Van Horn before the sun gets too low in the sky and blinds me."

He started his car and turned west down US 90.

Twelve

"I should be used to long drives after living in Texas all my life," Smidgeon mumbled to herself, "but these mountains are crazier than I like. North Carolina seems to stretch on forever."

US Highway 64 wound its way ahead of her, and the journey was starting to wear her down. She felt a wave of relief when she finally saw the Tennessee State Line sign.

"Now," she thought to herself, "all I have to do is find Lawrenceburg and the Bumpass cemetery before I can head back to Texas."

Whenever the ordeal of the trip began to drain her resolve, Smidgeon's thoughts returned to Sam, and she would flex her foot and press the gas pedal down again, squeezing a little more speed out of her sedan.

"I don't know if what I'm doing is going to help you, honey, but it's the only thing I got going right now."

As the miles sped past, she entertained second thoughts and wondered if she should have reported Sam's disappearance to the police. She and Lance had discussed this as one of the options before she left.

She remembered telling Lance, "I don't know if the police can do anything."

"Listen," he had said, "I don't have much use for the cops, not really, but I think this is one thing they're good at. They have the resources to look for him, or at least be on the lookout for him and maybe they can figure out what's going on."

"It's all about these notes," she responded, "there's a link, I know there is, and I'm sure Cerides is even more interested in them than we are. If we can understand what these notes are about, *we'll* know what is going on."

"But driving all the way to North Carolina—"

"I've got to go, Lance," she had said, "that's the simple truth. The police will just file a few papers and wait for a body to show up. They won't care about these notes or what they mean. I've made up my mind. I know in my heart I have to follow this trail."

Her memory of this conversation strengthened her resolve, and she pushed on with renewed energy. Smidgeon was relieved when the smaller road merged with an interstate highway for a while.

She passed Chattanooga and added a little more speed. She smiled as she remembered her mom and dad singing parts of the song "Chattanooga Choo-Choo" in happier times. When she saw signs mentioning Lookout Mountain, she thought she remembered something about it from movies about the Civil War.

"I wish I could see some of these places I'm passing, but..." her voice trailed off.

Soon Chattanooga was in her rearview mirror, and she continued until she saw an exit for US 64 and she continued onto the smaller road once again.

She meandered along for a couple more hours, exhausted but pushing forward, eager to get to her destination.

"I could plop down and sleep for a full day, but every time I stop," she said to herself every time she dared think about resting, "I'm taken a little farther away from saving Sam."

Her fatigue had put her on the verge of stopping for the night when she suddenly came upon Lawrenceburg. It took her four stops, asking at different stores, before she found someone who knew the location of Bumpass Cemetery. It was almost dusk. She wondered if she should wait until morning to visit a graveyard but decided she couldn't wait.

"Besides, late in the day is probably a good time," she convinced herself.

Smidgeon still had to find the right grave, and she had been worried about something else. If confronted, she felt she'd have to provide some reason for her to be in the cemetery, so she had picked up a small gardening hand trowel at one of the small stores where she stopped to ask directions. She also bought a silly-looking decorative ceramic flower in a pot. She began to formulate her plan as she negotiated the turns given to her at the last convenience store. She knew she'd have to find the grave quickly. Once she located it, she figured she could kneel as if she were praying and proceed to dig a small hole to find any clue. When she was finished, she'd place the pot in the hole and be on her way.

She found the cemetery in the center of a quiet residential area as the daylight began to fade. She was glad the few houses were fairly far apart. She turned onto the cemetery loop and was relieved to see a headstone with a familiar name right by the little road.

SAMUELS.

She parked the car, approached the marker and read "Michael Samuels, b July 26, 1923, d November 4, 1970." She stood in front of the simple stone as if deep in thought before kneeling behind it. She glanced around. All was quiet.

Smidgeon retrieved the small shovel and flowerpot from her purse. She pushed hard on the turf until the ground gave way. She probed down but felt nothing. She dug out a small divot of grass and dirt about three inches deep and prodded again. Again, she felt nothing. She dug and clawed another two inches of soil out of the hole. She tried again and the tip of the shovel hit something. She excavated the cavity until she came upon a hard and unnatural obstruction. She unearthed a small metallic square. A now familiar shade of green, red, and gold became evident as she recognized another Lucky Strike cigarette box. She dusted it off and slid it and the trowel into her purse. A glance in every direction verified no one was paying any attention to her.

Smidgeon quickly scooped enough earth back into the hole to allow the small pot to sit flat with the surrounding ground. She smoothed more topsoil around.

"I hope it's okay," she said, as she got to her feet, dusted off her hands and moved around the stone to the front once again.

"I'm sorry for disturbing you, Mr. Samuels. I don't know what connection you have to all of this, but hopefully, no one will disturb you in this way ever again. Thank you."

She somberly returned to her car and retraced the directions in reverse order, back to the highway.

"Best head on down the road in case somebody thought I was doing something suspicious," she said to herself.

She found a small motel down the road in Waynesboro and checked in for the night.

"Just passing through," she told the clerk as she checked in.

Inside her room, she retrieved the small box, placed it on a table and stared at it for a long time.

~ * ~

Sam dozed in the heat of the shack. He was sweaty and uncomfortable. A sudden noise startled him, and he twisted himself so he could sit up on the small, filthy cot. A young girl was standing in the doorway. Her dark eyes were like saucers, staring down at him. She was carrying a soiled canvas bag.

"Who are you?" he asked.

She didn't respond. Sam searched his limited knowledge of Spanish but couldn't find useful words. He finally managed, "*Comida? Agua?*"

She nodded but didn't move, preferring to stare at him with her wide eyes. Sam realized he must look a sight, dirty and handcuffed, so he tried to change tactics.

He maneuvered his restrained hands into view and motioned with his chin, expecting her to open the restraints. She shook her head and hesitantly stepped away from him, clutching the bag with both hands. She produced a large bottle of Coke.

"No *Agua*. Coke," she said. She put the bag on a nearby table and opened the bottle with a small church key style opener. She cautiously approached Sam and put the bottle to his lips.

He took two huge swallows. It was warm but tasted good because he was parched and dehydrated. He nodded, and she carefully withdrew the bottle and took half a step back where she continued to stare at him.

"*Gracias*," he said. "*Me llamo* Sam." She remained mute.

She lifted the bottle again, questioning with her eyes. Sam nodded, and she gave him another long drink. He was thirsty and was allowed several swallows. Some spilled on his chin, and she pulled out a worn cloth and dabbed at the droplets.

She pulled out a plastic bag and unwrapped what looked like two rolled tortillas. She offered one to him, and he nodded. He opened his mouth and took a bite. The tortilla was fresh and warm; he was pleasantly surprised to taste the wonderfully flavorful beans spread inside. She continued to feed him in this way until the tortillas were gone.

"*Mas* Coke?" he said, and she nodded, lifting the bottle to his lips until he drained it.

She placed the bottle in the bag and started for the door.

"Wait," Sam said, "*tu nombre?*"

She froze, turned back to him and slightly shook her head. Sam assumed Cerides had warned her not to talk.

"*Por favor?*"

She looked down at her feet and whispered, "Maria."

~ * ~

Mule pulled up to the Culberson County Sherriff's office and saw a deputy getting into his cruiser as he pulled into the parking lot. He waved to the officer and got out of his car.

"Howdy," Mule said.

"What can I do for you, Mister?"

Mule handed the deputy one of his cards, "Name's Mule Hollis," he said. "Got a minute?"

"Clay Dodge," the deputy said. "Private investigator, huh?"

"Yeah. I'm a former Mitchell County sheriff's deputy."

"Remind me, where's Mitchell County?"

"A bit northeast from here about halfway to Dallas...you know, county seat is Colorado City. Now I'm doing my own thing. Been following a guy named Indigo Cerides for the Mexican Federal Police. He's wanted for a ton of stuff down there, and they think he's active over here as well."

"I haven't seen him, but I've heard people say a little foreign feller has been showing up and asking a lot of questions."

"'Little foreign feller' would fit this guy's description."

"I know he's been seen around The Mossback Café."

"Mossback?"

"Yeah, little restaurant here, down on the main road a ways. Good food, nice folks."

"Thanks for the tip."

"What's he wanted for down there?"

"You name it, he's done it. Theft, kidnapping, murder...the list goes on and on. Mostly money laundering on this side, I think." Mule hesitated and added, "So far."

"The feds involved?"

"I'd like to find him first. If they get on his trail, they'll take over and I don't get paid."

"I hear you." Clay said. "Well, I'll call this number if I run across him."

"I'd appreciate it. I'll be sure to keep you in the loop."

~ * ~

Smidgeon opened the Lawrenceville box and found another folded piece of paper inside, wrapped in three small plastic sandwich bags like the others. She retrieved the note and recognized the block handwriting, a mix of printing and cursive like the previous one.

Ozark Ark. Highland Cem Hanson '70

"Another cemetery," she said to herself. "I guess I'll need to get another map."

She pondered the tins and tried to remember the old commercials for Lucky Strike cigarettes and absentmindedly mumbled, "Some catchy slogan, but I can't quite remember."

On the way back from getting some dinner, she found a small convenience store near the motel and picked up an Arkansas map.

"Heading to Ar-kansas?" the clerk spoke with an emphasis on *Kansas*.

"Huh?" Smidgeon had been caught up in her thoughts. "Oh, yeah, maybe."

The man leered at her, displaying an array of surviving teeth, discolored from years of coffee and cigarettes. "Pretty girl like you needs to be careful out that way."

"I'm sure I'll be fine." She paid and hurried back to the motel.

She unfolded the map, checked the index, and found Ozark. She immediately noticed something familiar about it.

"Right on US sixty-four. Again."

She retrieved her Tennessee map and followed the same highway from her present location, across to the state line where it continued on the Arkansas map.

"Weird, still following US sixty-four," she mumbled.

She tracked the highway across the maps and decided she could save time by crossing down to Interstate 40.

"They run pretty close most of the time, but Forty is a more direct route," she mused. "Oh, dear! I had better call the café before Lance leaves."

After Lance accepted the collect call, Smidgeon said, "Any word of Sam?"

"Still no word on Sam, but everything else is fair to middlin' I guess. Business is down a bit. I think the customers miss you."

"You're not being mean to them, are you?"

"No, ma'am, but it ain't rightly The Mossback without you. You find what you were looking for?"

"Somebody's playing games, Lance. I did find the clue, but it just points to another place, Ozark, Arkansas. Another cemetery."

"Really? It's like a danged scavenger hunt. So you're running down a bunch of clues. How long you reckon it's going to take? Sam's been gone almost a week, don't you think I should come clean with Clay? The cops can likely do more to find him than you can by gallivanting off all over the country."

"Give me two or three more days. If I don't find what I need by following this trail, I'll head back home. I'm betting it's going to lead me right back to Texas."

"Okay. I sure hope it don't lead to Alaska. Please be careful. I've got things under control here. As far as Sam goes, no news is good news, I think. I hope so anyway."

"Bye, Lance, and thanks for everything."

"No worries, Miss Smidgeon."

Tears welled up in her eyes after she dropped the phone into the cradle.

"It better not be a wild goose chase, Sam. I need to find you."

~ * ~

"Why are we here, Loot?"

Smidgeon cried on the bed beneath the hovering spirits.

"Don't rightly know, Slim. But I have a sneaking suspicion it has something to do with this stuff here."

He floated down to the floor and stood over the table and examined the objects.

"The writing seems familiar and the cigarette tin...something about it rings a bell. Ain't seen one of them in a coon's age. Had a buddy back in the army during the war who smoked those Lucky Strikes. Would get several of those tins in his mail every few weeks. After he smoked all the cigarettes, he used them for everything. Even saw him use one as a little frying pan once. If we saw something tucked away in a Lucky Strike can, we'd know old Babe had been there."

"Babe?"

"Big guy from North Carolina, a bit slow sometimes, but he'd give you the shirt off'n his back. Got shell-shocked and was sent back home. That wasn't too long after—"

"After what?"

"Never you mind. We've gotta be here for some good reason. Let's just keep watching, and maybe we'll figure out why."

"What about Sam?"

"I don't know, Slim. I really don't know."

Thirteen

Sam slipped out of a restless sleep and peeked through the slits of his barely open eyes. Chills ran down his spine. Cerides was watching him. He sat up and turned to face the Italian.

"Ah, Mr. Milton, so nice of you to indulge me."

"How long do you think you can keep me prisoner like this?"

"As long as I like, my friend."

Sam cringed at the last word.

Cerides continued, "No one is looking for you. Well, perhaps Miss Toll. I inquired about her, but she is away on what the black gentleman called a family business. You, I suspect."

"What is it you want?"

"What were you doing down that road near Valentine?"

"We've already been over this."

"I think it perhaps has some relationship to what I am looking for. I also think it is connected to the disappearance of your, ah, friend, Miss Toll."

"It was nothing. Nothing."

"You know what I think, Sam?"

"Enlighten me."

"I think you have recently found something, perhaps during the repairs at the café, or it could have been at Miss Toll's house or even Loot's house. It does not matter. What other reason would draw you out to such a remote location so early in the morning?"

"And you just happened to be there."

"Of course. I listened at the door at the café and knew you would be driving to Valentine, so I followed you."

"So, you *were* spying on us."

"Very perceptive. And I know there is something you're not telling me. I cannot get the information out of Miss Toll while she is not available. Yes, I procured you as a bargaining chip to help me extract information from her. Now, in her absence, I must, unfortunately, concentrate on you. I don't like to do this, but you leave me no choice." Cerides looked up. "Diego!"

A large Hispanic man with a broad mustache entered the shack and loomed over Sam.

Cerides got up to leave, but whispered to Diego, "*puedes vencerlo,*" before he exited the room.

Sam didn't understand the words, but he got a clue to their meaning when the big man suddenly backhanded him across the face. He tumbled from the cot to the floor, where he sustained a kick in the side. Diego lifted him as if he were a rag doll, stood him up and punched him in the stomach before backhanding him again. With his hands shackled, Sam was powerless to resist.

Sam could taste blood in his mouth, and he was out of breath but tried not to make a sound. This lack of reaction seemed to infuriate his attacker who reared back with a fist and hit Sam in the jaw. Sam saw black for a few seconds. He had crumpled to the floor.

"*Alto!*" Cerides had returned. "*Suficiente.*"

Diego rubbed his knuckles and stepped back from Sam as Cerides approached. The older man dabbed at the blood dribbling from Sam's mouth with a moistened cloth, helped him to his feet and directed him back to the cot.

"Distasteful as this was, I hope it served as an incentive for you to tell me what I want to know. I will leave you to think about it."

Cerides motioned to Diego, and both men left the small room. Sam evaluated his injuries while he contemplated his options. The cigarette box he had dug up was identical to the one from The Mossback. Sam had glanced at the note inside, but the cryptic words meant nothing to him; it was a scribbled bit of gibberish. Sam felt a cold chill as he grasped a stark reality: Smidgeon must have discovered his abandoned car, found the hidden tin and deciphered whatever secret it held. It must have directed her someplace else but, of course, he had no way of knowing where she might have gone.

He whispered to himself, "I followed cryptic clues for years, I know the signs. Smidgeon must think this will lead her to me, but there is no telling what sort of trail she's following." He reclined on the small cot. "It can't be good, though, and I sure don't want her showing up here."

~ * ~

Deputy Clay was waiting when Lance flipped the open sign of The Mossback and unlocked the door.

"Morning, Lance."

"Clay? You're here bright and early."

"Smidgeon back yet?"

"She's still away with Sam on a family thing. Back in Houston."

"So it's his family."

Lance didn't like lying; he nodded before adding, "Expecting them back in a day or two."

"Well, get me a coffee to go. Say, Lance," Clay said.

"Yeah?"

"You seen any more of that little Italian guy around here?"

"Not here," Lance said, pouring the coffee. "Noticed him walking down the road a few days ago, out by near my house." It wasn't a total lie, Lance thought to himself.

"Yeah, I had a report of him getting in a car off Tesoro. Just curious. You should also know there's another stranger in town asking questions, too."

"Oh?" Lance said out loud as he muttered to himself, "What else can go wrong."

"A private detective named Mule Hollis."

"Mule Hollis? Okay."

"Said he's tracking a fella by the name of Indigo Cerides for the Federales down in Mexico. I think he's this same Italian guy. Anyway, this Mule Hollis guy might come around. Thought you'd want to know."

"Appreciate the heads up." He tried not to show any recognition of Cerides' name.

"You think you could get me a biscuit with a little meat on it?"

"Sure thing, Clay. Ham okay?"

"Yeah, sounds good."

"For here or to go?"

"You don't need to bag it or anything, but I'm taking it with me."

Lance disappeared in the back for a few minutes and emerged with a small wrapped biscuit.

Clay partially unwrapped one end of the package and sniffed at the contents.

"I know you're only filling in for a while, but I've got to say you know your way around a biscuit..." he hesitated to examine the edges. "Square?"

"My mama makes them square," Lance said. "Less working the dough, no waste. Roll them out into a rectangle and cut them."

"Square biscuit, don't that beat all," Clay said as he reached for his wallet. Lance held up his hand.

"It's on me, Clay. Enjoy."

"Tell Smidgeon to call me when she gets back to town."

"Will do," Lance said.

Clay continued to examine his mini-meal as he went out the door and Lance could hear him chuckling to himself, "Square biscuits—"

As Lance watched Clay drive off, he said to himself, "So there *is* more to Cerides. Makes sense."

~ * ~

Smidgeon pulled off Interstate 40 in Ozark, Arkansas, and made inquiries about the location of Highland Cemetery. She was not surprised to see it was right on US

64. The last headstone she visited had been in the southwestern section of the cemetery, so she situated herself in the same direction this time. She was looking for someone named Hanson, who died in 1970. It wasn't long before she spotted the headstone: "Mark Hanson, died April 15, 1970." Smidgeon parked her car and gathered her things. It was late afternoon, and she had this section of the cemetery to herself. She slowly approached the headstone as she glanced all around. She stood in front of the marker and said a prayer to the unknown soul buried there.

"I'm sorry, Mr. Hanson. May God grant you continued peace."

She moved to the back side, knelt in the center of the stone and worked the small garden trowel into the soft dirt. After a minute of digging she recognized the familiar feel of the shovel on metal and scraped at the dirt with both hands until she uncovered a small green box.

"Lucky Strikes," she intoned as she quickly placed the box into her purse.

She had stopped earlier and bought another small potted decorator plant, and she placed it into the hole as she had done at the cemetery in Tennessee. She patted the earth tight around the imitation plant and dusted her hands before getting up, grabbing her small shovel and purse. She again lowered her head in front of the stone.

"Again, I'm sorry. I don't know what you have to do with any of this, but now I'll leave you with a flower and my good wishes."

She backed away and returned to her car.

"Still a couple of hours of daylight," she said to herself as she drove into the parking lot of a small nearby grocery store. "Guess I had better see what's in this one and decide what to do."

She pulled the box out of her purse. Like the other buried tins, it was a "Flat Fifties" box, and there were plastic bags wrapped around a piece of paper. She recognized the handwriting from the previous note.

Smidgeon read out loud: "Osage Oklahoma Osage Cem Ennis Seventy." She sighed. "Oklahoma, huh? I guess I'm going to need another map. She opened her Arkansas map and realized, "I'm really close to the Oklahoma border. Fort Smith isn't too far...I'll head over there and stop."

She replaced the note, shoved the tin back in her purse and started to drive west again.

In Fort Smith, she found a motel room and called the café. Lance accepted the collect call.

"Any news, Lance?"

"No word on Sam," he said. "Otherwise things here are about the same. Any luck?"

"No, just another clue. Osage, Oklahoma. Another cemetery. How are things there?"

"Clay was asking about you and Sam. I told him you'd be back in a couple of days."

"No other word?"

"He said there's an investigator looking for Cerides."

"That's interesting. I thought there was something suspicious about him." Smidgeon raised her voice slightly. "I'm about tired of this, Lance. I ain't committing to a long haul across the whole danged country."

"I'm thinking anything you find in Oklahoma will end up pointing you back down here. I hope so, anyway."

"I hope so, too. I hate all this driving. I've never been away from home this long in my life, and I'm missing Sam something fierce." Her voice wavered with emotion. "I'm sorry I had to leave you with the café. Are *you* doing okay?"

"I'm pretty tired. I'm doing stuff we usually split among the three of us, but I guess I'm doing okay. It's gotta be done. Manny and Chuy have been filling in by working extra hours, too."

Smidgeon said, "I'm pretty sure I'll be heading home after Osage. All these clues make it an interesting hunt, but I'm beginning to doubt it could have much of anything to do with Sam. We need to somehow concentrate on finding him."

Lance took a deep breath. "I didn't want to tell you this, didn't want to worry you, but Cerides came around to my house asking about you again. I didn't let on that I knew about anything. All he said was he needed to talk to you."

"Did you tell Clay you saw him?"

"Just mentioned I saw him walking Center Street. The truth is, he disappeared into the night after he came to the house. Clay said he heard he'd parked a car way down on the main road. He has to be up to no good if he is trying to cover his tracks."

"You said there was someone else looking for him."

"Yeah, Clay told me. Guy named Mule Hollis. I haven't seen him."

"Hmmm, name sounds familiar, but I can't place him. Well, I'll see what I find in Osage, and then I think I'm going to head south. I can't believe I've followed a trail from Texas to North Carolina, Tennessee, Arkansas, and now Oklahoma. For what?"

"I know I was against this from the start, but now I think it's best to let it play out. It's got to mean something."

"I guess you're right. I'll let you know what I find."

"If I see this Mule Hollis guy, should I tell him anything?"

"Use your best judgment, Lance."

"I was afraid you'd say that."

~ * ~

Loot, Slim, and Scamp hovered and watched.

"Babe was from North Carolina, but he hoboed to all those states after the war. He settled down for a while in Oklahoma...had him a fling with some woman from a reservation out there. After they broke up, he hit hard times and came down to Texas. Joe helped him get a job on a ranch over toward Marfa."

"So you figure he left a trail?" Slim asked.

"I don't know, Slim, I don't know. Getting hard to remember all this stuff, but he did come to see me. I think this all points to something bad, some big trouble. This may be why we're here now."

"What about Sam?" Scamp asked.

"I can't figure out what part Sam plays in all of this. I just don't know."

"Usually we pop up wherever he is, but we've been locked onto this girl. Why?"

Loot shook his head. "Like I said, Scamp, I don't rightly know."

Fourteen

Oklahoma became a new puzzle for Smidgeon to solve. She stopped three times to ask for directions to the town of Osage, and then twice more to locate the Osage Cemetery.

"Lordy," she said as she drove. "Still close to US sixty-four, but it's much harder to get to."

She was frustrated by the fact she had to travel US 64 through Cleveland, a larger town by rural Oklahoma standards, swing around to cross the Arkansas River and make another awkward loop back to the tiny hamlet. Shortly after she crossed the river, she noted a sign indicating she was on the Osage Nation Reservation.

"That might explain the roundabout way I had to take to get here," she mumbled.

It was the most desolate place she had visited so far on this journey. The cemetery was on the north side of town. It had been a short drive from Fort Smith, so it was before noon and the streets were for the most part deserted. She parked and started walking around. Earlier in the morning, she had stopped and picked up another small potted artificial flower in a pot. Again, she concentrated in the southwestern section. She was soon rewarded for her efforts as she spied a weathered, simple headstone: Benjamin Franklin Ennis, October 22, 1970.

After glancing around, she knelt behind the headstone and began to work. The wind whistled through the background of trees while she dug. The dirt was baked hard, making it exhausting work, but she continued to chip away at it, and soon the corner of a familiar green box came into view. She scraped at the hardened earth to loosen it. Once her prize was freed, she slipped it into her purse and made quick work of placing the flower pot. It was the only spot of color in that section of the graveyard.

"I'm sorry for the intrusion, Mr. Ennis. Take care. May God have mercy on your soul," she said, pausing briefly before trotting back to the safety of her car.

As she drove away, she realized something. "Every person passed away in 1970," she said.

She crossed back the way she had come, assuming whatever she found in the box would again take her down US 64. She pulled into a small local drive-in and bought something to eat.

"I'm not going to want another hamburger for a long time," she muttered. "I might as well keep moving, but I need to see where I'm going."

The box contained another plastic-wrapped note.

"Turpin Oklahoma Independence Cem Davids '70"

"At least it's still in Oklahoma," she said as she slurped her Coke and nibbled at her burger.

She reviewed her map and found Turpin was much farther west, out in the Oklahoma Panhandle. "Looks like about another four or five hours. I'm getting whatever I find there, and I think I'm heading back to Texas. I've had about enough of this wild goose chase. It better be something more than just another location." Her straw made an empty sucking sound. "No surprise, it's right on US sixty-four."

Driving west, she crossed miles of flat, endless desolation with only an occasional sparse arrangement of trees or dwellings breaking the monotony. She thought to herself, "It's such an empty place."

Oklahoma continued to confound her sense of direction as US 64 made several confusing twists and turns. Smidgeon had to pay close attention to the road signs to make sure she was still on the right highway.

"It's like road planners couldn't make up their minds," she said at one point.

In the late afternoon, she could see the smattering of buildings in the distance she assumed might be Turpin. As she approached the town, a small sign on the side of the road caught her eye. INDEPENDENCE CEMETERY.

She was past it before the words registered on her brain, and she had to slow down to wait for a grain truck passing the other way before she managed to make a quick three-point turn to go back.

"What luck," she said.

She pulled the quarter mile or so down a side road and found the tiny cemetery. She parked and immediately advanced toward the southwest side of the small enclosure, started walking, scanning the markers and quickly found what she was looking for.

Lorena Davids, died Jan 1, 1970. She blinked. It also said born Jan 1, 1970.

A tear went down her face. "Aw, she was just a baby. I'm so sorry for you, baby Lorena."

Smidgeon didn't have a flower this time. "I don't know what I was thinking."

The cemetery was deserted, but there were trucks passing nearby, back on US 64. The sun was low in the sky, so she knelt and hacked at the hard packed dirt behind the small headstone.

"I feel bad disturbing you," she said.

After several minutes of chipping away, she heard a faint metallic sound.

"Finally," she whispered, as she chipped small dirt clods away from the green box and slipped it into her purse with the other tin.

"Getting quite a collection of these," she joked.

She scooped the clumps of soil back in the hole and apologized as she gently patted the mound flat, "I wish I had remembered to get another flower, you deserve it," she stood and added, "I'm sorry for bothering you, Miss Lorena, you rest in peace. God bless you and your family."

Smidgeon hurried back to her car and continued down US 64. Turpin was a tiny collection of old and new houses and mobile homes. She couldn't find a store, so she settled on the empty post office parking lot and parked with the engine running. After opening the box, she unwrapped the three plastic bags and pulled out the latest note.

She blinked in surprise. This one was different.

Smidgeon read it out loud to herself. "Sixty-four West past Felts—NM—U-turn—right—dead-end—20 ft. center 18 down."

Her heart raced. "Maybe it's the end of the road," she mused.

She checked her map. Felts was on US 64, but it was barely a speck on the map close to the New Mexico border; a few miles east there was a bigger town, Boise City. "It'll be dark by the time I get all the way out there," she said, "so I better get a room in Boise City."

Once off the road, Smidgeon retreated into the latest of her cheap motel rooms. She wasn't hungry; the last burger sat on her stomach like a brick, but she sipped at a vanilla shake she had bought from a local frozen dairy stand.

She spread out the map and reviewed the latest note. "I better find something, I'm running out of Oklahoma," she quipped. She noticed something interesting. Beyond Felts, near US 64, there was a spot where the borders of Texas, Oklahoma, and New Mexico all came together at one point.

Smidgeon was happy. "This has to be where the note is directing me. Maybe I'm headed back to Texas after all."

She tried to call Lance, first at the café and then at his house. There was no answer. She glanced at her watch.

"Well, it's late, so the café is closed. But I wonder where he is."

~ * ~

Sam woke to see young Maria staring at him from inside the doorway. He was tired and dirty and hungry but he smiled at her.

She stepped back, wide-eyed with fear when he twisted himself to sit upright.

"It's okay," he tried to assure her. "*Comida? Bebe?*"

She nodded and took a half-step toward him when a slight noise outside stopped her abruptly.

Diego entered and glared at them both. "*Silencio!*"

The large man sneered down at him and said in perfect English, "Before you eat, you must tell me what *Señor* Cerides wants to know." He rubbed a closed fist in his other hand. "You talk, you eat."

"I don't know what he wants."

"Then you will be beaten again and eat nothing."

"All I know is I found a note directing me to a spot along the road where I found a box. I hadn't had a chance to open the box. I don't know anything. It was in my car."

Cerides emerged from outside the shack. He had obviously been listening.

"Interesting. You could have saved us all a bit of trouble by telling me that the first time I asked."

"What trouble? I don't know anything."

Cerides scowled. "Ah, but Miss Toll has no doubt found this box. As you said, it was in your car, no?"

"For all I know, the car is still there in Valentine."

"No, the car is in Van Horn, parked safely at your house. And Miss Toll is suspiciously missing."

"Wait, what?"

"Yes."

"Where?"

"No one knows, or perhaps your friend, the black gentleman, knows, the one now running the restaurant."

"He doesn't know anything about any of this."

"I am not so naïve. Mr. Norton has simply told everyone Miss Toll, and of course, you, are both away on a family emergency. It is perhaps time I visited him again, with Diego here, to see if he might be persuaded to be a bit more forthcoming. Ah, but I believe he is still recovering from certain injuries. This will perhaps be not a good thing for him, you think?"

"Leave him alone. Let me go and I'll find out where she went."

"You have let things progress too far. Even when I find what I am looking for, I cannot let you go."

"You're going to kill me?"

Cerides calmly shook his head, "I still need you, for now. We will leave it there."

He turned and left the room. Diego nodded at the girl and followed the smaller man out. She cautiously approached Sam, reached into her bag, and withdrew a small wrapped package.

Sam shook his head and whispered "*Bebe.*"

She replaced the package and withdrew another bottle of Coke. Sam nodded. She opened it and held it to his lips, and he drained it.

He tapped at his bonds and whispered, "*Por favor.*"

She lowered her eyes, shook her head as she put the empty bottle back in her bag, and she quickly exited the room.

Sam sighed. "I have to figure a way out of here," he quietly murmured. "Smidgeon and Lance have no idea how dangerous this guy is."

Sam put his head back down on the dirty pillow and closed his eyes.

~ * ~

After another long day at The Mossback, Lance was slowly guiding his truck back home when he was cut off by a dark sedan. He swerved to miss the car and ran off the road in a cloud of dust. The car angled in to block his way.

Another vehicle pulled in close behind and parked to prevent him from backing up.

"What the—"

Several men got out of both vehicles. Lance reached down and retrieved the small pistol from inside his boot. He flipped the safety and set a bullet into the chamber; he was sure some of the men must have heard the sound. He didn't move as one of the men approached him. Lance was not surprised to recognize Cerides' features materialize in the dim light.

"Mr. Norton, we must talk."

"No. I've told you everything I care to tell you."

"I feel I must insist you accompany us to a more private place that might prove more persuasive."

"Let me repeat myself in a very simple way, Mr. Cerides. NO!"

The door was quickly thrown open, and a hand grabbed Lance's left arm, pulling him outward. A large man had placed himself outside his truck door while Lance had focused his attention on Cerides. Lance quickly spun around as his feet hit the ground and he swiftly had an arm around the large man's neck. Lance held the gun to his assailant's temple.

"Maybe you don't care about this guy, maybe you do. But what say we forget this little incident. You go your way, and I go mine? I have nothing to share with you."

Cerides considered the situation for several long seconds before responding, "You are a resourceful and capable man. All right, perhaps we can speak here. Where are Sam and Miss Toll?"

"Let's get one thing straight, Mr. Cerides, I am sure you know exactly where Sam is. This little exhibition has convinced me, so you might as well skip the crap." Lance tightened his grip on both his gun and his prisoner.

Cerides again paused and stared into the darkness for long seconds while coyotes yipped and crickets chirped.

"All right. I might have some information about Sam, but Miss Toll—"

"She's trying to find Sam, okay?"

"There was something in his car, no?"

"A note. She is following a series of notes. I don't know the details. She's on a wild goose chase, if you ask me. She's gone halfway across the country. She doesn't call every day, so I have no idea where she is right this minute."

Again there was silence. Cerides waved his hand, and his men returned to the two cars. He nodded at Lance. "You may release him. We will go. I am content to let Miss Toll continue to do my work for me."

Lance released the man but kept his gun pointed forward.

"You are a competent man, Mr. Norton. Perhaps you would like to work for me? I pay handsomely for a man of your abilities."

"Not interested," Lance retorted. "I'm good right where I am."

"Perhaps later. You may soon find yourself without a job."

"What's that supposed to mean?"

"Nothing, Mr. Norton," Cerides snickered. "But the, er, economy is always subject to change, as you well know."

"What about Sam?"

"He will be released *after* I speak with Miss Toll. All in due time."

Cerides pivoted and entered the first car, and both vehicles turned and sped off. Lance took a deep breath. His heart was racing.

"What have we gotten ourselves into?"

~ * ~

Sam was dozing when a soft finger touched his lips in the center. In the dark room, he could see it was Maria. She made a faint "Shhh" sound. She was holding a set of keys and she busied herself with the handcuffs. She moved to his feet and opened the shackles on his ankles. Sam's heart was in his throat.

She took him by the hand to the doorway and handed him a knapsack with the image of what looked like a Cabbage Patch Kid on it. Sam was surprised because it had some weight to it. She held her index finger to her lips, indicating the need to be silent. Maria waved for him to follow her into the night. He shadowed her blindly, stopping when she paused, always stealthily proceeding when she began moving again. They crept a few hundred yards away from the small shed. There was no moon. She halted, then turned to him before she took both his hands and stared intensely into his eyes.

"*Via con Dios.*"

"*Gracias,*" Sam said.

She took his hand and turned him in a direction and pointed. "*El Norte ... treinta kilometros,*" she said.

Sam nodded, clutched the knapsack tightly, and headed into the night.

He rested after about a half hour and examined the contents of the bag. Inside he found several bean-laden tortillas, folded over and wrapped in wax paper, and two bottles of Coke along with a small bottle opener, and something else that completely surprised him.

"A child's compass! God bless her," he whispered to himself.

It was a clear night but quite dark, so he couldn't read it. He looked up and found the Big Dipper and Polaris. Sam smiled; he wouldn't need the little compass at night.

He remembered her instructions and started walking. "*El Norte,*" he whispered and he moved carefully but quickly down the desert trail.

Fifteen

Smidgeon returned to US 64 and headed due west on a bright and clear morning.

"I hope this is the end of this ordeal."

The note was specific but abbreviated. She drove through the small community she assumed must be Felts. After a few more miles, she passed the "Welcome to New Mexico" sign and pulled over. She checked for traffic before making a U-turn; the highway was deserted. According to the note, she needed to turn right after her U-turn. She had passed a small road immediately before she got to the state line and in seconds she was back at that turnoff.

"That must be it," she whispered.

It was not paved, and her car kicked up a lot of dust. After close to half a mile, it intersected with another road from the right. The note mentioned a dead-end; she hoped this was the correct spot.

"Anyway, it's kind of a dead end," she mused.

She let the haze clear after parking before exiting her car.

She aligned herself dead center with the first path and paced off what she thought was probably twenty feet. She paced it three times and hoped she was standing on the correct spot. She glanced around in all directions.

"I reckon this must be exactly where Texas, New Mexico, and Oklahoma all come together."

She crouched and dug down with her small shovel. There was a big rock buried a few inches down.

"Another marker, maybe," she mused.

She moved the rock and continued digging. The note had said eighteen. "I hope it's eighteen inches and not eighteen feet," she panted.

The ground was hard but the deeper Smidgeon dug, the more easily the dirt moved. Sweat formed on her brow as she continued to hack at the stony soil until she finally heard the scraping sound of metal on metal.

She scooped away the dirt and pebbles and uncovered a corner of a familiar green metal box. She dug with her fingernails and pulled it out of the small hole. She shoved handfuls of dirt back into the hole, picked up the box and returned to her car where she immediately opened it. Inside, she found another piece of paper, wrapped in three plastic bags. She unwrapped it and found an index card with block letters carefully printed.

LOOK AT WHERE YOU BEEN, WHO YOU MET, WHAT YOU DONE

Smidgeon blinked at the card. "It is almost like Sam's riddle. Look at where you been, who you met, what you done?" she repeated out loud. "I've come all that way for *this*?"

She put the card back in the tin and tossed it to the floorboard of the car in disgust and checked her map. "I'm going back home," she said.

She didn't have a New Mexico map, so she pulled out her Texas map and tried to figure out her best way to head toward home without going too far out of her way. Smidgeon could see a little into New Mexico and noticed Clayton, New Mexico, had a state highway leading due south.

"I can probably get a map in Clayton," she mumbled. "I'll go there. She squinted at the road she had just come down and looked to the west. "I wonder if this road angles back to US sixty-four? I guess the worst I can do is head back the way I came."

After about half a mile down the graded road, she saw a big truck in the distance moving at high speed, so she continued and soon intersected with the highway.

"Gotta be the right road," she said as she turned left.

Clayton was about ten miles away. Smidgeon found a store and bought a New Mexico map. She again saw the small state highway heading due south and made her way there. "Gonna have to dogleg a little, but this will be my quickest route," she said as she drove to the south and home.

"Where I been, who I met, and what I done..." she grumbled as she drove.

~ * ~

Lance slept fitfully, and finally, after lurching awake for the third time, he decided to get up.

"Man," he said. "I wish Smidgeon had called so I could warn her about Cerides looking for her." He lamented, "There ain't nothing I can do but wait."

Prewash was sniffing at the door, but Lance decided to be more cautious than usual.

"Wait, girl, let me take a quick look," he said as he unlatched the front door and glanced around in the early morning darkness. He heard coyotes yipping in the distance and crickets chirping but nothing else. While the dog did her business, he went into the bathroom and splashed some water on his face. He never worried much about coffee or breakfast these days because he knew he could get something at the café.

He was slipping his pants on when he heard the dog snuffling at the door. He opened it to let her in and was startled to see Cerides standing on the small porch. Prewash tentatively sniffed at the Italian.

"Your dog is friendly, Mr. Norton."

"Yeah, I'll have to have a talk with her."

"I wondered if you have heard from Miss Toll."

"She calls most days but didn't last night."

"I am sorry I am impatient. I have many affairs to take care of, but I have an urgent need to speak with her."

"None of my business, Mr. Cerides."

"Ah, but you see, it is your business. Your employer is involved whether she knows it or not, and of course, her involvement involves you as well."

"And Sam?"

"Yes, of course. Mr. Milton is what I would call a bargaining chip."

"And what would you call me?"

Cerides chortled. "You might be a bargaining chip as well, but you serve my interests best by doing what you are doing. A failure to run Miss Toll's small restaurant would likely draw attention to her, and for now, that would not be the best thing for me. I will be watching you, Mr. Norton. Most likely we can settle all of these matters quietly and then all will be well."

"Uh-huh. I tell you what, why don't you trot your sorry ass out of here?"

"Of course. But I will be in touch."

"Or maybe I will. I might just drop by the sheriff's office today."

"I have done nothing wrong."

"You think there's nothing wrong with kidnapping?"

"You have no proof, and search as you may, you would find no evidence of any crime. Sam has family in the eastern part of the state, and he has a history of short-term disappearances. And, of course, even if you do convince the police of a possible crime, you and Miss Toll have conspired to withhold evidence. I know something of these things. Such a groundless accusation would not play well for either of you. We are at what I believe is called an impasse."

"I'm telling you—get out of here!"

"As you wish. But I will be watching. I will know when Miss Toll returns, and I will deal with her separately."

Lance slammed the door and quickly peeked out the window, but Cerides had already disappeared. "How does he do that?" he whispered.

He glanced at the clock and knew he had to get to the cafe, so he finished dressing, put out food for the patiently waiting dog and cat, then went to his truck. As he reached to open the door, he felt a wave of paranoia and got on his hands and knees. He inspected the underside and wheel wells all around the truck. "Silly, I guess, but I think Cerides is capable of anything."

He got to the café a few minutes late. Manny and Chuy were waiting.

"Everything okay, boss?"

"I had to round up the dog. She had a mind of her own this morning," Lance said, nervously laughing.

The three of them busied themselves with their prep work for the new day.

~ * ~

Sam considered drinking one of the Cokes Maria had packed for him. "I better save the liquid a little longer," he mused, "sun's coming up."

He'd been hiking cross-country due north for several hours. "The girl had said thirty kilometers, a little less than twenty miles." He had no idea of the time, but he had a lot of experience hiking long distances in the dark. "I think I've been walking maybe four or five hours at a fast pace, so I figure maybe I've made up close to half the distance, maybe a little more."

Sam wondered where he might hit the Rio Grande or how far he'd need to go after he crossed. And he had no papers; he'd left his wallet in his car. He felt in his pockets. He still had his keys.

He put a finger into the watch pocket of his jeans and pulled out the small stone given to him by the old Bruja woman. "I also have *this*. I'd almost forgotten about it." He put it back in its place. "Not sure if it has given me luck this time," he mused, "but I escaped and I'm still alive."

There was an outcrop nearby where he thought he could get some shade. It was going to be another hot day, so getting out of the sun seemed to be a good idea. "I wish I had my pack and a map," he said as he settled into the sparse shadow. "And I wonder how long I've got before Cerides starts looking for me."

Sam dozed through the day and woke up thirsty. It was late afternoon. He poked through the bag and found one of the Cokes. "Not a good thing to drink out hiking, but it's all I've got. She meant well."

He sipped the drink and rummaged around to find one of the wrapped tortillas. It was stale, and the beans were cold, but he wolfed it down and drained the rest of the Coke. Sam found the small compass and checked it. It was a toy, but it seemed to work well enough. It agreed with his assessment of the sun's movement, so he fixed the direction of due north and started hiking. The terrain was rough, and he had no idea where he was going, but he continued, always pushing north. Occasionally he fell, but the thought of Cerides threatening Smidgeon and Lance kept him moving through the waning daylight and into the night.

"Luckily, I've got years of practice doing this," he grumbled to himself. "It's tough, but I have to keep going."

In a few hours, he found a small dry creek bed trending due north, and his instincts were to follow it. After about an hour, he could see some sparse water sparkling in the distance. He approached the reflection carefully and could see lights across the water in the distance.

"Gotta be the river," he said.

He scouted the bank and squinted in the distance. It was dark, and he had no idea where he was or if it was a good place to cross. He found a spot with some cover and settled down to keep watch. He ate the rest of his food and drank his second Coke. He pocketed the small compass and tossed the bag to his side.

"I'm going to have to chance it," he mumbled. "What are they going to do, deport me?"

He cautiously approached the water, looking intently all around, and walked across. Most of the water was hip deep, but he had to swim against the slow current in the center. He soon felt bottom again and walked across. He found some cover on the other side and waited. His clothes were wet and clammy. He took his shoes and socks off to let them dry in the desert air. All he had to do was figure out where he was and find some way of getting back home without crossing paths with Cerides again.

"I wonder if they've reported me missing."

~ * ~

Smidgeon was mentally exhausted after driving endless miles down an empty New Mexico highway, but she was even more frustrated by the last note.

"Where I've been and who I've met and what I've done," she kept mumbling to herself. "Let's see, been to Durham, then to Lawrenceburg, Ozark, Osage, Turpin. Those were the specific places. I figure it's only the last four. Durham means something, too, but I don't know what. The last one was even weirder, but it's more of a crazy crossroads, just a place where the states come together; nobody would have ever thought of trying to stand on that spot." She squinted in the glare as she tried to make sense of her thoughts. "A meeting place of three states, like it's supposed to tie things together?"

She came up to another turnoff she was expecting and continued her southerly journey.

"Who did I meet?" She thought long and hard while she drove. Miles passed before it dawned on her. "It has to mean the names on the graves!"

She searched her memory. "Samuels, Hanson, Ennis, Davids."

She ran the names through her mind again and again. "I've always hated riddles ever since I was a kid. I could never figure them out."

Smidgeon got a hamburger in Roswell before continuing her way south. She had been attracted to the café because it was not unlike The Mossback. She had brought a small notebook with her and had scribbled the town names and last names in two columns. She stared at the two lists while she ate.

"You need anything else, sweetie?"

Smidgeon broke her concentration and looked up. The waitress looked like her sister from another mother, complete with a stray hair she kept blowing out of her eyes. Her name tag said "HOLLY."

"No, thank you, ma'am. I'm good."

"What you got there? You look like you're trying to solve a puzzle." Holly asked pointing at the notebook, "What is it, some word game or something?"

"Yeah, sort of. I'm trying to make some sense out of these...place names here," she said pointing to the first column, "And names here."

She blew the hair out of her eyes as she bent forward and squinted down. "I'm pretty good at word games," she said. "It's always best to look at the easiest thing first. I'll try the first letters of each." Holly sat down and picked up Smidgeon's pencil. "May I?"

"Sure," Smidgeon said.

Holly began to write. "The most obvious is L O O T on this side and S H E D on the other."

Smidgeon blinked in disbelief.

"Loot Shed," Holly giggled. "Sounds like money in a tool shed. Does that mean anything to you?" As her eyes met Smidgeon's, Holly realized she had struck a nerve. "You okay, honey? It does mean something to you, doesn't it?"

"Yes, I-I-I," Smidgeon stammered. "I can't believe I didn't see it."

"I told you I was good at this kind of thing. Plus, sometimes it helps to have a second set of eyes to look at a problem, you know? It's why I always talk to my friends about my love life or lack thereof." Holly giggled.

"Yeah, thank you, Holly, thank you so much!"

"Glad I could help. Will there be anything else?"

"No," Smidgeon said as she pulled out a twenty. "Keep it."

"Really, no, it's too much, let me get you some change."

"No, I've been trying to make heads or tails out of those words for hundreds of miles. I'm a waitress, too. You keep it, okay? You just made my day."

"You're a waitress?"

"Well, more an owner, but I do most of the waitressing. Small café down in Van Horn." Smidgeon fumbled in her purse and handed Holly one of the café's business cards.

Holly looked at the card, "Oh, I see, down in Texas?"

"Yeah, little café a lot like this one. I've been away on some family business, and I need to be getting back. Thank you again, Holly," Smidgeon said as she stood. She turned to leave and came back and hugged Holly. "God bless you!"

In the parking lot, Smidgeon saw a pay phone and made a collect call to The Mossback.

"Lance? I'm in Roswell, New Mexico. I should be there in a few hours."

"You need to be careful," he said. "Cerides is looking for you."

Sixteen

Sam stirred awake when an early morning shaft of sunlight flashed across his face. He checked his shoes and socks; it hadn't taken long for them to dry in the desert air. He looked at his little compass and frowned; the swim had ruined it, so he tossed it away. He figured the morning sun was due east and he walked north. He found a small graded road and soon discovered the lights he'd noticed the previous night belonged to the small community of Langtry. It was a lucky break; Langtry was right on US 90, but it also meant he was a couple of hundred miles from home.

"I lost track of how far we drove after we crossed the border," he said.

He found a small store up on the highway and washed his face and arms in the restroom.

"You buying anything?" the clerk said as he exited.

"Sorry," Sam said, shrugging. He wasn't sure if he wanted to ask for help at this point. He was hungry but had managed a good long drink of water from the tap.

He started walking due west on the highway. He'd done a bit of hitchhiking in his youth, so when he heard a car, he turned and stuck out his thumb. He didn't hold out much hope for snagging a ride so far away from anyplace significant, so he was surprised when a white sedan stopped.

"Where ya headed?"

The voice belonged to the driver, a black man with a big smile on his face.

"Van Horn, several hours west," Sam said, "But I'll go as far as you can take me."

"Heck, man, I'm enjoying the scenery, hop in and I'll take you," he said, "Name's Jeffers, Jeffers Lincoln."

"Sam Milton."

All the windows in the car were rolled down, and they tried to talk above the road noise.

"Got three days before I need to get back to my job. I'm a postal worker in Kansas City. My first vacation ever! Trying to stay off the interstate. Heading up to Roswell now, to where they had those aliens."

"Aliens?" Sam asked.

"You know, the 1947 spaceship…it was supposed to have crashed there. Big government cover-up."

"Oh, right. I remember reading about that. Not sure what you'll find."

"Anyway, I been reading the map. I think Van Horn is where I turn north again, go up by the Carlsbad Caverns and on up to Roswell. I was checking out Judge Roy Bean back there."

"How was it?"

"Touristy. It was a place to stop on the road west, I guess. You weren't there?"

"I went there years ago. I'm passing through."

"You look a little ragged, you on hard times or something?"

"Yeah, 'or something' I guess. I got into a little mess and got stranded in Mexico."

"In Mexico? I mean, I know it's close and all...hey, you're not one of those—"

"Illegals? Not hardly, but I crossed the river, if that's what you mean. I live in Van Horn."

Jeffers kept quiet for a few minutes as he drove.

"I'm not going to get in no hassle having you in my car?"

"Don't think so."

"But you said you got stranded. Look, mister, I don't want no trouble."

"My problems were with one man, a criminal. He took me prisoner and was holding me in Mexico."

Jeffers blinked at Sam wide-eyed. "You mean like kidnapped? Seriously?"

Sam nodded. They drove on in silence; Sam glanced at him but said nothing as Jeffers kept his eyes on the road ahead.

The remainder of the time they engaged in small talk, and Sam told his benefactor a little about living in Texas. Jeffers added a few details about life at the post office in Kansas City.

Eventually, Sam saw the familiar contours of the mountains beyond Van Horn in the distance.

"Won't be long now, we're getting pretty close," he said.

"Anyplace good to eat there?"

Sam giggled.

"What's so funny?"

"I work at a place, a café I mean. It's called The Mossback. So yeah, I think we can manage a good meal. In fact, I owe you for the ride."

"Naw, you don't owe me a thing, man."

"A four-hour ride? I'll treat you to a good meal."

Jeffers pulled over at a small roadside store. "I need to call home and check in with my mama," he said. He got out and made a brief call on a pay phone.

"Just tell me where to go," he said when he returned.

~ * ~

A stranger opened the cafe door while Lance enjoyed a rare afternoon meal break with a couple of tacos. A tall man took off his Stetson and glanced around the empty room before sitting down with Lance.

Transfixed by the stranger's intense cold blue eyes, Lance held the last bite in his mouth as his guest placed the hat on a seat next to him and continued to stare at him.

"Go ahead and chew that danged thing before you choke yourself to death. I'll start. You must be Lance Norton. Local lawman by the name of Clay told me I should talk to you. I'm Mulvihill Hollis, but folks call me Mule."

Lance swallowed his bite and extended a hand. Mule shook it vigorously.

"I'm hoping you can help me."

"With what?"

"I'm an ex-deputy sheriff myself, but since I retired, I've been doing a bit of private investigating. I've been trying to track down an Italian guy I hear has been nosing around these parts. The Mexican federal police agency informally hired me...he has quite a crime network down there, and they'd gotten information he's expanding it up here. Wanted me to keep tabs on him."

"You're talking about Cerides."

Mule raised one eyebrow. "Yes. Indigo Cerides. That's not all. I didn't even tell Clay this. Before the *Federales* hired me, they asked the FBI about him. Our boys have a file on him going back to World War Two. He was a prisoner of war."

"POW?"

"Yep. He escaped from a POW camp near Marfa and was never caught. According to their file, they assumed he fled across the border. The Mexicans said he's spent quite a bit of time in prison while down there, too. Bad dude."

"So does the FBI still want him for escaping?"

"I don't reckon it's an active case, but since he's started working this side of the border, who knows? He has some way of crossing without being tracked."

"How?"

"It's not hard...there are places to ford the river and even a few local bridges. Heck, people vacation in Big Bend and the border is nothing but a river to them. You can pee or poop on whatever side is most convenient."

"I had a feeling about him when he was in here. He gave me the creeps, you know what I'm saying? He made my skin crawl."

"Mr. Norton, he is gen-u-wine bad news." Mule hesitated and pointed at Lance's plate. "Are you going to eat your other taco? I'm starving."

Lance pushed the plate across the table. Mule gobbled the taco down in three bites.

"What's your relationship to the police? Can I tell you something in confidence?" Lance asked while Mule chewed his last bite.

Mule swallowed. "Well, like I said, I'm a *former* officer of the law, but these days I got my own way of doing things, and sometimes they get in the way. Still, if you know something about this guy you're afraid to share with the locals, it's better if you tell me. It might work out for the both of us."

Lance rubbed his fingers across his mouth while deciding what to say. "There's something about Sam."

Mule pulled out a small notebook from his pocket and flipped a page. "Sam Milton? Works here, doesn't he? Good friends with the owner, one Smidgeon Toll, and by good friends I mean romantic. That Sam?"

"Yeah. He's been missing for several days. I think Cerides has him."

"Wait, you mean like kidnapped? Now why in tarnation would he kidnap Sam?"

"Well..." Lance thought about what Smidgeon said about using his best judgment. "We're pretty sure it has something to do with some stuff we recently discovered around here."

Mule Hollis tapped his fingers on the table and stared at Lance. "Kidnapping is pretty serious, but it's right in line with what this Indigo Cerides might do. Extortion, intimidation, and murder are all pretty common with this guy. But you don't have any proof, except for the fact that Sam is missing. What about the owner?"

A group of tourists hustled in the door.

"Look," Mule said, "I see you have to get back to work. We don't have any proof of an actual crime, so I can appreciate the fact that you don't want to involve the sheriff. I'll keep this to myself. Can we talk later?"

"How about later tonight? I close about eight-thirty."

Mule stood up, his hat in his left hand as he extended his right. "I'll be here."

"Smidgeon should be back sometime this evening as well."

"Well, tell her about this Cerides character, you know, how dangerous he is, okay?"

"I already have. You need anything else?"

"Naw, I'm good. Thanks for the taco."

Lance stared out the window as Mule Hollis left the parking lot in a cloud of dust.

"I knew it," he mumbled, "I could feel him almost oozing evil right from the start. We gotta find Sam, if'n he's still alive. Maybe this guy can help."

~ * ~

As she drove south, Smidgeon tried to visualize Loot's shed. She hadn't spent much time out there and for the most part only remembered clutter and weeds. Her thoughts returned to the note and she whispered, "what you done."

After ten miles or so, she suddenly screamed, "Southwest!" and slammed her hand on the steering wheel so hard it hurt. "Every grave was on the southwest side of the cemetery. I need to look outside the southwest wall of the shed." She thought for a minute. "Southwest...Van Horn is southwest and come to think of it, Loot's old place is sort of on the southwestern side of town, too."

She again tried to picture the layout of the house and shed, but her memory was too vague to figure out direction. She'd need to be there with Sam or Lance to get her bearings, but she was delighted to think she might have solved every part of the riddle. As she drove, she wondered about the person who had hidden so many clues and what the link was between that individual and Loot, "...and to Daddy," she added out loud.

She felt elated as she crossed the Texas state line and saw the Guadalupe Mountains looming ahead of her. As she meandered down US Highway 62, she passed the national park and thought about the first time she met Sam.

"He lied, said he'd been hiking up here." She smirked. "I've always had a thing about danged liars, but I guess he had his reasons." She stole some glances of the landscape. "Still, I've never been up in there. I'll ask Sam if we can do it one day."

Her heart fluttered a little when she saw the highway sign directing her to Van Horn fifty-five miles away. "Texas 54," she said to herself. She was still almost an hour away, but she felt as if she were just around the corner. Along the way, she recognized the spot where she had picked up Sam the morning he'd hiked out of the mountains. He had been beaten by MacGregg's ranch hands and barely escaped by walking across the desert. Although they had met before, she always considered it to be the day she first started falling in love with him. She began to cry again.

"Where are you, Sam?"

~ * ~

Lance was busing a table when two people came in; he hurried his work and barely looked up. The taller of the two caught his attention right away. Not many blacks came in The Mossback, and he casually nodded at him with his chin. Then he noticed the scraggly, shorter figure.

"Sam!"

Lance almost knocked a table over rushing to the entrance. He and Sam hugged and finished by shaking hands.

"So, did you miss me?" Sam laughed and pointed to the other man and said, "Lance, this is Jeffers, he was kind enough to offer me a ride today. He's hungry so let's feed him. Jeffers, this is my good friend and associate, Lance."

"Good to meet you," Jeffers said.

Sam said, "Sit down and make yourself at home. I'm going to go clean up a little. I think I might have something to change into in the back."

Lance said, "Yeah, I think you do. Or you could take my truck and head over to the house."

Sam retrieved a menu and handed it to Jeffers. "I'll be right back."

In the kitchen, Chuy was at the flat grill, and he dropped his spatula with a clang when he saw the familiar face. "Mister Sam!" He rushed over and patted Sam on the shoulder.

"Hey, Chuy."

"Where's Miss Smidgeon?"

Sam turned to Lance with a questioning glance.

"I'll explain in a few minutes...you go get cleaned up."

"Comp Jeffers, okay? I owe him for the ride."

"Sure thing."

Sam opened the bottom drawer of the file cabinet and found a change of clothes. "Holdover from the old days," he said. "Even have a change of socks and underwear." He sniffed at the shirt, "Just a hint of smoke, but it will have to do."

"So where you been?"

"Long story. Where's Smidgeon?"

"Trying to follow a trail. She's been all over. North Carolina, Tennessee, Arkansas—"

"What? Why?"

"It started with the note you found and left in your car in one of those Lucky Strike cans. Guess you found it out south of Valentine."

"Oh, right. Cerides wanted to know what I found out there. I told him I didn't find anything. I think he figured I was lying. In fact, I did open it, but it didn't make any sense. I didn't even remember what it said. I was headed back here so we could all try to figure it out together when he snatched me."

"Yeah, he's been back here a couple of times, snooping around. Where were you?"

"Someplace in Mexico. We crossed at a small bridge outside the park at Big Bend. We drove for hours after crossing. We made so many turns, I lost track."

"He's some kind of big criminal down there."

"I think he's some kind of big criminal everywhere."

"Escaped POW from World War Two, too."

"Yeah, he told me. Doesn't think anybody cares. So you've told the police about all of this?"

"Not really. Clay is suspicious of him but hasn't tied anything back to you or Smidgeon. Our story is you and Smidgeon are away on a family emergency. Then there's the private detective."

"That is a good story...it works for both of us. Wait, what? Private detective?"

"Yeah. He's looking for Cerides, too. I did tell him about you being kidnapped, but he's agreed to keep it quiet...doesn't seem to matter as much now. I'm supposed to see him again later."

"Well, maybe he can help. You mind if I go ahead and change?" Sam asked, already taking off his shirt.

"I'll leave you to your privacy. Let me go get this Jeffers fella's order."

Sam quickly changed his clothes, and as he began to leave the office, Lance met him head-on.

"Jeffers is gone."

"What do you mean?"

"Gone. Not in the restroom either. Vamoosed."

Sam rushed through the empty dining room and out the front door and scanned the parking lot. The car he arrived in had vanished. He returned to the restaurant.

"See what I mean?" Lance said. "Gone. Guess he changed his mind."

"He said he was really hungry. I have a bad feeling about this."

"What do you mean?"

"Cerides is crazier than you can imagine. How could I be so stupid? I think this Jeffers dude was sent there to pick me up. Man, he was *good*, too, talking all about his job at the post office in Kansas City."

"You really think so? Maybe you're a tiny bit paranoid."

"Lance, I was kidnapped, starved, and beaten. Cerides is looking for something, and he will stop at nothing. He wants Smidgeon. He must have set up my escape, and he knew right where I'd go."

"You better lay low."

"Yeah, but where? He knows the café, he knows your house, and he knows my house. Van Horn is too small."

"Motel maybe?"

"Again, he'd figure it out. And he knows my car and your truck."

"Loot's old truck maybe?"

"It still in the shed?"

"Yeah. It's been covered up for a while, though. I threw a tarp over it. Even if he had been nosing around out there, he might not recognize it. I think maybe it might be okay."

Sam looked down in thought. "You know, Cerides did say he read about the murders and the gold mine and such. It's what rekindled his interest in Loot and Joe."

"Well, this is a good time. Nobody has seen you but me and Chuy," Lance said.

"And Jeffers," Sam added. "But forget about him. I need to lay low for a few hours. I wonder if Marcy would put me up until you can close the café."

"I can close it right now. Ain't nobody here."

"But it might look suspicious."

They heard the tell-tale sound of tires on gravel outside.

"Somebody's here. You get into the back and hide out in the office while I deal with whoever this is," Lance said. He glanced out the window, squinting at the dust cloud. "Wait, where'd they go? Quick, you hide while I check this out."

As Sam passed through the kitchen, Chuy asked him, "You want something to eat?"

"Not right now, Chuy, thanks. Hey, don't tell anybody I'm here, okay?"

"You got it, boss."

There was a rattle at the back door, and Sam froze.

"Is somebody back there?" Chuy asked. "It's locked."

"Must be Lance," Sam said.

The deadbolt clicked, and the door opened. A blaze of afternoon light framed Smidgeon as she lingered in the doorway to let her eyes adjust. To Sam, she looked like an angel, despite her crumpled clothes and mussed hair.

"Sam!"

The embrace took long minutes until it was interrupted by Lance.

"This whole thing is getting better and better," he said. "Now *both* of you have to leave. Head out in Smidgeon's car, and we can figure out the details later. Just go."

"I've got a lot to tell everybody," Smidgeon said.

Sam hugged her again. "I'm sure you do, sweetie, but we're pretty sure Cerides is gunning for both of us, and we have to get out of here." He kissed her again, looked deep in her eyes, and added, "Now."

Seventeen

After parking on the back side of the Dolings Motel, Smidgeon got a key from her friend, owner Marcy Dolings. Sam kept out of sight in one of the rooms while she conferred with Marcy. He remembered the last time he had stayed in one of those rooms; it was the morning Smidgeon had picked him up on the highway out north of Van Horn.

About dusk, there was a light knock on the door and Sam peeked out the window; he saw it was Smidgeon and Marcy and let them in.

Marcy gave him a brief hug. "Sam, you do seem to have a flair for the dramatic, don't you?"

"Hi, Marcy. Yeah, I guess it seems that way."

Smidgeon interrupted. "We have a plan, Sam. Marcy's late husband Ed had a hunting cabin out north of Sierra Blanca."

"Up FM Eleven-eleven?"

"Yes. Do you know the area?"

"I nosed around up that way quite a bit."

"Well, it isn't much, but Ed loved going up there, and I've kept paying the taxes and utilities just in case. I don't know why...I guess it's another part of him I wasn't ready to let go of."

"I understand. But it's remote?"

"Oh, yes. Only a few people around here know about it. I go out and check on it now and then but haven't been there in over a year. It should still have power and water, though."

Their conversation was interrupted by another knock.

Sam looked out the window and saw Lance, so he opened the door.

"Evening, folks. Miss Smidgeon called and told me the room number, so I closed up a little early and walked over. I didn't want it to look too suspicious. It sounds like we got a few things to do."

"I already told Lance about the cabin," Smidgeon said.

"I've been checking on your house while you've been away," Lance said to Sam and Smidgeon, "so I can go by like I've been doing, but this time I'll grab a few things."

"I've made a list," Smidgeon said.

"Right. Even if Cerides shows up, it's a good cover."

Marcy continued and turned to Sam. "After dark, you and Smidgeon can go over to Lance's place and get Loot's truck."

Lance said, "Key is hanging on the hook right inside the door. I think you'll be safer in his truck than in her car. They'll spot the car, but I doubt they'd be looking for the truck."

Sam liked what he was hearing. "What do you think, maybe park the car in the shed?" he asked.

"Right," Lance said. Park it in there and cover it with the tarp. Don't know how much gas is in the truck, though, but I have most of a five gallon can in the shed. Throw it in the back and use it if you need it. Should we alert the police?"

Smidgeon said, "Officially, no. But Marcy is going to talk to Clay privately."

"He isn't going to like it." Sam chuckled.

Marcy broke in. "He should be used to this kind of thing from you three by now."

"What about this private eye?" Sam asked.

"Mule Hollis? I was supposed to see him later, but this is more important," Lance said. "I'm sure I'll catch up with him at some point."

"After you get the stuff from the house," Sam said, "where should we meet?"

"Head out First Street and keep going."

"The old road that goes to Allamoore?"

"Right. Drive out two miles and wait. I'll be along."

Smidgeon added, "We can follow the same road most of the way to Sierra Blanca."

"That's great. The interstate would be pretty risky," Sam said.

"So what are you going to tell Clay?" Smidgeon asked.

Marcy said, "Pretty much the truth. You are both in danger. From what Lance has said, they're looking for this Cerides character. So this can fit in with the plan. Since Cerides is looking for you two, maybe he'll surface long enough for them to catch him."

"What about directions and a key, you know, for the cabin?" Sam asked.

"It's all in this envelope," Marcy said, handing a packet to Smidgeon. "It's a little involved, but you should be able to find it. Lordy, we drove out there in the dark for years."

Smidgeon squeezed Sam's arm. "I'll find it," he said.

~ * ~

Several hours later, Sam and Smidgeon made their way over to Tesoro Road.

"Do you think anyone is following us?" Smidgeon asked.

"So far so good," Sam answered.

In Loot's shed, he uncovered the old Jeep truck. "I hope this thing starts. Everything hinges on it."

"What will we do if it doesn't?"

"Well, I guess we'd have to take your car. Cerides knows about it, but with us going down back roads and driving out there in the dark, it's a chance we'd have to take. The truck was running a few months ago, so we'll see."

He retrieved the keys from the wall.

"Sam, I need to ask you something."

"What?"

"Which way is southwest?"

He pointed to the side wall. "I'd say this is the southwest wall." He stood in the doorway and looked at the sky. "Yeah, I'm pretty sure. Why?"

"Just something I've been thinking about. I'll tell you later."

He had a puzzled look on his face, and answered with a tentative, "Okay," then continued. "We don't have time for anything else right now anyway. I've got the key. If it starts, I'll pull it out, and you pull your car into the shed."

"Okay," she said.

He flashed the lights momentarily. "It's got power." He turned the key. The starter groaned its disapproval.

"Nothing," Sam pumped the accelerator twice and held it to the floor while he tried again. The engine coughed but it died. He tried again, and the truck rumbled to life.

"Great," he said. "The fuel gauge shows half full, but I don't know whether to trust it."

Sam got out, found the gas can Lance had mentioned, and put it in the back; he returned to the cab, moved the truck out of the shed to the street, and waited while Smidgeon eased her sedan into the shed. Sam parked behind her. He let the truck idle while she gathered her suitcase and the few things she had accumulated on the trip. A paper grocery bag clinked as she carried it. She put the bag next to her purse on the passenger side of the truck.

"I think this is all I need from the car."

"Okay," Sam said. He picked up the tarp, spread it over the car and closed the shed doors; they both got into the truck.

"Here goes nothing," he said, and he backed to the street and pulled away.

First Street ran parallel to Broadway, so they had to double back toward town far enough to get to a side street so they could pass over the railroad tracks. Once they turned, that road would take them west out of town. A few blocks away, they heard sirens and saw at least one vehicle with flashing lights heading somewhere in a hurry.

"Wonder what's up?" Smidgeon asked.

"No time to find out, we need to head west," Sam said.

The pavement veered to the right which they knew indicated the end of town, but the road continued unpaved to the dark horizon.

"So far, so good," Sam said as they rattled and bumped on their way.

"Two miles," Smidgeon said.

"Odometer doesn't work on this clunker," he said. "I figure five or ten minutes... thirty miles an hour would be only about four or five minutes at best."

"Let's stick with five. I think we're going about thirty," Smidgeon said.

After five minutes, he pulled as far to the right as he felt was safe and turned off the lights.

"Should I leave it running?" Sam asked.

"Shut it off. I need some quiet."

Sam turned the key, and they were both bathed in a wave of silence.

"That's better," she said.

~ * ~

Lance glanced out the window periodically while he filled Smidgeon's list. He felt like a burglar except for the suitcase. He packed it feverishly with spare underwear, socks, and extra clothes for both Sam and Smidgeon.

"Ain't got time to coordinate outfits," he mumbled. "Hope all this stuff fits."

He spotted Sam's wallet on the dresser and slipped it in his pocket. In the kitchen, he filled a grocery bag with things like Spam, Wolf Brand Chili, rice, beans, a few cans of vegetables, various soups, and crackers. He looked through a drawer for a can opener and found a military-style opener.

"Betting this is Sam's. He'll know how to use it."

He peeked out the window again.

"The same car," he said. "I'm sure of it; that's three times!"

After the car was out of sight, he quickly put the bags and suitcase in the bed of his pickup. He locked the door, got in the truck and waited.

"I'll give them a few minutes and then I'll high-tail it out of here after their next pass," he mumbled.

Two minutes later, the car came by again. It was circling, going right to left. As soon as it was out of sight, he eased the truck out the drive and slowly followed in the same direction with his lights off.

"It's dark...they might not notice me. They're circling counter-clockwise so I'll try to zig-zag my way over to meet Sam and Smidgeon without them seeing me."

Lance slowly made the first turn. He didn't see the car, so he continued at the same pace and got to the next cross-street and turned right. There were no headlights in his rearview mirror so he turned on his lights. He sped up and quickly zig-zagged his way across town.

He only saw two other vehicles, but he was sure no one was following him.

"They'd probably figure I was heading back to my place anyway."

He eased his old truck up to forty, but it rattled so loudly he dropped the speed back down until it stopped shaking.

"It's about all the old girl can take on this road. Sam and Smidgeon shouldn't be too far ahead."

After a few more minutes he spotted a slight reflection from what he hoped was a tail light lens and he slowed down. The old truck loomed on the right, and he pulled alongside it and turned off his headlights.

Sam exited the Jeep truck's cab.

"You made it."

"Barely."

"What do you mean?"

"Somebody was casing the house. I'm sure of it. I saw a car circling around."

"Did they see you?"

"I think I got out of there with them not knowing which way I was going." Lance looked back. "Doesn't look like any headlights following me anyway."

"Yet," Sam said. "Smidgeon says she thinks she can get us over to FM eleven-eleven on the back roads, but I suggest you wait a few minutes, continue this same way, too, and head back on the interstate."

"Right." Lance nodded.

Smidgeon got out of the Jeep. "After you swing back from Allamoore, I think you should head down to Michigan Flat so you can go back into town from that direction."

"Good idea. There's too much open country for them to cover it all," Sam said. "We might actually pull this off."

"Oh, found this at the house, figured you might need it," Lance handed Sam the wallet.

"Hah. I forgot I had left it in my car when Cerides nabbed me."

Lance quickly moved the suitcase and food from his truck and said, "You best be on your way. Good luck." He shook Sam's hand while Smidgeon secured the suitcase and bags as best as she could.

"Looks like you did good, Lance," she said. "Tomorrow at the café, it's business as usual, right?"

"Right."

Sam and Smidgeon got in their truck, and started it with no trouble. Sam moved forward about a hundred yards before turning on the lights.

Smidgeon squinted into the distance. "My memory is pretty sketchy about these roads, but keep heading this way for now."

"Maybe we better go ahead and hit the interstate after Allamoore?"

"I'm wondering," she said. "It would be faster. I'd hate to get lost. I know I can get us most of the way, but we stand out like a sore thumb out here, too."

"Plus, they don't know they're looking for an old Jeep truck," Sam said.

"At least we hope they don't. Can you see any lights behind us?"

Sam glanced in the rearview mirror. "No. Even if we did, it would likely be Lance."

"So we could head west long before he gets here to go east."

"Let's do it," Sam said.

There wasn't much of anything in Allamoore except a big talc mine.

As they passed the entrance, Smidgeon said, "It starts and stops all the time. Allamoore is hardly a bump in the road." She added, "Turn left here."

Once they were heading west on the interstate, Sam looked in the rearview mirror. "I think we're still clear." He continued, "I'm pretty familiar with that farm road," Sam said.

"I know you are, sweetie, and I've got the rest of the directions once we get there."

Sam kept his eye on the rearview mirror, but the traffic seemed to be mostly big trucks; a few honked because he was having a hard time keeping his speed up.

"Speed limit's still fifty-five, but some of these trucks are doing seventy or better."

"I've listened to truckers complain about the speed limit ever since they lowered it. I reckon in a couple of years they'll raise it again."

In Sierra Blanca, they exited and made their way north.

After fifteen minutes or so, Sam mused, "I used to park around here, pretend my car was broken down," he explained, "then I'd hike off to the east."

"From here?"

"Yep."

"It's got to be twenty or more miles!"

Sam shrugged. "I figured my car was safer on the bigger road than on the back roads. It was usually a couple of days over the weekend, and this road was less traveled than Texas 54."

"I still can't believe you did that so many times."

"I had the *fever*, as Loot used to say."

"I'm so glad you got it out of your system, honey."

"Did I? They say it gets in your blood and doesn't let go. I hear Tim MacGregg is having a heck of a time trying to dig out what's left of the mine."

"It's what I always said. They'd find you out and knock down the mountain trying to get at the gold. He's letting the ranch deteriorate while he spends a fortune digging. He hasn't found a danged thing."

"I never was a hundred percent sure it was the right place, I mean, it seemed to fit the clues but—"

Smidgeon gently touched Sam's forearm. "Speaking of clues, in all this rush we haven't had time to talk about what happened to you."

"Cerides waylaid me by preying on my good nature...he pretended his car was broken down. When I went back up the Brite Road, I stopped to help and he pulled a gun on me. You found the car?"

"Local sheriff's office found it and contacted Clay. Lance and I went and picked it up."

"I figured the police were on my trail the whole time."

"No, there hadn't been enough time to file a missing person's report at that point. When we got to the car, we found the Lucky Strike tin with the clue, and I decided I couldn't wait for the law to decide if you were in trouble or not."

"We have two of those boxes now, I guess."

Smidgeon howled. "Lordy, two? Add five more, plus a smaller one. All Lucky Strike."

"Wait, what? Eight cans?"

"Yep. The one you found out Old Brite was only the *second* one. That one led me to a bunch of others."

"I barely peeked at the note. Didn't understand it at all."

"So we figured. It sent me all the way to Durham, North Carolina."

"North Carolina?"

"Yes. It said 'Duke Chapel.'"

"Right, now I remember. I had no idea what it meant. Something else, too. I thought we'd figure it out together."

Smidgeon continued, "Lance knew Duke University had a Duke Chapel, so I figured I had better go there and figure out the other word on the note."

"I remember it sounded foreign."

"Yes, it was." Smidgeon said. "Savonarola. I had to ask when I got there—it's some Italian guy. They have a bunch of statues in a small entryway to the church. One was this Savonarola. There was a smaller can stuck to the back of his statue with a note sending me to a cemetery in Tennessee."

"Tennessee?"

"Lawrenceburg, Tennessee. It's a long story, Sam. I've got all the tins and notes. Easier to explain all the details when you can see it all together. But to make a long story short, I think it all points back to Loot's shed."

"Loot's shed? A note sent you halfway across the country only to have you come back to Loot's shed?"

"I know it doesn't make any sense, but it sure looks that way."

"We've been driving what, about thirty minutes?"

"Probably. Oh, Marcy's directions?" She examined the small sheet of paper in her hand with a flashlight.

"Yes. Should come across a row of mailboxes with two roads intersecting sort of catty-corner from each other. About thirty miles, she said."

"Well, we aren't doing anywhere near sixty, so we probably have a few more minutes."

Smidgeon looked out the window. "It's really dark tonight. Anything behind us?"

"Nothing. Just black road back there."

"Anyway, that's why I was asking you about the southwestern wall of the shed."

"The note said something about the southwestern wall?"

"No. But I noticed every single tin was at a grave on the southwestern side of the cemetery. The first one seemed sort of random, but I realized after I found it, the way the cemetery was situated, the grave was on the southwestern corner. I pretty much assumed the direction would be southwest and quickly found all the other graves."

"I have to see these notes. So there were six, all except the first in cemeteries?"

"No, the last one wasn't. It was in a strange place, right where New Mexico, Oklahoma, and Texas all meet. It had a riddle."

"Not another riddle," Sam laughed, shaking his head. "What was it?"

"Look at where you been, who you met, what you done."

"Wow. Much worse than Slim's."

"It's a puzzle. I'll show you when I can lay it all out for you."

"Wait, I see some mailboxes on the right. Are they supposed to be on the right?"

"Yes, on the right. There should be a graded road coming from the right about fifty feet before the mailboxes and another road going away on the left right after the mailboxes."

Sam slowed down and said, "There's a road and...here are the mailboxes; and there's the other road on the left."

"Okay, turn here. It's about ten more miles," she said. "There should be a fork after about four miles, take a left, and look for another after two miles, take a right. After three miles at a dead end, take another right. The cabin will be on the right after about a mile. It's marked with boulders on either side of the driveway."

"If this is the right road, it shouldn't be too hard as long as you keep me on track."

"How did you hike out in places like this?"

"I got used to it," Sam said. "It was what I thought I needed to do. Kinda like right now." Smidgeon repeated each of the directions for every turn, and soon they spotted two boulders on either side of a small cutoff on the right. Sam turned, and his headlights illuminated a small building.

"Cabin is right," he said.

"Marcy said it has power and water, but we have to turn everything on at the fuse box on the back."

"I was thinking about pulling around there to block any view of the truck from the road, but if we turn on lights, it will be pretty obvious somebody is here. I'll park here close to the door so we can unload." He looked off into the distance. "There's a smattering of lights out there...one more won't mean much."

He got a small flashlight, and they walked up to the door, Smidgeon holding the key. Once they were inside, Sam surveyed the cabin with his flashlight.

"A bit dusty, but it's cozy," he said. "I'll see about the power."

He walked around the back and spied an outhouse.

"Great," he said. "We're going to be roughing it for sure."

He found the fuse box and opened it. He flipped the main switch on and walked around to the front; everything was still in the dark.

"I guess I expected something to be on," he said as he looked around the small area. He saw a light hanging over a small round table with a dangling cord, which he pulled; the cabin was bathed in light.

"What a relief," Smidgeon said as Sam went to get the rest of their things out of the truck.

Eighteen

Mule pulled into the darkened restaurant's parking lot. He had been driving around hoping to spot one of Cerides' vehicles but had been unsuccessful.

"Odd. That Lance fella told me he'd be here. Guess something must have come up." He looked all around. "I wouldn't think a place like this would close early...doesn't smell right." Mule turned around and scanned the main road. "I don't like it."

He pulled out of the parking lot.

"Might as well get me a place to stay," he said, as he spied the Dolings Motel nearby. He parked and walked into the office; it was empty. The hair on the back of his neck bristled as he looked all around before exiting the office. Mule looked up the row of doors in the front of the building. All was quiet. He walked around to the back and saw a light shining from the open door of one of the rooms. He pulled out his forty-five and approached the room.

"Oh, Lord," he said, as he twisted into the doorway, gun extended.

Mule paused at the body on the floor and quickly inspected the small bathroom to make sure the room was clear before he returned and dropped to one knee to check for a pulse.

"Guess I won't be staying here tonight," he muttered as he trotted to the office to call the police.

~ * ~

Lance could see two cars parked at the end of Tesoro Road as he approached his house. His heart began to race as he pulled into his driveway; he knew what was coming. He heard car doors open as he walked up to his front door. He visualized his shotgun leaning against the wall inside the doorway, so he hurried his limp and unlocked the door.

"Prewash, come on, girl," he said as he opened the door. The dog tarried in the doorway and growled. Lance reached in behind her to grab the barrel of the shotgun and with one swift motion he had it ready as he spun around.

Three men were facing him, two large and one smaller.

"Good evening, Mister Norton. We are so sorry we must disturb you." Lance recognized the voice as Cerides.

"If you will excuse me, I need to let my dog out to do her business. She's been cooped up all day." Prewash continued to growl. "You go on, girl, go pee."

The dog's fur bristled as she cautiously moved past the figures into the yard.

"Ah, yes, of course. Now, Mister Norton, there is no need for a gun, is there?"

Lance eased into the doorway and flipped on the porch light. Cerides was flanked by two men he recognized; all three were armed. "Pot calling the kettle, don't you think?"

Cerides glowered as Lance surveyed his visitors. One was the man he had held at gunpoint in his last meeting with the Italian; the other was Jeffers, the driver who had brought Sam to the café and disappeared.

"We are, as you have likely surmised, looking for Sam and most probably Miss Toll as well. My associate here," Cerides pointed at Jeffers, "who I believe you have already met, informs me that he brought Sam to the café this afternoon. You were at Sam's house this evening as well. We were watching. I applaud you for your skill in attempting to elude us. I assume you were collecting things for the two of them. I am no stranger to such actions myself. It is precisely what I would have done."

"Exactly what is it you want?"

"Can you put the gun down so we can go inside and talk?"

Lance scoffed at the three guns pointed in his direction. "You gotta be kidding me. I know only two things that might interest you right now. You ain't coming inside and I ain't putting the gun down."

"Another of my associates is sure he saw Miss Toll arrive at the café, and he was sure he spotted her later at a local motel but he lost track of her. Now your two friends seem to have vanished. Where are they?" Cerides spoke in a low but stern tone.

"Seems to me, when you wanted to talk to Sam you ended up kidnapping him and holding him prisoner in Mexico. He says you had him beaten."

"Ah, an unfortunate misunderstanding, no? I had to learn if he had the information I needed. I let him go."

"He escaped!"

"I wanted him to think he escaped. Like you, Mister Norton, Sam is an extremely competent man. I played upon his resourcefulness as a means of furthering my own goals."

"You expect me to believe you?"

"How else do you think my man Jeffers here was on hand to pick him up?"

"I have to admit, it was unexpected."

"By you, but not by me."

"But why did Jeffers leave?"

"To report to me, of course. I have trained my people well. I assumed I would soon be able to query Miss Toll. My mistake was in underestimating all of you." Cerides raised his gun, and the others inched forward. "Where are they, Mr. Norton?"

"I really have no idea. They hightailed it east somewhere, far away from here. I don't know where."

"Ah, this is what the motel owner said as well. Miss Toll, who works almost every day of the year and is beloved in this community, has a safe house? I do not believe it."

"The motel owner?"

"It is well known they are good friends. Miss Toll's car was seen there late this afternoon. Sadly, Mrs. Dolings did not survive our discussion. I think she may have had an undiagnosed heart condition. It was most unfortunate."

"You killed Marcy?"

Cerides sneered. "As I will you, Mr. Norton, if you do not tell me what I need to know. Again, where are they?"

Lance tightened his grip on the shotgun and pointed it at Cerides, who took a step back, allowing his two companions to move in front of him.

"You have only two shots, Mr. Norton. You most likely cannot take all three of us with two shots. A shotgun can be most effective against one, or perhaps two assailants, but three? I am afraid you are at the disadvantage here."

"I met them east, south of Kent."

Jeffers leaned over and whispered in Cerides ear.

"Jeffers here confirms he saw you return to town from the east. Mrs. Dolings also said something about the east. It is too easy. I do not believe you. You see, Mr. Norton, when you try to deceive a person whose very life has been a long series of sometimes quite elaborate deceptions, you are almost certain to fail. Drop your gun and come with us. I must insist."

The two henchmen had each taken one step forward when the night was pierced with a scream and a gunshot. Cerides crumpled to the ground, grabbing his leg in pain, and his two shocked companions turned and bent over to help their leader, who had released his gun. The shot had gone high when Cerides' leg buckled and the bullet had imbedded itself in the doorframe just to Lance's left.

"Good dog, Prewash!" Lance stepped forward, kicked the weapon to the side, and motioned for the three men to move back.

"Blasted dog," Cerides said. He was bleeding from the ankle where Prewash had bitten him.

Lance gestured again with the shotgun. "Pick him up and get out. I forgot to tell you, she's old and looks slow but she's still a heckuva watchdog. Don't blame her, she was protecting me. She knew you was going to try to hurt me. I'm telling you the truth: I really don't know where they are. Now get up and get out."

"We'll get him and his wretched dog later," Cerides said, trembling in pain. "She dies, Mr. Norton. Understand that. Before all this is over, she dies."

Lance held his temper and gestured with the business end of his shotgun again. "Never mind your threats. She's had her shots. Now, get out. The neighbors down the road don't like gunfire out here. Cops are probably already on their way."

Cerides turned and glared at Lance as he limped to one of the cars. The other two followed, and they all drove away in a rush.

Lance put a plastic bucket over Cerides' gun.

~ * ~

Smidgeon arranged all of the old cigarette tins on the small table, taking care to put them in order.

"This is the one from your car," she said, pointing to the first one on the left.

"The one from Old Brite Road."

"Yes," she said as she opened it and handed Sam the paper it contained.

He read it out loud, "Duke Chapel—Savonarola—lower back." He blinked at Smidgeon. "Tell me again, how did you know what it meant?"

"Lance guessed it was the Duke Chapel at Duke University in North Carolina. He'd been there, I guess...he has a cousin in Durham. With you gone, it seemed the best thing to do to help find you was to, you know, follow the clue."

"Savonarola?"

"Some Italian religious guy from a long time ago. There are a bunch of statues in the entryway of the chapel. One of them is this Savonarola."

Sam stared quizzically at Smidgeon for several long seconds. "How would you know that?"

"A man wandered by when I was at the chapel. He said he was a divinity student and asked if he could help me. He knew all about the chapel and this Savonarola. This tin," she said, holding up the smaller one, "was stuck up on the back side of the statue. I think it was stuck up there with gum."

"Gum? Seriously? And it never fell off?"

Smidgeon shrugged her shoulders and said, "Like Lance said, ever try to get gum off the bottom of one of our tables?"

"Good point," he said as he opened the tin, unfolded the paper, and read, "Lawrenceburg, TN, Bumpass Cem. Center back Samuels Seventy. So you went there next?"

"Yes. I headed west on US sixty-four because Lawrenceburg, Tennessee, is right on the highway. Let me tell you, it was quite a drive. North Carolina is a really long state."

"So, you found Lawrenceburg and Bumpass Cemetery."

"Yes, the grave of Mr. Samuels was on the southwestern side, and I dug up this tin," she said, tapping the next one.

"Whoever left this trail sure loved their Lucky Strikes." Sam opened the tin and read the next note. "Ozark, Arkansas, Highland Cem Hanson Seventy. So, you went to Arkansas?"

"Yes, but after looking at a map, I realized I could connect with Interstate Forty and save some time. Driving the old highway is dreadfully slow when you're in a hurry."

Sam said, "I was thinking, maybe the interstate didn't exist yet, but these graves were both in 1970, which doesn't work."

"Maybe all of Interstate forty wasn't finished."

"Another thing to consider is some old-timers don't like driving the interstates, so they stuck to the smaller roads,"

Sam said as he picked up another tin. "Did you ever wonder why they always used cemeteries?"

"I figured maybe they thought the graves would be undisturbed over the years."

"Except to follow the clues, you must disturb them."

He opened the tin and read the next note. "Osage, Oklahoma, Osage Cem Ennis Seventy."

"That one was harder to find because it was on an Indian Reservation. I had to ask for directions several times," she said. "Seemed like a really old cemetery."

"Yet there's a grave in 1970."

"Yes, and on the southwestern side, of course."

Sam opened the next tin. "And another note sending you to," he said reading, "Turpin, Oklahoma, Independence Cem Davids Seventy."

"It was a little baby, not even a day old," Smidgeon said.

"Still in 1970." Sam replaced the note in the tin.

"I thought about it a lot while I was driving. Whoever was putting those notes picked only fairly recent graves."

"Right. Easier to bury the tins, not as noticeable maybe because the ground was freshly disturbed."

"Yes, for them, at least. I had a hard time with most of the digging, especially in Oklahoma. Thirteen years is plenty of time to bake the earth."

"You didn't worry about it? I mean digging around the graves?"

"I always stood, lowered my head, and apologized with a small prayer; then I would leave a small flower in a pot for most of them. It wasn't anything fancy, something I bought at a five and dime, but I figured it at least looked like I had a reason to be there in case somebody asked me what I was doing."

"What a great idea. You were thinking on your feet."

Smidgeon reached out and touched his arm, "Yeah, in the beginning I thought I was being clever, but it became something I needed to do. I realized I was disturbing somebody's grave."

Sam leaned over and kissed her on the cheek. "You're right." He continued, "And this one led you to..." Sam opened the next tin, "Sixty-four West past Felts, NM, U-turn right dead-end twenty feet center eighteen down." Sam looked up, wide-eyed. "Wow."

"I know...it worried me when I read it. But it made sense once I got there. It's where the borders of Oklahoma, New Mexico, and Texas all meet. I drove to the New Mexico state line, where I had to make a U-turn. The small road was in the middle of nowhere, so it was a good way to identify it."

"I see. Whoever wrote this was pretty clever. So it was a dead end?"

"Well, there was another road extending off to the right; I thought maybe it was a dead end back in 1970. I stepped off twenty feet from the dead center of the first road and dug down eighteen inches...it was rock hard."

"Temperature extremes compacted the dirt, I imagine, but you found this, the last tin?"

"Yes. The last tin." Smidgeon picked it up and read it. "Look at where you been, who you met, what you done."

Sam took the paper and silently read it for himself. "Another riddle! I hate my life."

Smidgeon poked Sam in the shoulder, "Hey!"

He laughed. "Not you, of course. These silly riddles seem to keep following me. What the heck is this supposed to mean?"

Smidgeon opened her small notebook. "It was all I could think about on the way home. It was driving me crazy. I had the clues all written down together and when I stopped to eat in Roswell, I was just sitting staring at them. My waitress noticed the town names all spelled—"

Sam interrupted, "LOOT!" Then he saw the rest for himself. "SHED!" He looked at Smidgeon. "Loot's shed! That's why you were asking about the southwestern side."

"It all kind of fits."

Sam thought for few seconds, tapping the last Lucky Strike tin. "Babe," he said.

"Babe? Who's Babe?"

"Remember the letters we found in your dad's box of mementos?"

"Oh, I forgot about those. Several of the letters mentioned someone named Babe."

"There's more. Cerides was chatty sometimes. He told me about Babe."

"What did he say?"

"Cerides is tied to all of them...Loot, your dad, Babe and a couple of others, Scooter and Delbert. It all goes back to the war in North Africa."

"I remember the name Delbert...he wrote some of those letters. He was from Van Horn, too, joined the army along with Loot and my dad. Mildred told me about him."

"The group of them found a cache of gold coins."

"The coins!" Smidgeon cried.

"Yes, the coin we found and Lance's. I'm sure they were part of it. They decided to split it, but Cerides was an outsider, a prisoner, and he said he thought they were going to cut him out. And they did, I guess, but only after he tried to take it all for himself. Later, Delbert and Scooter somehow got mixed up with Cerides in Mexico, teamed up or something. Judging from what I know of Cerides now, it must have been a criminal enterprise. I think they double-crossed him."

"Again," Smidgeon said.

Sam raised his eyebrows. "Yeah, again. I'm pretty sure the cache of cash in Loot's house was theirs. Thankfully, I don't think Cerides knows about that. But they had told Cerides Babe felt guilty about the money and never spent it. The other shares, theirs, Loot's, your dad's, had all been squandered by that time, but they told Cerides Babe had hidden his."

"And Babe was friends with both Loot and Daddy," Smidgeon said. "He must have been hanging around, and at some point, he hid the box in the wall."

"It's got to be what happened. And Cerides found out about it."

"What? How?"

"He said people talk about unusual things. It was the coincidence of it all, the murders, the mine, and the fire. It made the news, and he heard about it. He recognized your last name in the paper and read about Loot's murder. It drew him here. And now, he's obsessed with you. He seems to think you know a lot more about this than you do."

"Well, I didn't, *until now.*" She tittered nervously.

"So the trail leads back to Loot's shed," Sam said. "And we're stuck out here because this lunatic is chasing us." He shook his head in disgust. "Yet *another* lunatic."

"How long do you think we need to hide, Sam?"

"Until Cerides is out of the picture. You, at least. I think I need to go back and deal with him and find out what this last clue means."

"Uh-uh," Smidgeon said, shaking her head. "No way. If you go, I go. Who do you think has been putting her life on the line for weeks, figuring out all of this?"

~ * ~

Mule Hollis stood in the background and watched as the local deputies worked the crime scene.

"What have I gotten myself into?" he thought.

In the twenty-five years Mule had worked for the Mitchell County Sheriff's office, he had never seen such a cold-blooded killing.

He stayed out of the way while Clay, the senior deputy on duty, supervised the investigation. To Mule, it had all the earmarks of a robbery except for one thing: the cash in the office was untouched. According to Clay, the victim was Marcy Dolings, who was, as Mule had suspected, the motel's owner. She was shot at point-blank range behind the right ear.

"Execution," Mule thought, and his mind wandered as he watched the familiar workings of an active crime scene.

He had been a detective for the last ten years of his career. Crimes were generally simple in and around Colorado City. The murders he had worked were either crimes of passion or they involved robberies.

His wife Grace had passed away five years earlier. If she had lived, he might not have chosen to run for sheriff, but losing her after nineteen years of marriage had devastated him. He found himself in a dark place. Friends urged him to enter the race, and he begrudgingly did so. It did manage to break him out of his rut by getting him out, talking to people. Losing was always a possibility, but he never imagined he'd be out of a job if he lost. His opponent let him go the minute he took office.

A Texas Ranger friend had suggested he get certified as a private investigator, and after doing a little investigation himself, he decided it might augment his pension enough to keep him interested in life. His friend had also kicked this opportunity his way. The Mexican Federal Police were tracking Indigo Cerides, a foreign national who had long been a thorn in their side. Mule was intrigued by the case. Cerides had served a long term in prison followed by deportation, but he escaped before leaving Mexico. Most of his operations centered on smuggling, and he seemed to straddle the border with ease. With the drug trade so prevalent, he managed to fall between the cracks since he appeared to dabble in everything *except* drugs.

Mule had spent months checking on Cerides' suspicious activities between El Paso to Eagle Pass. Every tip and encounter had led him here, to this grim scene in a Van Horn motel. He knew in his gut this was the work of Cerides.

Clay approached and broke him out of his trance. "Hey, Mule, got a second?"

"Sure, Clay, what can I do for you?"

"We're all tied up here, but maybe you can help us out with a call I just received, and I think it may involve the guy you're looking for. Can you go check it out and let us know what you find out?"

"Are you sure? I'm just a citizen, not the law. I have no jurisdiction."

"I know, but I think he only needs to make a statement, you could check out the scene and see what happened, and maybe when I finish up here, I can follow up. It's Lance from the café. Sounds like maybe it might be your guy anyway."

Mule stroked his mustache. He had been on the way to talk to Lance when he found this murder scene. "Sure, I'll see what's going on and get back up with you later. I'm pretty much in the way here anyway."

"I hoped we were through with this sort of stuff for a while."

"Looks like an execution to me. Money's still here."

"Well, I thought maybe they panicked and took off."

"They killed her in a room on the back side. They had plenty of time to take the money."

Clay looked back at the body. "I guess you're right. I might be here longer than I thought."

Mule got the directions, made the short drive to Tesoro Road, and parked out front. Lance Norton, brandishing his shotgun, met Mule on the porch as he walked to the door.

"Saw the headlights. I was afraid they'd come back with reinforcements. Didn't expect you."

Mule lifted his hands. "Yeah, sorry I missed you at the café. Clay and his men are all busy working a little unpleasantness back in town."

"Let me guess, Marcy at the Dolings Motel."

Mule was surprised and suspicious. "How could you know about that?"

Lance sighed. "Cerides. He said he was questioning her and she had a heart attack."

"Well, I'm not a doctor, so I can't rightly say if she had a heart attack or not. Do you think a bullet to the back of the head is one of the symptoms?"

"She was shot?"

"Execution style, in one of the rooms on the back side. Now, what happened here?"

"Cerides showed up with two of his goons when I got back from work. I was letting the dog out when they approached me."

"Seems a little late for you to be getting home, considering the fact that I got to the café at closing time and it looked like you had left early."

Lance hated talking to cops, even ex-cops. "The devil is always in the details," he silently reminded himself.

Mule pointed at a dark hole in the door frame. "What happened there?"

"Cerides," Lance said. "He pulled a gun on me. It's only fair...I already had a shotgun on him and his men. They'd threatened me once before."

"You report it?"

"No, sir. I'm not much in favor of threats, but he hadn't done anything against the law, at least to me. He was asking about Sam and Smidgeon. He can threaten me all he wants, I ain't afraid of him."

"Oh, did they get back like you thought?"

"Yes, and given the way things have been going, they decided to hide out for a little while longer. Anyway, I had nothing to share with him and told him so in no uncertain terms. Then he started to make a move, and my dog chomped down on his leg bone. He freaked and fell and shot wild."

Mule pulled out a small knife and dug at the hole in the frame.

"Sorry, but if what you say is true, I need to retrieve this slug intact."

"I understand. Evidence."

"It very well may be connected to the other murder."

"Oh, right, didn't think about that."

Mule worked the bullet free and asked Lance, "you got a baggie or envelope I can put this in?"

"Sure thing," he said, and he disappeared back inside. Prewash was just inside the doorway. She wagged her tail as she gazed up at Mule.

"She likes you," Lance said when he returned with the bag. "I think Cerides left a bad taste in her mouth. I hope she didn't catch nothing."

Mule placed the bullet in the bag.

"You want some more evidence? I got a spare bag here."

"What do you mean?"

Lance stepped off the porch and turned over the bucket revealing Cerides' gun.

"Cerides dropped this when my dog bit him." Lance handed Mule the other bag.

As Mule retrieved the firearm he turned to Lance. "I think we both need to go down to the station so you can tell the sheriff everything. I've heard about the mess y'all had a while back, and here you are, getting shot at again. I think we need to know everything that's going on."

Lance knew Mule was right. If they were going to stop Cerides, he had to disclose what he knew. "Okay, let me feed the cat and lock up."

~ * ~

Later, at the station, Clay got three cups of strong coffee, and they all sat together in a small interview room.

"What do you know about this man, Indigo Cerides?" Clay pushed a picture toward Lance. Mule sat to the side and observed.

"He came in one day asking questions. Sam talked to him. He seemed harmless. Asked about Smidgeon's dad, too. He's also been out to see me a couple of times, mostly looking for Sam and Smidgeon."

"But they've been away on some sort of family business."

Lance fidgeted in his seat. "Well, Clay, that's not entirely true."

The deputy sighed. "Big surprise, considering it's coming from you three. Okay, where have they been?"

"Well, you told us about Sam's car in Valentine."

"Yeah, you acted like it was nothing...like he was on another wild goose chase based on something you found. I never heard another word about it. I assumed you found Sam and everything was okay."

"Yeah, well, we went and picked up the car, and we figured no news was good news. We supposed he was maybe out in the desert or something, you know?"

Mule leaned forward to interrupt. "I worked in law enforcement for quite a number of years and I can tell you...no news is rarely good news."

"Yeah, I suppose you're right. Anyways, we found an old cigarette tin in the car. We reckoned Sam found it out there. It was identical to one we had found in the café during the repair work."

"So there were two tins?"

"Yeah." Lance repositioned himself in his chair. "The first one had the clue to something out south of Valentine. That's why Sam went out there. The second one had another clue. I don't rightly remember exactly what it said, but it mentioned Duke Chapel, and I knew it probably meant the one in North Carolina. Smidgeon decided to go there to see if she could figure it out."

Mule's eyes widened. "North Carolina?"

"Yeah. She hoped it would help us find Sam."

Mule shook his head. "But Sam came back, or so you said. Where was he?"

"Well, we didn't say anything. We let you assume. He was actually abducted and held prisoner...by Cerides."

Clay stood up, placed both hands on the table, and leaned forward. "Wait, are you saying he was *kidnapped*? And you didn't think to call the police?"

"Well, at the time we didn't *know* he was kidnapped. Cerides took Sam across the border to Mexico."

"Lovely. So now we have a major crime involving two international jurisdictions." Clay shook his head in disbelief.

"Well, according to Sam. Anyway, he said he was taken someplace in Mexico. He was held for several days of beatings and questioning, but at some point, he managed to escape. He made his way back north and wandered back across the Rio Grande near Langtry. Sam's an experienced hiker, so I believe him. He started hitchhiking and managed to snag a ride back here."

"How did they cross the border in the first place?"

"He said near Big Bend, on the far side of the park."

"Oh, I know about the little bridge near La Linda," Clay said.

"Yeah, and I'd already heard Cerides uses it a lot to move back and forth," Mule added.

"The guy who happened to pick him up turned out to be an associate of Cerides. He dropped Sam off and then disappeared. That's when things started to get really crazy because minutes later, Smidgeon showed up."

"Oh, and you said she went to North Carolina? Better than Mexico, I guess. What did she find there?"

"I don't know all the details about her trip, but I think she found a series of notes, each one leading to the next, making a sort of trail across the country. It all led her back here. But like I said, right after she returned, we realized Sam's ride was working with Cerides and we knew they were both in great danger. So she and Sam hid out at Marcy's place while we worked out a plan."

"So Marcy was involved?"

"The café wasn't safe, and we couldn't go to my place or to Smidgeon's place either. It seemed a good option at the time."

"You should have called me, and I would have put them in protective custody," Clay said.

"Maybe. But knowing what I know about this guy, I think Cerides could probably get to them if they were in jail," Mule said.

"Basically what we thought, too," Lance added.

Clay shifted his eyes between Lance and Mule and cleared his throat. "I have a little more faith in what we can do. So, anyway, you said you all cooked up a plan. Where are they?"

"Marcy has a place. Well, it was her husband's place. A little hunting cabin out Farm Road Eleven-eleven, north of Sierra Blanca."

"Hudspeth County. I can get up with them and see if we can bring them in."

"If it's well-hidden that might be a bad idea, Clay," Mule said. "Cerides has a wide network. If he has no reason to suspect what direction they took, they might be safer for the short-term if we leave them be."

Clay frowned and rubbed his face with both hands.

Lance added, "I seriously doubt Cerides knows where they are...we all covered our tracks pretty well."

Clay shook his head. "Don't be too sure. We're still looking at all the clues, but if Cerides killed Marcy Dolings, he is ruthless. I'm pretty sure Marcy was tortured first."

"Before our little altercation, he mentioned he talked to Marcy, said he thought she had a heart attack. But think about it. I don't think he would have wasted his time coming to see me if he thought he knew where they went."

Mule said, "I imagine he said heart attack because he figured you'd be more cooperative if you didn't expect to be shot. Still, you may have a point, Lance. If he wanted Sam and Smidgeon and already knew where they went, why would he waste another few minutes trying to get information out of you?"

"Hah. He didn't figure on my dog, though. I was letting her out like I always do when I get home from work. He came up with his two underlings. One of them was the guy who gave Sam the ride. Sam introduced him as Jeffers. I don't know if that was his first name or last. Anyway, I pulled out my shotgun, and we talked. The conversation got to the point where I think it was probably headed the same way as it did with Marcy. Prewash was still out there, patiently watching all this time, but when Cerides and his men started moving toward me, she sensed the danger and chomped down on Cerides' ankle like it was a ham bone."

"She bit him?"

"Hell, yeah, she bit him. Hard. He began to fall, and his gun went off. Freaked him out, if you ask me. Sort of surprised me as well." Lance chuckled. "I hope she don't get sick."

Mule asked, "Think he'll need medical attention?"

"I'm sure. She can bite through a tin can."

"So I can alert medical centers all around the area to look for a dog bite," Clay said.

"I figure he might have something available down south of the border," Mule said.

"It's a long drive, but Mexico is his regular stomping ground, too. If he uses the same bridge on FM twenty-six/twenty-seven..." Clay stood. "I had better alert Brewster County. If he's headed that way, it could take him a while to get there...we might be able to cut him off. Did you get an ID on their vehicles?"

"No, it was dark, so all I could see were two cars. One was light colored, maybe white. The other was dark. I have no idea if it was black or blue or green or something else."

"There's one other thing, Clay."

"What?"

"He threatened to kill my dog. Seriously. Said she was going to die."

Clay said, "Ain't nobody killing your dog if I can help it, Lance."

Nineteen

Sam woke up rested after the best night's sleep he had enjoyed in more days than he could remember. The stress of his captivity combined with the uncomfortably warm conditions had left him exhausted—the snatches of sleep he'd managed after his escape hadn't helped either. He was still tense, but being reunited with Smidgeon was like a tonic to him. He surveyed the landscape after inspecting the outdoor facilities and was surprised to see the sun high in the sky.

"Must have slept ten hours, maybe more," he mumbled.

The scrubland on the western side of the little mountain ranges stretching north of Van Horn to the Guadalupe Mountains was quite familiar to him. He walked around, inspecting the building. It had been unoccupied for quite a while, and the weathered exterior was in need of some minor repairs.

"Nice retreat from the real world," he said as he walked over to the water supply for the cabin, a hand pump. He tried the handle a couple of times and could hear air gurgling out the spout, so he continued to pump at it like he was trying to jack up a car. Soon a rusty colored liquid emerged. He continued to pump until it came out somewhat clear and splashed some into his left hand. He sniffed it and said, "I hope it's safe."

He returned to the cabin, saw Smidgeon stirring under the covers, and smiled. Snuggling with her had been the most pleasant experience he'd had in days. Sam started rummaging through the supplies Lance had gathered.

"Good," he said out loud. "Instant coffee." He scrounged a small pot and went outside to fill it with water; he put it on the hot plate.

"What are you doing, Sam?" Smidgeon blinked up at him from the small bed in the corner.

"Going to make us some coffee," he said, holding up a jar of instant.

There was an odor of scorched dust as the hot plate element began to glow. Sam scrounged a couple of mugs from a makeshift cabinet and winced after looking in them. He decided to fill a worn plastic dishpan at the pump to rinse and wipe the cups.

"Well, at least the cabin has most of the comforts of home. A hand water pump, an outhouse, and a hot plate."

"Why didn't you start a fire in the little pot belly stove?" she said, pointing to the corner.

"Lights at night are bad enough, but smoke would be a dead giveaway," he said.

"I didn't think of that."

Sam added, "Besides, all the wood I could find was old and rotten."

He poked around in the bag from the house, "Here's a handful of single packets of sugar."

"He must have scrounged them from The Mossback," she said. "No creamer, I guess."

"Can of evaporated milk."

"Better than nothing. This is really roughing it."

"Well, water and electricity are a plus. Rural people made do with evaporated milk for generations. Why do you think so many biscuit recipes are for two thirds of a cup of milk?"

"I've always wondered...oh! One small can of evaporated milk!"

The water began boiling, and Sam clicked the buttons on the hot plate and turned it down to medium. "Pump hasn't been used in a while. I had to let the water run a bit to run clear, so I think to be safe we should boil it for five minutes."

"I don't care how bad things can ever be, Sam. I always feel safe with you."

"I wish I'd asked Lance to pack a gun or something."

Smidgeon reached over, fumbled in her purse, and pulled out her .45. "I wasn't driving cross-country without my daddy's gun." She rummaged around in the purse and pulled out five cartridges. "All I could find. Eleven shots including the six already in it."

"Well, it will have to do," Sam said. "We can't fight a sustained gun battle, but something tells me we won't have to. If we run into any trouble with Cerides, I'm sure it will be short and sweet. Probably won't come to that...he needs us, or thinks he does."

"Right. He thinks we know the location of Babe's missing treasure, or what's left of it," Smidgeon said, pouring hot water over the instant coffee powder in the cups.

"Yeah. And maybe we do."

"Loot's shed?"

Sam stirred the liquid in his cup. "That would be my guess, according to the clues you found."

"Well, then, we should find it before he does."

"But Cerides doesn't know where it is."

Smidgeon face broke into a sly smile. "Exactly."

~ * ~

"Nice place."

"I have been here before, Slim. Once. A long time ago."

"Really?"

"Dolings needed help installing a new roof on this cabin. Got mad at me fer gitting drunk before the job was finished."

"Oh, been there, done that," Slim said laughing. "So there's more treasure at your place?"

"Don't rightly know. Maybe. I recollect Babe staying at my place back in 1970, Christmastime."

"So ya think he buried a treasure there, outside your shed?"

"Could be. But it was Christmas, and I was drinking almost the whole time he was there. Of course, Christmas didn't have anything to do with me being drunk."

"Hey, same here, I was on a awful bender that year."

"Stop it, you two ornery cusses," Scamp said.

"Babe only stayed a day, maybe two. He wasn't drinking, so I didn't pay much attention to him. He seemed to have other things on his mind...the war, I think. He didn't let it go like most all of us. Babe bottled it up and kept fighting the war over and over again in his head."

Slim hovered closer to Loot. "Merchant marine warn't no picnic either. Always worried we'd get a torpedo up the—"

"Slim!" Scamp swatted at his friend.

Loot continued, "Babe had worked a little at some ranch over toward Marfa until his mama got sick and died; I think he was heading back there to work again. He didn't seem well, didn't seem right in the head."

"What do you know about being right in the head?" Slim chortled.

"Not much I guess, but boys, I got me a terrible bad feeling about this."

~ * ~

Lance opened the café on time. The three of them had agreed to keep up the ruse about Sam and Smidgeon's absence, and when one of the cooks arrived, he decided it was an excellent chance to test the ploy. Chuy had seen both Sam and Smidgeon the day before, so Lance hoped he would believe his cover story.

"So still no Miss Smidgeon or Mister Sam today?"

"No, Chuy, they both drove all day yesterday to get here, so they're taking one more day off. I guess you're stuck with me again."

"I bet I know what they's doing."

"Stop that!"

Chuy giggled, and Lance glared at him, but inwardly he knew his plan had worked and he'd be able to tell anyone who asked the same thing.

After a long day at work, Lance went back home and slept with both his pistol and his shotgun within easy reach.

He woke up to a sharp crack of thunder.

"Rain. Great for the ranchers but bad for business," Lance mumbled under his breath.

He dragged himself out of bed and looked at the alarm clock. "Fifteen minutes before the alarm!" He briefly thought about returning to bed but reconsidered; Prewash was rattling her tags so he quickly pulled on his jeans.

"You don't care about no thunderstorm when you need to go out, do you?" She looked up at him with her big eyes. He absent-mindedly let her out the front door and surveyed the dingy clouds, momentarily silhouetted by flashes of lightning.

"You're lucky, no rain quite yet."

He went to the kitchen to start some water boiling for a cup of instant coffee before returning to let the dog back in. He immediately regretted leaving his guns in the bedroom. Cerides was standing in his living room, holding a small pistol.

"Mr. Norton. Unfortunately, our previous conversation was interrupted, so I am now here to continue. One of my associates has already taken your dog."

"You leave my dog alone, you—"

"Come now, Mr. Norton. My threats were made in haste. Surprise and pain have a way of combining to replace rational thought, don't you think? I think it is, how do you Americans say it? It is rather cute you are so attached to your dog. Still, this is useful to me, no?"

"Cerides—!"

"It is simple. I have no grievance with you...or your dog. All I want to know is the location of Sam and Miss Toll. Simple, no?"

"I told you, I don't know where they are."

"Such an emphatic declaration has the ring of truth, but, well, I am a keen student of the human condition. I will concede, you may well not know the exact location, but I think you know the *general* location. It is quite a different distinction, you see? For a man of my means and will, even a general location will be most useful since it limits the extent of my pursuit. At present, I have to search everywhere, but with more specifics, I can narrow the scope. I will locate them either way, but finding them quickly is better for me, it is better for you, and... it is perhaps better for *them* as well, Mr. Norton."

Cerides waved a hand in the direction of the car, and Lance heard Prewash whine.

"Go to hell, you bastard!"

"Perhaps I will, but I *must* know where they are."

Headlights flashed down the road and outside the doorway; a voice interrupted the conversation. "*Policia!*"

Cerides ducked out the door and two figures ran to the waiting car. It sped past the oncoming vehicle. Lance ran out the door so quickly he forgot he was still barefoot. He briefly looked around his yard, but Prewash was not there. The approaching car made the circle at the end of Tesoro Road and stopped as Lance advanced at a trot just as the rain started. Mule Hollis rolled down the window.

"I was following Indigo Cerides but lost him. Thought I'd check over here and danged if I wasn't right. You okay?"

"You just missed him! He took my dog."

"Why would he—?" Mule glanced down the road and saw the car make a left turn. "Well, I better keep following!" Gravel flew as Mule Hollis sped back down the road, leaving a damp Lance Norton standing in the rain.

~ * ~

"I still think we should stay here, at least until it gets dark."

"Smidgeon, if there really *is* something buried outside the shed, we need to find it first."

"But, Cerides doesn't have the clues. He needs us, and he doesn't know where we are."

Sam's mind was racing, but he paused to gather his thoughts. He remembered the time he thought he had solved the first clue of Slim's riddle and he was in a rush to get back out and renew his search. Loot had cautioned him to slow down by telling him he had '*the fever,*' and Sam realized it meant he would stop at nothing to pursue his goal. This was almost the same feeling. He wiped away beads of sweat from his forehead and took a deep breath.

"You're right, Smidgeon. We have the clues. Rushing off would be a big mistake. Besides, it's raining. We have no idea how many people Cerides has working for him. He could have people watching roads all over the area."

"I guess you're right. Look at how lucky he got with his man picking you up."

"I'm not so sure that was lucky. I'm beginning to think he set me up. The escape was just too easy."

"You really think so?"

"Yeah, and I fell for it. At first, I thought maybe I had struck a nerve with the girl, but he probably told her to let me go, to point me in a particular direction."

"So he would send you out into the desert?"

"He said he had heard all about the incident with the mine, with the murders. Locals have pretty much left me alone about my past here, but even knowing a few details, it's pretty easy to reach a logical conclusion. He had to have figured I'd spent a lot of time tromping out across the desert on my own. Let's face it...most people would have been intimidated by the notion of a cross-country hike, but not me. For years I would set my course and start walking. This was easy. All I had to do was head north."

"I see what you mean. So Jeffers, the guy who picked you up, didn't just happen by; he was waiting for you."

"Exactly. And if I didn't make it, say, I died in the Mexican desert, well, Cerides' hands are clean there, too. I'd be another anonymous gringo adventurer who messed up. But this all means he's desperate to find what he's looking for."

"Of course he is, but where does that leave us?"

"He thinks we are the key, but that means everybody we know is in danger, especially Marcy and Lance."

"We were very careful, Sam."

"Careful isn't ever enough when you're dealing with a maniac."

Smidgeon looked worried. "So you think Marcy and Lance are in danger?"

"Yes. I wish now we hadn't left."

"Me, too. What were we thinking?"

"At the time, all I could think about was getting you to a safe place."

"Well, I think we are pretty darn good at taking care of ourselves."

"The trouble is, I don't think they know how evil this guy really is. That's why I think we need to go back."

"So we need a plan. Night is the safest time, but if Cerides is really looking for us, I think we should try to ease our way back into Van Horn the back way."

"The back way?"

"Yeah. He is probably expecting us to come in by way of the interstate."

"Clever girl. You're right. So you think we need to go the long way round?"

"Yep, go north, up FM eleven-eleven and circle back over to Texas fifty-four, then back down to Van Horn. It ain't too far out of the way when you think about it."

"If we've got enough gas."

"We've got the five gallon can Lance sent along."

"Well, that should help."

Smidgeon yawned. "You hungry, Sam?"

Sam stood and said, "You get the crackers, and I'll heat up a can of Wolf Brand Chili...we can listen to the rain while we eat."

"We've got a lot of time to kill and a long night-time drive, so we should probably take a nap. I swear I could sleep for a week, and besides...ain't nothing like a rainy day for some serious cuddling," Smidgeon said, with a wink.

"Talked me into it."

~ * ~

Business was down. Lance didn't know if it was the rain or if it was the absence of Smidgeon. He assumed it was likely the second reason because almost every customer who came in asked about her.

"When's Miss Smidgeon coming back?" was a common refrain. Sometimes they'd add Sam into the mix, too.

But today, all Lance could think about was Prewash. He had heard the unmistakable vengeance in the Italian's voice when the dog bit him. Lance's eyes began to tear up every time he remembered her cry out as they stuffed her in the car. His heart was not into the work of running the restaurant, but he had promised Smidgeon he would take care of the place in her absence. He had been elated when she returned, but now, everyone was in danger, not just his dog. Cerides was ruthless, but he wanted something from Lance, and it was the only thing that was possibly keeping Prewash alive at this point.

"Storm's keeping it quiet, Mr. Lance."

"Except for the thunder, Chuy."

Chuy laughed. "*Si*, but I meant the customers. It's never busy on a rainy day. Maybe we better close early, eh? I don't think Miss Smidgeon will mind."

Lance considered Chuy's suggestion. He had worked there as a cook for a long time. The famous Mashed Browns had been his inadvertent invention. They were one of the most unusual things on the menu, and Lance could eat a mountain of the odd mixture of mashed potatoes and hash browns.

"Let's give it another hour. If things don't pick up for dinner, maybe we can shut down early," Lance said.

"Okay, Mr. Lance."

Lance looked at the sky and thought, "It's going to be a long hour."

~ * ~

"We should probably leave most of our stuff," Smidgeon said. "We can come back and collect it when everything has settled down."

"Right." Sam thought it was optimistic to think things might settle down, but he didn't want to alarm Smidgeon. "Still wish you'd stay here where it's safe. I can handle this."

"You can take *that* bee right out of your bonnet," she said. "I'm going."

"Looks like it'll be dark in about half an hour, which will give us time to get through those confusing back trails and get on the highway," Smidgeon said, climbing into the passenger seat of the old truck.

Sam finished pouring the gas from the spare can into the tank and looked at the sky. "Hopefully the rain is over for now. I hope these little roads are passable. I've never tested the four-wheel drive on this thing."

They bumped and rattled down the roughly graded trails following Marcy's directions in reverse. It was almost pitch black by the time they got to the paved road and headed north.

"Seems like old times," Sam said.

"I bet it does. Take it easy, okay? We're not in a hurry."

When FM 1111 dead-ended, they turned right on US 180. After a little over twenty miles, they turned right on Texas 54.

Sam turned to Smidgeon and said, "A little over an hour to Van Horn."

"Hope everything is okay down there," Smidgeon said.

"Me, too," Sam said, adding in a reassuring tone, "I'm sure everything is okay." But deep inside, he knew the drama was far from over.

Twenty

Lance eyed the empty parking lot and muttered, "Three customers in the past hour."

Chuy joined him. "So, what do ya think?"

Lance glanced at his cook. "You got someplace to be I don't know about?"

"Naw, Mr. Lance. You said maybe we gonna shut down early. I'm already almost ready in the back. I don't like just sitting around, you know?"

"I know. Makes me nervous, too. Yeah, let's close," Lance said, and he flipped the sign and locked the door.

Chuy returned to the dining room a few minutes later while Lance was totaling the day's receipts. "Finished, boss. I got us all set up for tomorrow."

"Good job, Chuy," he said, unlocking the door. "Have a good evening."

He paused after he re-set the deadbolt and watched Chuy drive away, then returned to his work. He was nervous; he always felt vulnerable when he had the register open while balancing the day's totals, so he hurried through his figures.

"It never comes out right on the nose," he mumbled to himself, "but today it did. Pretty rare event." He decided to take an extra few minutes to double-check his calculations. After he re-counted the cash, he shook his head. "Perfect. Weird."

He took all the bills into the back, and in the little office, he worked up what he was going to drop at the bank as a deposit. He stored the rest of the cash in the small floor safe.

"Deposit's a little low," he mumbled. "Be glad when Smidgeon's back. I'm convinced she is one of the reasons people come here. No Smidgeon, no Mossback."

He put the bank bag on the coffee counter and did a walk-through while he mentally verified his usual closing checklist. "Ketchup, sweeteners, salt, pepper, napkins, dining room swept and mopped, coffee ready to go, towels...oh, towels." He had forgotten to restock the clean towels, so he went into the kitchen to get two fresh bundles.

Lance stopped abruptly, allowing the swinging door to hit his back.

"Mr. Norton."

Indigo Cerides was standing in the kitchen holding a gun, flanked by his two armed henchmen. Lance quickly glanced at the open back door.

"I didn't hear you come in."

Cerides smirked. "It takes a bit of finesse, but forcing a door can be done quietly. Do you think this is the first establishment any of us have entered like this?"

"I guess not," Lance said. "What do you want?"

"A silly question...what do I always want from you?"

"I've got a less silly question. Where's my danged dog?"

"Ah, your dog. The dog is safe. She still doesn't like me very much."

"What's to like?"

Cerides sighed deeply. "I am a reasonable man. Quite reasonable. Why must you make this so difficult?"

"They're hiding from *you*, but I don't know where. Judging from what you did to Marcy Dolings, I think they had the right idea."

"That was a most unfortunate incident, but, seriously, there is a lesson there for you. It is a constructive example, no?"

Lance glared at the Italian.

"Now, we must go. Please." Cerides indicated the open back door with his free hand.

Lance did not move; he knew it was an invitation to his own death.

"I don't think so," he said, and he began to ease backward against the dining room door. He doubted Cerides had noticed it, but Lance had heard a faint but familiar sound. His heart was racing, and he knew if he was wrong, he was a dead man. He threw himself back against the door, and as it swung open, he ducked and scurried toward the coffee station. As he crouched, he pulled the small handgun from his boot. He was relieved to see he had guessed right.

Smidgeon Toll was quite a sight, standing with her .45 in a classic firing stance with her legs spread apart and her long hair flowing around her shoulders.

Cerides had a shocked look on his face as she fired once through the wildly swinging door. She turned and shouted, "Come on, Lance!"

They both rushed through the front door. Once outside, Smidgeon fired again, this time into the air. The Jeep truck was at the front door idling as Sam came running around the side of the building.

"Get in," he said, and they all bounded into the cab.

As they sped out of the parking lot, Lance said, "They won't be far behind."

"I spread some of the crap back there in their way. Maybe it'll slow them down a bit. Oh, they might have a couple of flats, too!"

Smidgeon saw Lance was still gripping his gun in one hand but had something in his other. "What do you have there?"

"The deposit bag. It's not much, but I didn't want them to have it."

"Oh, Lance..." Smidgeon shook her head.

Lance panted. "I *knew* I heard the front deadbolt and thought, 'who could be opening the front door with a key?' I knew it had to be you guys."

Sam said, "We pulled up along the side of the building, and I recognized Jeffers' car sitting in the back. Your truck was parked in the front, so we figured you were in trouble. Smidgeon insisted on going in the front with her .45, so I went to the back to see what I could do to mess with their car."

"Where we going?"

"Sheriff's office. Smidgeon, why'd you fire a shot outside?"

"I dunno, to attract attention, or to maybe freak him out. I shot at him when the door was swinging. He looked pretty shocked when he saw me holding my big gun."

"You think you hit him?"

"I had a good bead on him but didn't hang around long enough to find out."

Lance turned and looked out the back window. "Don't see anybody following us either," he said, still breathing hard.

"Did you get a plate or make on their car?" Lance asked.

"Light-colored Impala, it looked fairly new. Didn't get the plate except for the first two letters 'GD' that's all I remember."

Lance said to Sam, "Why did you let Smidgeon go in with the gun?"

Smidgeon poked Lance in the ribs. "Hey, don't go all sexist on me, Lance. Ain't nobody using my daddy's gun except me. Besides, I'm a better shot than Sam."

A patrol unit was in the driveway of the sheriff's office, and Sam flashed his lights to stop them as he approached. He pulled in and rolled down his window. Clay was driving the other car.

"We had a report of a possible gunshot down near The Mossback," he said.

"Yeah, we just came from there. It was Cerides," Sam said.

"Everybody okay?"

"Yeah, we're fine...they have a light-colored Impala, and the license plate starts with 'GD.' Okay?"

"Y'all go on in, and I'll go have a look. I'll radio that you're here."

~ * ~

"Come on, Loot, we should follow them."

"Hold on, Slim."

"What are you doing?" Scamp asked.

"Concentrating, trying to foul up something on Digly's car before they get away."

"Digly, you mean the Italian feller?"

"Yeah."

They floated overhead as three startled men stumbled out the back door of the café and got into their car.

"Jeffers, get a flare out of the back and light it...throw it into the restaurant. Quickly, we must go."

Slim hovered over the car. "They gonna try to burn it down...again?"

Jeffers had run around the back of the car but tripped over one of the obstacles Sam had placed there. He got up and opened the trunk.

Loot came close, and a glow developed as he focused enough energy to slam the trunk lid down on Jeffers' head.

Both Scamp and Slim hooted as Jeffers screamed and jumped back.

With another flash of light, the trunk slammed shut.

Jeffers glanced around wide-eyed and ran back to the car.

"Good one, Loot. Got him smack dab on his punkin haid," Slim said.

A loud voice came from the car. "Why did you not do what I told you?"

This was followed by a pitiful, "Something strange, boss, we gotta get away from here!"

Slim slapped his spectral thigh and guffawed wildly. "Hah! Look, Loot...they're trying to drive on two flat tires, bumping and rattling over all the stuff Sam put out there. Ya done good, Sam!"

"Yeah, the boy done all right for hisself."

"You done good, too, Loot," Slim said, as they watched the car rattle away with sparks flying as it dragged part of a bakery rack to the end of the parking lot.

~ * ~

Sam, Smidgeon, and Lance sat on a bench in the sheriff's office. It was dreadfully quiet. Mule Hollis sipped at a cup of coffee and kept a wary eye on them.

"So why'd you two come out of hiding?" Mule asked.

"We had a lot of time to think out there at Marcy's cabin," Sam said. "We decided everybody else was in just as much danger as we were and we were worried, especially for Lance and Marcy."

"Guess we're safe enough here, at least for now," Smidgeon said. "He's not likely to attack anybody in a police station."

Mule glanced nervously around. "Maybe, but I wouldn't put anything past this guy."

Lance said, "Yeah, I'm with you, mister. Listen, you two, there's something you need to know." He glanced up at Mule.

"What?" Sam asked.

Mule looked down at Sam and Smidgeon and gravely said, "Apparently Cerides had info you were seen at the motel, and he went over there to question Marcy Dolings. She's dead."

Smidgeon gasped. "He killed Marcy?" Her eyes teared up. "Marcy," she repeated in a low tone, weeping. Sam consoled her as she buried her head in his shoulder.

Lance spoke up. "I don't know all the details. Cerides told me she had a weak heart and had died while he was interrogating her, but Clay said she'd been shot."

"Yeah, she was most definitely shot," Mule said. "More like executed, I'd say."

Smidgeon looked up. "I can't believe it. The bastard!" She continued weeping.

Sam consoled Smidgeon as best as he could. "I'm just...well, I hope they can pin it on Cerides."

"Well, later, Cerides came by my house again, and his gun went off. Mule here took great care to dig the bullet out of my door frame, so maybe it can match up. Cerides dropped his gun, too.

"Clay sent both the gun and the slug I dug out of Lance's door frame down to the DPS crime lab. They'll compare them to any bullet they get from Mrs. Dolings."

Sam turned to Lance. "Wait, Cerides took a shot at you?"

"In a manner of speaking. He had a gun on me. I had a gun on him. He came up on me while I was taking Prewash out. While we were talking, the conversation got a might heated. I guess I was maybe in more trouble than I realized, but dogs, well, they sometimes have a better instinct about such things, so she chomped down on his ankle like it was a soup bone. I guess Cerides was so surprised he lost his balance and squeezed the trigger."

Sam grinned. "Good dog! She stopped the conversation cold. It's not funny, he might have hit you."

"I know. I guess I feel pretty lucky. His buddies picked him up and hurried off. I shoulda blasted them all with my shotgun right then and there."

"What a relief," Smidgeon said, stifling a sob and wiping the tears from her cheeks.

"Short-lived though. They came back later, early in the morning and took her. He threatened to kill her after she bit him. He tried to reassure me by telling me it was an empty threat made in the heat of the moment, but I figure he means to use her as a bargaining chip. I don't think Cerides makes empty threats."

"Oh, Lance." Smidgeon tried to stifle her crying and turned to Lance. "I hope she's okay."

Lance looked down at his feet. "I ain't so sure. She bit him pretty darn good. I mean, she can bite through a can. A man don't forget something like that."

Sam put a hand on Lance's shoulder. "We've got him on the run now."

Mule said, "Maybe, but you best not underestimate this man."

They all looked up when some lights flashed across the windows.

In a few minutes, Clay came in. They looked up at him hopefully, but he just said, "Nothing. Found a witness who said they were rattling away on a couple of flats. Can't imagine they got very far, but they somehow disappeared. This guy is slippery."

"Exactly what I was telling them. Cerides has a lot of tricks up his sleeve," Mule said.

Sam said, "I think he's been at this sort of thing for a long time."

Mule drained his coffee cup. "You don't know the half of it, young man. Cerides' escapades go back at least to the war. Maybe even longer."

"He told me a little bit about his life when he had me prisoner," Sam said.

Clay spoke up. "We can compare those notes later. First things first. Sam? I think we need to have a little chat."

"Oh, the kidnapping? I think that's the least of our problems right now."

"Let me be the judge of what's important to this case. I can at least add something to the charges. Let's go into an interview room."

Mule put his hand on Sam's shoulder. "It's something solid we can hang on him, Sam."

Sam nodded, and he walked down the hall with Clay following. Sam recognized the same small room where he had been questioned before. He sat at the opposite side of the table from the deputy.

"So tell me what happened."

"We found something during the renovation, a box with a note. It said something about Old Brite Road south of Valentine. Some kind of clue."

Clay chuckled. "Something an old prospector like you couldn't ignore, right?"

"Maybe so, but we were *all* curious. It seemed like it was a harmless enough idea to go check out."

"And you found something...I mean, after you poked around where it told you to go?"

"Yes. A small box like the first one."

"What was in it?"

"Another note. Something about a Duke Chapel. I figured I'd bring it home and work on it with Smidgeon. I wrapped everything back up and stuck it under my car seat and headed back."

"Presidio deputies found your car at the end of that same road, right off US ninety."

"He was parked there, alone."

"Cerides?"

"Yes, I thought maybe somebody had car trouble or something. I was an idiot for stopping, but by the time I got out of the car, he had a gun on me and forced me to leave with him. I was able to lock the car, but in minutes we were headed east with me driving."

"To La Linda?"

Sam seemed surprised. "How do you know?"

"Lance mentioned it. But please go on."

"We crossed at a little bridge. It's downriver from Big Bend National Park. Then we drove all night down crappy Mexican roads for hours with too many twists and turns to keep track of until we arrived at a small settlement. We parked at a shack on the edge of it, and he bound me. He spent quite a bit of time interrogating me."

"About what?"

"He's obsessed with some supposed treasure. He was an Italian deserter during the war in North Africa, where he knew both Loot Meldings and Joe Toll. A whole group of soldiers sort of adopted him. I think he was just a kid drafted into the Italian army who ran away when he decided he was tired of the fighting. They found a hidden cache of gold coins. The group of them was supposed to share it, but he's convinced they decided to double-cross him and turned him in so they could get his share, too, but you know what?"

"What?"

"I figure he wanted it all for himself. Money does strange things to people. I have first-hand knowledge."

"Go on."

"I was beaten, I was starved. He's certain Joe must have told Smidgeon something about it. I kept telling Cerides he didn't, I didn't know where Smidgeon was, and neither of us knew anything about any coins. Of course, I had no idea she was driving all across the country. I wasn't entirely truthful to him, though. We found one coin at her house, and Lance found one coin in Loot's house."

"But you got away."

"I befriended a young local girl Cerides had hired to bring me food. She helped me escape. I'm not sure, though.

It might have been a ruse on Cerides' part. Now it seems like it was way too easy. Either way, she gave me some supplies, pointed me north, and I got the heck out of there."

"So you blindly hiked cross-country from Mexico to the United States."

"Well," Sam said, "I do have a lot of experience doing the very same thing."

Clay smirked. "Oh, you mean like when you were looking for your danged mine."

"Yeah, pretty much. At first, I was happy to get away, but now I realize Cerides would never have allowed me to get away so easily."

"Why do you think that?"

"Just a gut feeling. Plus, I got really lucky when I crossed over. It was near Langtry. I crossed and hid out to make sure I wasn't being followed across the river, and I made my way up to Highway Ninety and hitch-hiked. Got picked up pretty quickly."

"Getting a quick ride *would* be a lucky break out there."

"Yeah, and now I can see it was probably *too* lucky. The guy brought me right to The Mossback. He had an entire backstory about Kansas City, and he kept telling me how hungry he was and, heck, I was going to feed him, too, but he flat out disappeared."

"Whoa. First he says he's hungry, then he disappears before he has a chance to eat? You're right, that's suspicious."

"He told me his name was Jeffers Lincoln. He was driving a light-colored Impala. I rode in the car for several hours. It was the same car we saw at the café tonight."

"We had reports of a gunshot near the restaurant."

"It was Smidgeon. There were two. One inside and one outside."

Clay left Sam alone in the small room and returned with Smidgeon.

"Sam here says you fired a gun? Where is it?"

"In the truck. It's my daddy's old .45. I fired it twice. Once at Cerides in the kitchen, once outside after we ran out the door. He broke in and was threatening Lance in the kitchen; Sam and I saw their car in the back. He went to the back to try and do something to maybe slow them down. I went inside to make sure Lance was okay. I unlocked the front door and crept in and listened at the kitchen door and could tell he was in trouble, so I stood there trying to decide if I should push in there, guns-a-blazing or not. When Lance suddenly backed his way out the door and dropped to the floor. I saw Cerides through the swinging door and fired once at him."

"Lordy, if this keeps up, I'm going to need a bigger room, excuse me," Clay said, rising. He soon returned with Lance and another chair.

Clay continued, "So Cerides had you in the kitchen."

"Yeah, he had me covered. He was trying to force me to go with him. I was sure I was a goner if I left with him. I was figuring my best bet was to duck out the door, and I was sure of it when I heard the front door deadbolt."

"You heard it and Cerides didn't?"

"Guess so. You get used to the sounds in a place."

"That's right, Clay," Smidgeon agreed.

Lance continued, "Actually, I was hoping it was you guys, Clay, but I was pretty sure I had locked the door, so figured it had to be Sam or Smidgeon."

Smidgeon laughed. "You know, Clay or Sam would have made a lot more noise, Lance."

Lance continued, "So, anyway, my back was against the door. I carry a piece in my boot, so my plan was to push my way out and drop, roll toward the coffee station, grab my gun and cover the kitchen door just in case I was wrong about the front door. Either way, I assumed I was already dead...I figured on going out fighting."

"And you, Smidgeon, fired at Cerides. Sam, what were you doing again? Why didn't you have the gun?"

Smidgeon's face flushed. "Now you listen here, Clay. It's *my* gun, and I'm a heck of a lot better shot than Sam."

"Yeah, she's got a point there. I'm not much of a gun person. City boy, remember?" Sam said. "I ran to the back and moved some heavy garbage cans behind their car and I slashed two of their tires. We had some bakery racks out there, too, so I scattered those around. Figured if we made a run for it in the old truck, it might slow them down a bit. Seemed to work."

Clay nervously tapped his fingers on the table as he tried to process all of the details of the stories he had heard. He asked Smidgeon, "You said you fired twice?"

"Yes, once inside through the swinging door and once outside, when we ran out the front door; I fired into the air. I was hoping to attract attention."

"And it did. I was responding to a call about a gunshot when you first saw me tonight. So you both are still armed?"

Lance and Smidgeon answered at the same time. "Yes."

Clay took a deep breath and let it out slowly, his cheeks billowing like Louis Armstrong blowing his horn.

Smidgeon elaborated. "Well, Clay, not this minute. We both stashed them under the seat in the truck before we came in."

"Given the circumstances, I guess that's okay. Now, I need to get back out and look for this Cerides character. He must have either a place he can hide out close by or another vehicle. Where are you all going to be?"

Sam, Smidgeon, and Lance all exchanged glances.

"Not sure," Sam said. "Lance? We might have better visibility at your place. It's more out in the open, and it's at the end of a dead-end road. One of us can keep watch."

"Sounds like a plan to me," Lance said.

Clay stood. "Go there and sit tight until you hear from me."

As they walked down the hall toward the door, Lance said, "I need to get my truck from the cafe and lock up. Sam, you still have a key to the house, don't you?"

"I do. We'll drop you off and meet you at the house."

"No," Clay interrupted. "I'll take Lance to the café. I want to look around a little. You two go on."

Sam and Smidgeon looked at one another, and Sam said, "Sure."

"Where's Mule?" Clay asked.

"I guess he took off," Lance said.

~ * ~

The Mossback Café was quiet when Clay and Lance arrived. Lance's truck was still out front.

"Light's still on in the kitchen," Lance said.

"You get your gun out of the other truck?" Clay asked.

"Yes, sir...got it right here," he said, patting his leg.

"Boot holster?"

"Yep."

Clay shook his head and pulled around the back. There were wire racks scattered around along with two dented garbage cans. Trash was scattered all over the place.

"What a mess," Lance said.

"Just leave it tonight. The place probably can't open tomorrow anyway."

"I better put up a sign," Lance said. "Family Emergency or something."

"Let me go in first. Think the back door is open?"

"I forgot about the back door. They broke in. I need to take a look at it."

"You didn't mention that at all."

"Sorry, Clay, so much happened in such a short time. We need to fix it right away, or we can't lock the place up."

"Well, like I said, I need to check it out first, and if the place is clear, I'll wave you in. You can maybe grab your gun and stand watch."

"Okay."

They exited the cruiser with their guns drawn. When Clay cautiously opened the door, the back area was suddenly bathed in light. Lance waited a long couple of minutes before Clay appeared at the doorway again.

"It's clear," he said. "This door jamb doesn't look too bad if you have a few long screws you can put in there. Don't see any blood in here, so I don't think Smidgeon hit him when she fired."

"Well, the door was swinging," Lance said as he inspected the doorframe. "You're right, if we have a minute, I've got a few tools in the office. I'll get the drill and some screws. Sam has a hardware can full of screws and such. Gonna go lock the front door and do a quick repair on this."

While Clay kept watch, Lance carefully drilled some holes and drove long screws into the jamb to squeeze it back together. He closed and opened the door several times, and it snagged in a couple of places, but when he tested the deadbolt, it seemed to work.

"Good enough for the time being," he said.

He flipped off the light, and they closed the door behind them. Lance tested the door again with a strong push after locking it.

"Good enough?" Clay asked.

"Seems solid," Lance responded. "Guess I'll go join Sam and Smidgeon."

Clay said, "I'll be in touch if I find out anything. You call it in immediately if he shows up there or if you see anything suspicious. Don't confront him."

"Will do, Clay. Thanks."

A haze of dark dust settled around him as Lance watched the deputy drive off and he opened the door of his truck.

Twenty-one

Loot's old garage loomed in front of them as Sam parked the truck; Smidgeon shivered a little. "This place is really spooky at night."

"Oh, it's not too bad. It's not like there are ghosts or anything."

"Maybe, but I'm not so sure," she said. "You think my car's still okay?"

"I'm sure it is," Sam said. "Let's get inside and wait for Lance. Where's your gun?"

"Got it here in my purse."

"Maybe I should take it while we check out the house."

"What, so you can shoot yourself in the foot? I'll take it. Grab the shotgun when you open the front door. Lance told us it's just inside the door."

"Let's go," she said as she pulled the .45 out of her purse and held it with both hands, pointing it forward as Sam unlocked the door. He pushed it open and waited a moment before he reached inside and felt the cold steel of the shotgun barrel. He grabbed it and brought it around. He hoped Lance kept it loaded. He indicated with his chin for Smidgeon to move behind him and he proceeded to enter the house.

"You think I should hit the lights or should we keep it dark?" he whispered.

"Lights," she answered, and he flicked a switch in the entrance.

There was a rustling noise from the right, and they both turned, ready to shoot. A small figure came out of the shadows.

"Mrrrow?"

"Oh, MamaKat. Come here, sweetie," Smidgeon said, reaching down to pet the cat.

Sam moved through each room in the house and returned. "It's empty," he said. "I suggest we sit and wait for Lance." As an afterthought, he checked the shotgun. "Both barrels are loaded," he said.

Smidgeon sat on the couch and cuddled the cat. "I wish this was all over, Sam," she said. MamaKat rubbed her head against Smidgeon's chin.

"Me, too."

"And we left a lot of stuff out at Marcy's cabin," Smidgeon began, but her eyes teared up. "Oh, my God, I forgot about Marcy. Why does everything we do end up with people we care about getting killed?" She put her face in her hands and sobbed.

Sam sat and put one arm around her. "It's not us, Smidgeon. It's not our fault."

"I want all this drama to be out of our lives. First the gold mine, then all the stuff with Moll, and now...who knows what this is all about? We don't even really know, do we?"

"Just what we found out from your cousin, the notes you found, and what Cerides told me."

"I've been on the run for almost two solid weeks and you...you've been beaten and tortured and—"

"We've got the upper hand, Smidgeon. I'm sure this will be over soon."

They saw the headlights before they heard the familiar rumbling of Lance's truck as it pulled into the driveway. Sam got up and started to the door.

"Sam," Smidgeon said. "The shotgun, don't forget the shotgun."

"It's Lance," he said.

"Sam? Come get it."

He recognized the tone in her voice and experience had taught him any debate was over, so he returned to the couch and retrieved the gun.

Once outside, Sam's eyes took a few seconds to adjust to the dim light. He thought it was strange Lance had not exited the truck. The passenger door suddenly popped open. Sam raised his gun.

"Hold it." Jeffers emerged and pointed a pistol at Sam.

Beads of sweat formed on Sam's forehead as the driver's door slowly swung open. He saw Lance ease his feet to the ground. A shorter figure holding a gun followed him; it was Cerides.

"Ah, Sam, we meet again. I am gratified to find you have safely made it back to Van Horn."

"I'll bet you are."

"Come now, after we conduct some minor business, I will be on my way." His gold tooth gleamed through his smile even in the darkness.

"I've told you again and again, we don't have what you're looking for. Let Lance go."

"I have fewer cards than before, so I think I will hold onto this one, thank you very much."

"Don't mind me, Sam. Blast these jokers."

Sam fingered the two triggers on the shotgun, considering his options. He only had two shots; if Sam shot at Cerides, he was sure to hit Lance as well. If he tried to shoot Jeffers, Cerides would probably shoot Lance, and there would be a pause before Sam could aim his second shot.

At that distance, the shotgun might or might not kill either man, but he'd be out of ammunition, while the two others would most likely still be able to shoot. Either way, Lance would be killed or wounded. The only other option was to surrender and hope he could talk his way out of it.

Sam was startled as another voice emerged from the darkness.

"Give me your gun or I swear I'll splatter your brains all over the truck."

Sam saw Jeffers go wild-eyed and lower his weapon and slowly turn and hand it to the figure behind him. Internally he was screaming "Smidgeon!" but he held his tongue. She stuck Jeffers' pistol into her belt and moved the big man over to the front of the truck.

"Let Lance go or—"

Cerides scoffed, "Go ahead and shoot him. I will kill your friend, then kill you and Sam. You cannot defeat me."

For the moment, Sam considered the fact that at the café there had been three of them. "Where's the other guy?" he thought.

"In my line of work," Cerides said, "the people I employ are generally expendable. Take the other associate you met this evening. After we drove away, it was soon apparent the car had been rendered inoperable. When another car approached, we ran into the night. We could see this other car circling and we assumed it was searching for us. My other associate chose that moment to terminate his employment. Well, to be more specific, he ran away, so I had Jeffers here dispatch him. I could not risk him being captured and perhaps talking. I assumed his body would divert whoever was looking for us. I remembered the truck back at your café, so we returned to see if we could perhaps appropriate it. We hid in the shadows when Mr. Norton here returned."

Jeffers towered over Smidgeon, so she poked him in the back of his head with her .45 and said, "On your knees, and cross your feet. Hands on your head." He complied.

Cerides laughed again; the sound sent a chill down Sam's spine.

"You are a most proficient adversary, Miss Toll. Perhaps when our business is concluded, you would consider joining me?"

"Don't listen to him," Lance said. "He said the same thing to me!"

Smidgeon sneered. "After what you just said about your employees? Listen, I run a business, and I know you need to treat your workers a lot better than you seem to."

"I'm paying you a great compliment, my dear," Cerides said. "You stood your ground and fired at me. Your shot grazed me through the swinging door, giving me yet another scar I will wear like a badge of honor. As a warrior, I cherish those moments."

"Warrior? You were a deserter," Sam said. "You said so yourself."

The smile dissolved and Cerides countered, "I was trained as a warrior, and I have fought many battles, and not only in the war. Working for those useless men was a waste of my time and talents. I prefer to fight for myself. This was as true then as it is now. Do you think my decade in a Mexican prison was a picnic? I fought for my life every day and eventually earned respect. Those who opposed me or turned on me died."

"You are nuts," Smidgeon said.

"You confuse insanity with survival. I have learned to do what I needed to do in order to endure."

Sam interrupted. "Yet, here you are. A bitter and lonely man, in search of revenge for something that happened decades ago. You are waging a vendetta against people who are all dead. Think about it, all of them are long gone: Joe, Loot, Scooter, Delbert, and Babe."

"Yet you know all of their names. This tells me you are a liar...you always knew more than you said."

"*You* told me. You told me the whole story."

Cerides hesitated like he was searching his memory. "Perhaps I did. I sometimes get too talkative, but no matter. You know more than you think you do... and you," he momentarily turned to Smidgeon, "*You* have been away, traveling. For what?"

"Family business," she said.

"Lie!" Cerides tightened his grip on Lance's arm and pushed the gun hard into the back of his neck. "Tell me! You found something in Sam's car. I knew I should have searched it, but I thought he was the prize that would get me what I needed."

"So you aren't perfect. Give it up. We have the both of you covered."

Smidgeon and Sam both failed to notice Jeffers uncross his feet while they were watching Cerides.

Jeffers spun from his kneeling position and momentarily knocked Smidgeon to the side and grabbed for her weapon. She struggled, but she was stronger than he expected; she would not let go of the gun.

With Cerides' attention momentarily diverted by the struggle, Lance made his own move and grabbed for the pistol. They both fell to the ground as they fought.

Sam looked on helplessly but finally chose to go to Smidgeon's aid first. Jeffers ceased struggling when he felt the cold steel of the shotgun barrels pressed against the side of his head.

"Move aside," Sam said. "Lie face down, feet crossed, hands outstretched." Jeffers complied, and Smidgeon again pointed her gun at his head.

Sam turned to Lance and Cerides, who were rolling around on the ground.

"Dang, you're strong for a little fella," Lance grunted as he tried to both wrest the gun from Cerides' grip and at the same time keep it pointed away from his head.

The smaller man was showing his age, though, as he panted through the struggle. Sam moved to help his friend. He figured the shotgun was useless at such short range, so he leaned it against the truck, dropped to his knees and grabbed the Italian's wrist, pressing hard with a thumb underneath the joint. Finally, Cerides' grip loosened and Sam pulled the gun away. He pointed it at the Italian.

"That's enough. Stop. Get up," Sam shouted.

Cerides panted and didn't move for a minute as he caught his breath. Lance brushed himself off as he slowly rose and stood next to Sam.

Sam said, "Get the shotgun."

As Lance was reaching for the shotgun, Cerides suddenly jumped to his feet and lunged at Sam to shove him back. He spun around and ran into the darkness, down Tesoro Road. Sam aimed the pistol and tried to pull the trigger.

"Safety's on," Lance yelled.

Sam examined the unfamiliar weapon and found the switch, but Cerides had disappeared. "Lance, did you see where he went? You could have shot him."

"Nope," he said. "He was out of range before I could get a bead on him."

A car came rushing down the road and skidded to a halt. Mule Hollis came running up to them with his gun drawn. He pulled out some handcuffs and put them on Jeffers.

"Found their partner shot back in town. I decided to go looking for them, but they had skedaddled. Figured I'd check here. Where's Cerides?"

"We were just tussling with him," Lance said, "but he ran off. You didn't see him on the road?"

"No, he must have veered cross-country when he saw my headlights."

"We're trying to figure out which way to go," Sam said.

Smidgeon shouted, "Wait, over there!" She pointed with her gun. "What's that light?"

~ * ~

"Loot!" Scamp said, "He's getting away!"

"No, he ain't," Loot intoned, and he left a faint vaporous trail as he followed the running figure.

He landed a couple of dozen feet ahead of his target in an expanding glimmer of light.

Cerides was brought to a standstill. *"Madonna mia santissima! È impossibile!"*

Loot glared at the trembling figure and pushed out and focused his energy with an intense luminous flash.

Cerides catapulted backwards, but his eyes never left the ominous visage of Loot; he was transfixed by the vision but somehow managed to stumble to his feet. He stood, quivering, immobilized by fear.

"It's a trick, it cannot be you! Go away!"

The apparition again lashed out, and Cerides toppled again, crumbling into a weeping heap on the ground.

His energy spent, the radiance around Loot faded.

~ * ~

Sam raced toward the light with Mule close behind. Smidgeon handed Lance the gun she had taken from Jeffers, and he stuck it in his belt while he continued to point his shotgun at the shackled man.

"Go on, follow Sam," he said. He turned to Jeffers, "don't you get any wild ideas."

Sam paused and stared at the end of a circle of bluish light. There was a sudden bright burst and Cerides' body lunged backward. Mule and Smidgeon joined him, and the three of them watched as Cerides started to rise; they began to approach Cerides but paused when there was another flash and they saw the small man hurdle backward again.

"Sam, d-d-do you see...?" Smidgeon said, pointing.

At first, Sam was too mesmerized to answer. He managed a meek, "Loot?" as the hazy figure faded into darkness.

The spell broke when they realized all they could hear was the sound of weeping. They rushed to Cerides who was on his hands and knees, sobbing and hysterically declaring over and over again, "Forgive me. I know I have sinned, forgive me, forgive me, please forgive me—"

Sam tapped the Italian's shoulder with the toe of his boot. "On your feet."

Cerides groveled at Sam's feet and continued to sob uncontrollably, "Take me away from this evil, please, I'll do whatever you want, but take me away from here."

Mule bent over and grabbed both of Cerides' shoulders and lifted him. "Okay, let's go back."

Lance was still guarding Jeffers when the four figures returned.

Smidgeon said, "I'll go call the police," and she ran to the house.

"How'd you catch him?" Lance asked.

"Not sure," Sam said. "He stumbled or something."

"It was strange, like he fell backward or something," Mule added.

"What about the light?"

"You saw it?" Sam asked.

"I saw something flickering out there. I thought maybe it was the police but it vanished. What was it?"

"Don't ask," Sam said. "I need to think up a good answer to that."

"The night plays tricks on your eyes sometimes," Mule said.

"It was the face of evil. A devil," Cerides said, and he started to sob again.

"What's he getting on about?" Lance asked.

Mule said, "We got him, which is all I need to know at this point."

Sirens wailed in the distance.

"Finally," Sam said.

"I just wanted what was rightfully mine," Cerides said. "But now I understand...it was always a thing of wickedness, and I want nothing more of it. Take me to the police. I want to get far away from this place. It carries an aura of wickedness," he continued with a wavering voice.

"I agree with Lance. What *is* he talking about?" Mule asked.

"Who knows," Sam said. "I think maybe he hit his head when he fell."

"You saw it, too," Cerides accused. "I heard you. There is something not right about all of this. It must be some trick. How did you do it?"

"Do what?" Sam said. "We turned the tables on you, that's all. You've turned the tables on us a couple of times."

"You've summoned spirits from the great beyond to haunt me with memories from my past. How?"

"What do you mean?" Sam blinked at his prisoner.

"You didn't catch me. It was Loot. I felt his icy fingers of death clutching my throat. There was no escape."

"I'd go easy on such talk, pardner," Lance said. "They throw folks in the looney bin for talking crazy. Or maybe that's your angle."

Cerides glared at Lance. "Do not make such light of what I say. I'm serious. You people are all evil."

Lanced said, "Sounds like another big heaping spoonful of the pot calling the kettle, if'n you ask me. You want to talk about evil? Where's my dog?"

Cerides spit at Lance, "Curse your stupid dog!"

Lance took a step toward the Italian.

Mule put a hand on Lance's shoulder. "Hold it; the police are coming. Don't make things any more complicated than they already are."

Two patrol cars rushed down Tesoro Road and screeched to a halt in front of the house. Clay got out of the lead car, followed by another deputy from the other cruiser. Both officers had their guns drawn.

"So the gang's all here," Clay said as he cuffed Cerides.

The other deputy took control of Jeffers. Both men were separated into the two patrol cars. Clay returned to the group of people in the front yard.

"We've got another body on the far side of town. And we found a sedan nearby, broken down with shredded tires. It looked like he tried to run away." Clay turned to Mule. "You know anything about it?"

"He was that way when I found him."

"Cerides said he told Jeffers to kill the guy after the car stalled and the dude tried to run away. After shooting him, those two returned to the café to steal my truck," Lance said. "They were hiding there when you dropped me off."

"My fault," Clay said. "I should have thought to recheck the entire area, not just inside."

"I didn't think about it either," Lance said. "They snagged me when I started to get in my truck."

"It was a standoff," Sam said. "Cerides held a gun on Lance, and Jeffers was holding a gun on me. I had a shotgun on the both of them. Then Smidgeon went out the back door and circled to the front and got the drop on Jeffers."

"Jeffers grabbed for my gun, but I was a lot stronger than he thought I was," Smidgeon snickered.

"In the confusion," Lance said, "I started for Cerides' gun. Sam had gone to help Smidgeon, but once Jeffers was under control, he came back and, between the two of us, we got Cerides' gun. At that point, we had the two of them, but before we could call you guys, Cerides took off, running, trying to make a break for it. He ran off into the dark," he continued, pointing. "When Mule suddenly showed up, Sam, Mule, and Smidgeon took off after him while I covered Jeffers."

"We ran down and caught up with Cerides when it looked like he fell," Sam said. "He fell again before we got him."

"Cerides is going on and on about some kind of evil and sinister presence."

"Yeah," Mule said. "We figure he hit his head when he tripped."

"He's nuts," Lance said. "I think he must be laying the groundwork for an insanity defense. Give me a few minutes alone with him. He still has my dog, if she's still alive."

Clay turned to Lance. "Oh, I completely forgot in all this excitement. Your dog was found at a motel near Marfa. She was in a room alone, howling. One of the Presidio deputies took her to his house."

Tears welled up in Lance's eyes. "Oh, sweet Jesus."

"So we'll get him on dog theft, and we're also building a strong case against him on Marcy's murder here. The FBI has a whole string of crimes along the border they want to ask him about."

Mule spoke up. "The *Federales* will want a big chunk of him, too."

Clay continued, "Heck, the FBI said he's still got an escaped prisoner of war charge on his record. I doubt they'll prosecute on such an old charge, but we have plenty of stuff to hold him indefinitely."

"Good," Sam said, "maybe we can all relax."

"You ain't kidding," Clay said. "That would be fine with me."

Sam handed Clay a handgun. "This was what Cerides was holding on Lance. Jeffers had Lance's gun, and of course, Smidgeon had her own .45."

"Oh, Cerides had another gun? Great. If the other one isn't the murder weapon, then this one probably is. Good enough for now. You folks need to watch your backs. We don't know if he has any more people working for him around here."

"Based on what he did to his other man, I think they'll all be in the wind," Mule said.

Sam started to walk with Clay toward the cruiser. "One more thing, Clay."

"What?"

"When Smidgeon had her gun on Jeffers, Cerides said she could go ahead and shoot him."

"Good to know. It will surely help turn Jeffers. I'll get a more detailed statement from all of you later."

"Exactly what I thought," Sam said.

"You folks get a good night's sleep. I'll be in touch."

Cerides watched Sam from the back seat of the patrol car; he had a confused look of terror on his face. Sam returned the stare and shook his head in disdain. "Sure thing," he said to Clay as he turned and slowly walked back to the house.

Twenty-two

Lance set a kitchen chair in front of the couch where Sam and Smidgeon were sitting. He returned to the kitchen and came back with three mugs of steaming coffee. "Sorry it's just instant," he said.

Smidgeon took a sip from her cup. "It's fine. You know how I like it, too."

"So sweet no one else can touch it. I reckon I've been working at the café long enough now to know what you like." Lance took a sip before continuing. "I called the deputy over in Marfa...Prewash is doing fine. I've got to head over there first thing in the morning to pick her up. I'm still trying to wrap my head around everything that's been happening, Now that Cerides is out of the picture, I'm wondering what's next?"

Smidgeon and Sam exchanged glances. "Lance, do you have a shovel?" Smidgeon asked.

Lance raised an eyebrow. "I think there's an old one out in the shed."

"Good. I need to get my car out of there anyway—after we finish our coffee."

Sam interrupted. "So, you really want to do this now?"

"After all of this, I have to see if I'm right. I want to see if there's anything there."

Sam sighed and sipped his coffee. He knew better than to argue with her.

"Whoa," Lance said, "What the heck are y'all talking about?"

"It has to do with everything I found on my trip," Smidgeon said. "We've all been in such a tizzy ever since I got back, I've never had a chance to tell you all the details."

Lance responded, "I hope my heart can take it."

"We left all the stuff out at Marcy's cabin, but in a nutshell, everything fits together like a puzzle. If you take the first letter of each town I had to go to, and the first letter of the last name of each tombstone where I found the next clue, they all spell out 'L-O-O-T-S-H-E-D.'"

Sam added, "We think there is something buried somewhere around your shed."

"Well, it's really your shed. I'm a renter."

Sam laughed. "I forget sometimes."

"How do we know where to dig?"

Smidgeon said, "The last clue said, 'Look at where you been, who you met, what you done.'"

Lance covered his face with both palms and rubbed his eyes. "Another riddle?"

"Crazy, isn't it?" Sam responded.

Lance sipped the last of his coffee and swallowed. "So I see where you got the links from the where you been, and the names from who you met, but what does the last bit mean."

Smidgeon said, "I noticed everything seemed to be on the southwestern side. The graves I needed to find were always on the southwestern side of the cemeteries. I bet even the clue I found at Duke Chapel was on the southwestern side."

Lance paused in thought for a moment. "I'm pretty sure the wall closest to the house is the southwest side."

"I thought so, too," Sam said, putting down his empty cup. "I think it's time to do a little digging."

Lance grabbed two flashlights, and they all headed out the door to the shed. Sam pulled the tarp off Smidgeon's car while he was getting the shovel.

Smidgeon surveyed the side wall of the shed. "I think right here in the middle," she said. "All the boxes were in the middle of the tombstone." She pointed down. "At least it isn't a grave."

"We hope." Sam laughed as Smidgeon glared at him.

"I wonder why the boxes were always in cemeteries," Lance pondered.

"I wondered the same thing," Smidgeon said, "and I thought about it a lot while driving. I think maybe because whoever buried the clues figured they'd all have a better chance of being left alone."

"Seemed like they were all recent graves, too," Sam added, "so it was probably easier digging."

Sam positioned the shovel where Smidgeon had pointed. The ground was rock hard. He chipped at it and worked hard for every inch he scraped away. Lance went back into the shed and returned with an old post-hole digger.

"Here, Sam, let me hack away at it with this."

"Okay."

Lance chiseled the hole Sam had started with the twin blades of the digger until he had a hole about eight inches deep. On the next try, they all heard the sound of metal on metal. Smidgeon shone her flashlight down the hole and thought she could see a familiar shade of green. She got on her hands and knees and clawed at the ground with her bare hands.

"Needs to be dug around. My nails will never be the same."

"Wish we had one of those little gardening shovels," Sam said.

"We do!" Smidgeon jumped up and ran back to the house. She returned with her purse and fumbled around in it until she dropped it, clutching something in her hands. It was her car keys. Sam and Lance looked at one another, confused, as she ran back to the shed. They heard the trunk open and close, and she reappeared brandishing the garden trowel she had used on her trip.

"Here we go," she said, and she knelt, working hard inside the small cavity until she was able to pull the tin from its resting place.

"Another one for our collection," she quipped as she carried it toward the house.

Sam and Lance dropped their tools and followed her. Once inside, they all sat around the kitchen table and stared at the weathered cigarette tin.

"Go ahead and open it," Sam said.

Smidgeon popped the front of the hinged lid, and they could all see sheets of yellowed folded bits of paper wrapped in three plastic bags. She pulled the bundle out and unwrapped it.

"Baggies," Lance said. "Haven't seen those in a while."

"Yes, every note was wrapped in three bags like this," she said.

Smidgeon unfolded the paper and found several handwritten pages. The other notes had been more hastily scrawled, but this one was neatly written as if the person had been able to take their time and think about what they wanted to say. Smidgeon began to read out loud.

My name is Thaddeus Melvin, but people have always called me Babe. If you are reading this, then you must have solved my puzzle.

This story starts far away in North Africa in 1942. War changes people, and that goes especially for me, my four best buddies and an Italian kid we picked up along the way. Words can't even describe the hell and death of battle, but we were all also affected by something else. We found a box of coins buried in the desert. The six of us swore to share it. And we were going to do it, too, we all shook on it. But one night, the Italian kid, Digly we called him, decided to take it all. We should have figured it, but we thought he was a good kid. We knew he was a deserter, but we took him in anyway. One night, Joey Toll was on sentry duty, spotted him lugging that heavy box away, and yelled at him.

The shouts woke me up. I was right there and jumped up and saw it all for myself. The kid shot him with a pistol he'd been able to hide from all of us. By then, Loot and the others were on their way, too.

Delbert shot the kid in the leg and knocked him flat.
Loot and I grabbed the kid while Delbert helped Joey,
and Scooter ran to get the corpsman. Joey survived,
but he was hurt bad and it was his ticket home. Delbert
had just winged the kid, and the medic patched him
up.

In spite of all the commotion, Loot was able to
hide the box again, but the racket attracted attention
and the truth about Digly was out. The thing was, even
when we were waiting for the MPs to take him to the
prisoner compound, even with him trying to steal the
whole box and shooting Joey, he still expected his
share.

We all just shook our heads, and he screamed
something in Italian. I knew from the tone of his voice
he was swearing vengeance on all of us.

We figured we'd never see Digly again, so we split
the gold among the five of us. I shipped mine back
home, told my mama to hold it for me. Everybody did
the same. We shipped Joey's home, too.

Not long after that night, another battle was
heating up, and we were providing armored support. I
was dug in but good, and at some point, I watched a
corpsman working on a fella when a German 88 shell
landed right on them. They just wasn't there anymore;
everything was gone excepting for one boot and a pile
of rubble and smoke. I froze.

Later, the major took one look at me and knew I
was done. I ended up being sent home on the same
hospital ship as Joey. Honestly, it was the one thing
that helped, having Joey to talk to. After going home, I
was a lost soul. I stayed with my mama in Durham,

North Carolina, for a goodly while, but it didn't help me. Every night I dreamed about the explosion.

After a couple of years, I headed to Texas because Joey had told me so many good things about it. He wrote me and told me he had used his share to open a café. Loot was there, too, in the same little town, but he was drunk all the time. I wavered back and forth with drinking myself, which I know now was the reason things were especially hard for me. I got what work I could, mostly as a hand at various ranches, but I always managed to binge my way out of the job. I liked the Brite place most of all, though, down near the border, isolated, quiet and it was far enough from Marfa and Valentine to keep me from getting into too much trouble, at least most of the time.

Everywhere I went, I lugged the small box with my share. I never could let go of it, but I felt guilty about it, too, and couldn't bring myself to spend it; well, unless times got tough and I'd pull out something to help me get by. I'd bury what was left whenever I stopped long enough to think maybe in time things would work out.

When Mama got sick in 1970, I had to leave the Brite place and head back to Durham. Truth be told, I never rightly quit, I just left. Mama was in such a bad way. Lung cancer. She was miserable and in a lot of pain.

Docs said it was because she'd smoked all her life. I grew up a smoker, too. She sent me tins and tins of Lucky Strikes when I was in the army. She had old Lucky Strike tins everywhere in her house, too, stacks of them she'd saved. Our family all worked at the cigarette factory in Durham. You could see the factory smokestack and water tower from her bedroom window, out to the southwest, with the Lucky Strike logo painted on them. I looked at the cans and tins stuck all around, some empty, some with my letters she'd saved or with buttons or rubber bands or whatever. In my grief, all I could see were the relics of what had killed her.

Then I remembered the Brite Ranch; I had buried my box near an old well. I used to like to stand next to it and I'd daydream of home. I returned to Mama so quickly, I just left my box right there. I hadn't thought much about it at the time, but now I realize why I was drawn to that well. It was called the Lucky Strike Well. When I looked out the window and saw the smokestack again, I remembered the box and the well and a plan all fit together in my head like the pieces of some crazy jigsaw puzzle.

I'd always liked a good joke, so I thought I'd pull a big prank. If you're reading this, you now know the joke is on you, since you've followed a long trail in a loop.

Loot is drunk and passed out, so I'm taking the opportunity to write and bury this last note. A few days ago, I did Joey a favor at the cafe, helping patch a hole in a wall in his kitchen. A cook had gotten mad and punched it. If you followed the whole trail, that was the first clue. This is the last one.

It's my legacy of greed, betrayal, mistrust, sorrow, grief, and regret. I hope you do better with it than I have. I've told you what you need to know. I'm heading off into the sunset as soon as I bury this. My legacy is now your legacy. Be careful how you handle it.

Babe

Christmas 1970

~ * ~

"Good old Babe," Loot said. "We failed him, all of us. Shoulda been a better friend to him, but we was all about us. I remember that Christmas when he came to stay with me, and I remember him going to see Joe. I got drunk on my ass and passed out. I woke up and he was gone."

Scamp added sadly, "I remember it, too. It was the week I found out my sugar was off, never ever felt right from then on."

Slim hovered close by and mused, "Me, too. I was on a horrible bender, the last one of my life."

"Did you quit drinking after that?" Loot asked.

"Well, not officially," Slim said. "At the end of the week, I met Sam and died in his arms."

~ * ~

Smidgeon dropped the papers as she tried to stifle a sob and looked up at Sam and Lance. They both had tears in their eyes.

"Man," Lance said. "This is one heck of a note." He picked it up and reread each page carefully. "There's a novel in there if anybody could figure out how to write it. The question is, how do we go about checking it out? Or do we even care?"

Smidgeon took the papers from Lance. "Oh, *we* care. I ain't come this far to stop now."

"I'm in," Sam said. "Been almost killed too many times to ignore it now."

"You and your treasure hunts." Lance chuckled. "But I'm a treasure hunter, too. I'm in."

"We've all known this was basically a treasure hunt from the get-go. The clues, the gold coins. And Cerides was after the same thing," Sam said.

"Yeah. Babe couldn't have known it, but we could add vengeance and murder to his list of legacies," Lance said.

"Amen," Smidgeon said. "So, I think the best thing to do is to go back to work in the morning, almost like nothing happened. I'll ask around to see if I can find out something about the Brite Ranch. I've heard of it...it's one of the old spreads, but I don't know who runs it these days. I remember hearing stories about some sort of doings back around World War One."

"Yeah, Billy told me about it," Sam added. "A raid by Mexican bandits. You know, with Pancho Villa. I think a lot of people were killed."

Lance said, "A long time ago. Still, people don't easily forget that sort of thing."

"All the more reason for me to ask around," she said.

Twenty-three

Smidgeon and Sam returned to the café the next day. Neither had worked in almost two weeks. To Lance, it had seemed like a lifetime. They had all been up late, but Smidgeon still opened up on time.

When the morning rush slacked off, she blew a strand of hair out of her eyes and turned to Lance. "I'm exhausted," she said. "Has it been this busy all this time?"

"Lately? Nothing like this. I'm telling you, it's *you*, and the word is getting around." he said. "Our customers come here to see you, not some scraggly outsiders like me and Sam."

"Oh, come now," she said. "You did great."

"I tried, but I think folks were uncomfortable with me running things. I know I was."

Sam joined them and said, "Business is booming. I could have done with a slack day. I woke up tired."

"Me, too. We were just talking about that, Sam," Smidgeon said. "Lance thinks it's me."

"He's right," Sam said. "You think I kept coming here for the food?"

"Oh, stop it. Hey, did you see Gil from the feed store?" she asked.

"Noticed him as he was leaving," Sam said.

"He knows some of the folks over at the Brite Ranch. The feed store does business with them from time to time. He's going to call me back with a contact as soon as he looks them up."

"It's a pretty strange request," Lance said. "They ain't likely to be too interested in us snooping around. I can tell you from experience, a large working ranch doesn't have time for much foolishness."

"All we can do is ask," she said.

The phone rang during an afternoon lull in business, and Smidgeon flagged down Sam after she finished the call.

"That was Gil. He gave me the number of the foreman at the Brite Ranch. He suggested I call him this evening."

"Sounds promising," he said.

After they closed, Smidgeon called the number Gil had given her. Lance and Sam kept an eye on her while she talked on the phone.

The conversation was brief, but she hung up with a smile on her face.

"He said we could come out tomorrow. He has some time between nine and ten...he'll show us around."

"Guess I'll stay here and run the café, like usual," Lance said.

"Oh, Lance."

"No, really, it's all right. Somebody's gotta do it, and I'm still a bit stove up."

"You sure?"

"Smidgeon, you're the local, you talked to the guy. People *like* you. If it was just Sam and me showing up alone, they'd likely to think something was off."

~ * ~

It was a crystal-clear morning as Smidgeon's sedan rattled down the Old Brite Road south of Valentine, kicking up clouds of dust in its wake.

"So what did the guy say?" Sam asked.

"He seemed a little skeptical," she said.

"Been there, done that," Sam laughed. "Understand, even if we find anything, they probably won't let us keep it. It's on their property, so it's theirs."

"Sam, honey, I'll just be happy to figure it all out. You don't know what it's been like, wondering where the next clue would lead me, not knowing what was at the end."

"You forget, this is what I did for over ten years."

"I guess you *do* know what it's like."

"You bet I do."

They approached the small fork where Sam had found the clue. He slowed so she could see where he'd dug up the second clue.

"I think it was on the southwest side, too," he said.

"Of course it was."

"I love it out here," Sam said. "Look at the cattle," he said, pointing.

"Herefords," Smidgeon said. "Really nice ones."

They eventually approached the end of the road and drove into the ranch compound. The plumes of dust kicked up by the car had acted as an early-warning system, and a man approached them on horseback.

He dismounted and walked up to the car. Sam and Smidgeon got out to meet him.

"You Miss Toll? I'm the foreman here, Gabe Lodge. I think I've been to your place."

"Pleased to meet you," she said, pointing, "and this is Sam Milton."

"Oh, wait, you're *that* guy, the one who found the Sublett Mine and got mixed up with all them murders. I read all about it. I should have recognized your name, too, Miss Toll."

"Smidgeon, please."

"Drive on down this way to the right. I'll follow. Veer right at the first fork you come to and keep going, and you'll find yourself at the Lucky Strike Well. Take it easy or you'll snap an axle."

Smidgeon rolled up her window and drove slowly on the roughly graded road.

"I'm not used to ranchers being so welcoming to me," Sam said.

"Well, don't forget, Gil vouched for us. Gillet Osmond never met a stranger in his life."

"Yep, he's the best."

They eventually came into a rough clearing with two circular features. One was full of water.

"That's got to be the well," Sam said. He pulled out his compass, glanced at it and pointed. "Move to the left, and pull over near the edge."

Smidgeon steered the car where Sam indicated.

"This is good. I'll get another bearing when we move away from the car. Let's go."

A few minutes later they were joined by two men riding down the same road on horseback. They dismounted next to Smidgeon's car.

"This is one of our hands, Fred," Gabe said. "He's been here longer than just about anybody. Miss Smidgeon, you mentioned somebody named Babe. Fred here says he knew somebody named Babe years ago."

"You knew Babe?" Sam asked.

"Yes, sir. Nice guy. He was quiet and a good worker, but ever so now and then, well, let me put it this way: he liked his liquor. Known a few like him in my life...never quite finished fighting the war, you know, like in his head."

"Ever say anything about this well?" Sam asked.

"I'll tell you this...he liked to stand out here and stare at it. He'd park himself right about where you're standing. Yes sir, right there, that's about right." He laughed and shook his head. "I hadn't thought about that in years. He said something about it made him miss his mother or some such nonsense. I remember him telling me she was sick right before he disappeared. Didn't say nothing, just took off."

"Totally out of the blue," Smidgeon said.

Fred took off his hat and scratched the back of his head. "I mean, we figured it was because of his mom. He didn't even collect his pay. Heck, they would have let him go and would have kept his job for him. I mean, if'n his mom was dying and all. But like I said, he was tetched by the war, he wasn't never a hunnert percent there, if you know what I mean."

Gabe interrupted. "So, what's this all about? You said you think he buried something? You figure it might be right here?"

"He left a clue, well, we think he left a bunch of them. We've followed his clues all over the place."

Fred said, "I can see that. Babe liked his jokes, especially riddles and puzzles and such."

"Yeah," Smidgeon said, "exactly, like a big puzzle of clues and they left a trail...led us right here. Well, the last one led here," she added as she pulled the last tin out of her purse and popped it open. She handed Gabe the last letter. "He mainly tells his story, but this part here," she shuffled the pages, "mentions Brite Ranch and Lucky Strike. He liked working here."

Fred eyed the tin. "Lucky Strikes...hain't seen one of those cans in years."

"Yeah, in the note he says his mother had a lot of these," Sam said. "He grew up in Durham, North Carolina. His family all worked for the tobacco company. I think the Lucky Strike Well must have made him think of home. He says something in there about a smokestack with the words 'Lucky Strike' on it."

Gabe shook his head and scratched his chin. "If that don't beat all, but I guess I can see it."

Sam said, "Everything we have found so far was due southwest. So we think it might be about here somewhere."

"Like I said, it's pretty much where I remember him standing. I probably wouldn't be so sure excepting he did it a lot. We all thought it was pretty strange."

"So can we dig?" Sam asked.

"Go for it," Gabe said. "It'll be tough, though. This is pretty well packed down. We run cattle through here and vehicles. It gets baked solid in the summer."

"I'll be careful," Sam said as he started chipping away with the point of his spaded shovel.

Gabe read through Babe's note while Sam worked. "This is quite a story," he said.

"Isn't it?" Smidgeon said.

"You're right, it's awfully hard," Sam said. He returned to the car. "I borrowed this from Lance," he said as he pulled a pick-ax from the trunk.

Chips began to fly as he chipped at the hard-packed ground. About a foot down he hit something. Both Gabe and Fred were wide-eyed.

"Lucky Strike lives up to its name," Sam joked. He carefully whittled with the pick and crouched to scoop out handfuls of debris. It was a small wooden container, about six inches square and maybe two inches deep. By the time Sam unearthed the box, they could see it was screwed shut all around.

"Lordy, I never thought you'd actually find anything," Gabe said.

"Me either," Sam said. "Not really."

"We could take it back and get some tools to work on it," Fred said.

Sam thought for a second. "I think I'll whack it with the pick." He placed the box on the ground and hit it with the broad side of the pick. The wood splintered. He hit it once more, and it fell apart. Gold coins gleamed in the bright sunlight.

"Well, I'll be..." Gabe said.

Sam dropped and picked through the fragments. "It's hardly a fortune," he said, "but there's maybe a dozen or more coins here." He scooped them up and handed one to Smidgeon.

"It's like the one from the frame," she said.

"There's others?" Gabe asked.

"It's a long story, but my daddy had hidden one back at our house. We found it not too long ago."

Sam said, "This is all tied to some war booty a bunch of soldiers found in World War II."

"Like he said in the note," Gabe said.

Fred backed away from the group. "That's enough for me. I'm not saying I'm superstitious, but I don't want no part of no dead man's hoard," he said. "I told you what I knew about Babe but I'm done. Y'all have a nice day." He looked to the sky, "God Bless you, Babe, rest in peace now, ya hear?" he whispered as he mounted and rode away.

Smidgeon turned to Gabe. "I reckon this belongs to the ranch."

"I don't know, Miss Toll. I was being nice because Gil asked me to help you out. Never in my wildest thoughts did I think you'd find something."

Sam had filled the hole and was smoothing it down and tamping it with the shovel.

"So what do you want to do?" he asked.

Gabe poked at the spot with the toe of his boot. "I don't rightly know. The owners are at an auction and left me in charge, so they don't know anything about any of this. I tend to agree with Fred, and I really think they will, too. This Babe fella even mentions in the note all the trouble he figured was attached to this, his legacy he called it. We've done fine all these years not knowing anything about it, and it ain't worth that much, not really. It's gold, sure, but you weigh it out you get what, a few thousand at most? I reckon since y'all went to so much trouble...you keep it. You heard Fred, he ain't interested, and neither am I. I'll just figure it was a dry hole. Why don't you nice folks pick up your stuff and be on your way. Okay?"

Sam held one coin out. "You sure you don't want one, as a keepsake?"

"It's tempting, but I got me a weird feeling in the pit of my stomach. I think it's sort of tainted or something. Thanks for the bit of adventure, but I've got work to do." Gabe mounted and followed Fred down the trail.

Sam dropped the coins into Smidgeon's purse and loaded the tools in the trunk.

"We shouldn't leave all this splintered wood," she said as she scooped up the fragments and put them on the floorboard behind the passenger seat.

They exchanged waves with Gabe as they turned left and headed north on Old Brite Road.

"He was right, you know," Sam said.

"About what?"

"It really isn't that much money."

"I don't care about the money, Sam."

"I know. Weird though; so much trouble for such a small amount," he said. "Maybe I should go visit Cerides in jail and tell him."

"I don't think he cares either, Sam."

"Why?"

"Both Babe and Cerides didn't care about the money. They each tied it into their own sense of right and wrong, and I think it drove both of them crazy. Seriously, it changed all their lives. My dad put together something good with it, but everyone else had nothing but bad come from it."

"I can relate, honey, believe me, I can relate," Sam said as the dust kicked up by the little sedan settled behind them.

~ * ~

As Loot, Slim, and Scamp watched the car leave, another vaporous image joined them.

"Good morning, Loot."

"Babe! Everything okay?"

Babe waved as the car disappeared in the distance, and their images all began to fade. "It's perfect, Loot, just like it's supposed to be."

Meet Thomas Fenske

Texas native Thomas Fenske currently lives in North Carolina with his wife, nine cats and a dog. Somehow he still manages to write despite the chaos.

Other Works From The Pen Of Thomas Fenske

The Fever
In the late 1800s, Ben Sublett was already known for his secret gold mine in the far reaches of west Texas. When Ben died in 1892, it was thought his secret died with him. Eighty years later in a central Texas jail, a dying, homeless wino named "Slim" Longo whispered a long-held family secret to twenty year old Sam Milton.

A Curse That Bites Deep
After years of frustration and sacrifice, Sam Milton's life seems to be on track. In The Fever he got the girl, he found the mine, and he hopes he'll soon have the gold, but he forgot one minor detail: the curse and its ripples are affecting almost everyone around him.

Lucky Strike
A bitter, decades-old grudge surfaces with a vengeance in a small west Texas town.

Penumbra –
Reluctant treasure hunter Sam Milton and his girlfriend Smidgeon Toll find themselves immersed in the search for a missing man they have never met and end up on the trail of a cache of ancient gold in the desert southwest.

The Hag Rider

This Civil War memoir explores a fifteen-year-old cavalryman's transition to manhood, complicated by the spectral manipulations of a hoodoo witch sworn to protect him.

Harmon Creek –

When political candidate Earl Swanger ended up stabbed and dead next to a bridge in rural Texas it looked like a case of homicide, right? Then why was it ruled an accident within two days? This fictional account revisits the 1930 cold case and the possible skullduggery behind the coverup.

www.ingramcontent.com/pod-product-compliance
Lightning Source LLC
Chambersburg PA
CBHW071548110726
47908CB00007B/2033